NO MERCY

LAWMEN SERIES BOOK 2: NO MERCY

Cheyenne McCray

Published by Pink Zebra Publishing.

Formatting by Bella Media Management.

Cover by Scott Carpenter at www.pandngraphics.com.

ISBN-13: 978-1507592847

LAWMEN SERIES:

NO MERCY

CHEYENNE MCCRAY

CHAPTER 1

November rain fell from the Arizona sky and thrummed on the tin shed's roof in a steady rhythm, but Dylan Curtis's throat was as dry as the usually parched desert.

A special agent with the Department of Homeland Security's Immigration and Customs Enforcement, Dylan had witnessed a lot of bad shit. But seeing one of his closest friends hanging from a noose was one of the worst things he could remember experiencing.

The pain eating at Dylan was like a chainsaw cutting through his gut. He adjusted his Stetson while he surveyed the gut-wrenching scene as the rope around Nate O'Malley's neck was cut down from the rafters by police officers.

After the body was lowered, the remains were put into a body bag on the floor of the storage shed. It was all Dylan could do to watch as the officers zipped the body bag until he could no longer see Nate's corpse.

Corpse. Fuck. Dylan dragged his hand over his stubbled jaw as he tried to digest the fact that Nate was gone. *Suicide.* No matter how he tried, Dylan couldn't comprehend that Nate had taken his own life.

Through the shed's open door came the scent of rain and the sound of water dripping from the eaves. The smell wasn't nearly enough to ease the sickly odor of death.

"I know O'Malley was a good friend of yours." Lieutenant Liam Marks of the Bisbee Police Department approached and rested his hand on Dylan's shoulder a moment. "Thanks for coming down to identify the body."

Dylan said nothing. His heart and gut ached too much to speak.

Marks gave Dylan a sympathetic look before releasing his shoulder and going back to doing his job.

Nate's face had been swollen and purple, his light blue eyes bloodshot and bulging. There had been enough of a resemblance for Dylan to confirm Nate's identity.

If it hadn't been for G.I. Joe, Nate's German shepherd, barking for hours in his dog run, the neighbors wouldn't have called the police department to complain. The body likely wouldn't have been found for days.

Before going into the shed, Dylan had stopped by the dog run to check on Joe. Even though the dog run had a shelter on one end, the German shepherd stood out in the pouring rain. Because Joe knew Dylan well, the dog had calmed, but Dylan could tell he was still agitated. As Dylan had headed to the shed, Joe stood behind the fence, his keen eyes taking in everything that was happening. He was a highly intelligent dog that Nate had rescued some time ago. Joe had been incredibly loyal to Nate ever since.

It had been two months since Dylan had last seen Nate. Dylan had been working a case undercover and hadn't been able to communicate with anyone outside of his job. He'd gotten home a few days ago, but hadn't had a chance to get together with his friend.

And now Nate was dead.

Dylan attempted to distance himself emotionally from Nate's death, as if this wasn't so damned hard to take. Dylan knew he had to compartmentalize the fact that Nate had been one of his closest friends from the time they were in elementary school. Dylan knew he had to focus on what had happened and why, and make some kind of sense of it, if only for his own sake.

Conversation around him faded to background noise as he moved past the overturned bucket Nate had been standing on before he'd knocked it out from beneath himself. Dylan wanted to aim one of his boots at the bucket and kick the shit out of it, but he controlled the urge and continued toward his destination.

A suicide note had been scrawled on ledger paper and lay on a workbench. Dylan pulled on a surgical glove before taking the note off the bench to study the writing. Even before becoming a federal agent, he'd always had an attention for detail. He hadn't seen Nate's handwriting for a while, but he recognized it. Nate had written the note.

The shakiness of the writing was likely from nerves over what he'd been about to do. The ledger paper made sense since he'd been an accountant. Even in this day and age of computer technology, Nate hadn't completely been able to give up scrawling figures by hand on paper. He'd said it helped him think.

What didn't make sense to Dylan was the fact that Nate had committed suicide. He'd been so damned stable. A rock. It was true that lately he'd seemed a little off, but Dylan had attributed it to the fact that Nate had been facing a federal tax audit on his own business. Was that why Nate had killed himself?

Dylan barely kept from crumpling the note in his hand, and the paper shook with the effort it took to restrain himself. He hooked one thumb in the pocket of his Wrangler jeans as he stared at the paper without seeing it.

Out of the Circle of Seven, Nate had been the one Dylan had remained close friends with, even after all these years. Dylan had bumped into Marta De La Paz and Tom Zumsteg in Bisbee at separate times, and they'd filled him in on how Leon Petroski and Christie Simpson-Reyes were doing. Leon owned a water well drilling business, and Christie did clerical work in her husband's office. Marta worked hard as a stay-at-home mom of two children. Tom had taken a position as a physician at Copper Queen Community Hospital in Bisbee after working at Tucson Medical Center for a number of years.

It was a wonder how most of them lived in close proximity, yet they never got together.

As far as Belle…no one talked to Dylan about her. They knew she was too painful a subject to bring up, even after all this time.

Now Dylan would have to call Belle to tell her about Nate. He'd have to call every one of the Circle, but it was Belle who caused his stomach to churn even more than it already was. Through his work connections, years after she'd left, he'd kept track of but never contacted her. Still, he hadn't been able to help himself from making sure she was all right. He knew she was in the restaurant business, but hadn't delved any deeper.

Here it was, twenty-three years after she'd run away from home… and from him. He still couldn't forgive himself, and he still couldn't forget or put aside what they'd once had, no matter how young they'd been.

The suicide note came into focus as Dylan clenched his jaw and read it once again.

My friends,

Today I take my own life due to my guilt over the many wrongs I have committed against myself and against all of you. I am sorry for any pain I may cause you by my actions.

CoS always,

Nate

"Agent Curtis, does CoS mean anything to you?" A female BPD detective spoke, drawing Dylan's attention from the note.

He looked at Detective Teri Jensen, who was all of five foot one and thirty-five years old, if that. "Circle of Seven," Dylan said. "A group of seven who have known each other since elementary school." Dylan let out a slow breath. "They bonded when they were young and referred to themselves as CoS."

"You were one of the seven." Jensen spoke quietly, with certainty and understanding in her voice.

He gave a slow nod. "Yeah, I was."

"It's a terrible way to lose someone you care about." Her smile was sad. "I lost a family member to suicide a few years ago. You never get over it. All losses of family and friends are difficult, but there's something terribly personal and painful about suicide in a way that's different from any other kind of loss."

"Yes." Dylan had never experienced it for himself before, but from the pain now in his gut, he knew her words were true.

"I know it's tough, but do you mind if I ask you some questions?" Jensen pulled out a smart phone with a large screen from a holster on her hip and detached the stylus from where it was secured.

Dylan had expected this, just hadn't known who would be the detective doing the questioning. "Go ahead."

"He states guilt over wrongs he has committed." She studied Dylan. "Do you know what wrongs he's talking about?"

Dylan shook his head. "Nate's always been a stand-up guy. I can't imagine him doing anything serious enough to take his own life, much less committing wrongs against his friends."

Jensen made a note on her device. "From what I understand, Nate had no immediate family members."

Dylan thought about Nate's rough past. "He was sent to live with his grandmother at an early age after his parents disappeared. His grandmother died after he graduated high school, leaving him with no family."

Jensen held her stylus over her screen. "Tell me what you know about his parents."

"Not much." Dylan thought back to the early days when Nate and the others had come together and named themselves the CoS. "Law enforcement tracked his parents to the Mexican border where they crossed and vanished. They could have been dead for all Nate knew."

Jensen made another note on her device. "He mentions the CoS in the letter. Why do you think that is?"

Dylan pushed up the brim of his Stetson. "Those of us in the CoS were Nate's only real family." Dylan thought back to the past when the seven of them had truly bonded. "That's my best guess. I'm going to have to give it more thought."

The detective asked a few more questions and Dylan answered each one even though he'd rather have been left to his own thoughts and conducting his own investigation.

Jensen clipped her stylus back in its place and put away her phone. "If you come up with anything, here's my number." She pulled a card out of a pocket on the inside of her blazer and handed it to Dylan. "Office and cell number are both on it."

"I'll do that." Dylan took out his billfold and tucked the card inside for safekeeping with his credentials before pocketing them again.

He set the suicide note back on the workbench as Jensen walked away. Since photographs had already been taken before Dylan had touched the note, an officer came and bagged and tagged it. He pulled off the surgical glove and stuffed it into his pocket.

Dylan didn't look back as he walked out of the shed and into the rain. Water pounded down, soaking his overshirt, T-shirt, and jeans. His boots squished in the mud. The Stetson protected his head and water dripped from the brim.

Several law enforcement and emergency response vehicles were parked around the scene. Dylan focused on walking from the shed and the short distance toward Nate's home, which he had inherited from his grandmother. Dylan jogged up the stairs to the door that had been left open for the BPD to make sure no evidence of foul play could be found. When he reached the porch, he wiped his muddy boots on the welcome mat and shook the rain off of his Stetson.

The first thing that hit Dylan when he walked into the house was the smell of paint and new carpeting. He took off his hat and stood just inside the doorway as he surveyed the room.

Nate had always been a disaster when it came to his home, which was at total odds with his perfection when it came to accounting. He had worked out of his home and visited clients rather than having clients come to him. His office had always been more organized than the rest of his house.

Dylan had thought of Nate as something of an enigma. He hadn't looked like a stereotypical accountant—no pocket protector and no button-down shirts or slacks. He'd been all about jeans and T-shirts unless he had to meet with the IRS to handle an audit or visit clients' offices.

Nate had been more compact than Dylan and not quite as muscular. He'd stood just four inches shorter than Dylan's six-three. Nate had been popular with the ladies and liked to party, but had never married and had never had kids. After high school and the CoS drifting apart, Nate hadn't let anyone get close to him but Dylan. Even then he knew Nate had kept secrets.

But secrets big enough to commit suicide over?

Dylan let his gaze drift over the living room. The place was messy, but the carpet was new, the walls freshly painted, and the surfaces dust-free. The mess didn't seem natural, though, as if things had been somehow arranged to look out of place.

He frowned. A mess that looked intentional didn't make one damned bit of sense, but neither did the new carpet and painted walls, or lack of dust. Not too long ago, Nate had made a comment that he wanted to dump his grandmother's house. He'd even said he didn't plan to put in any work into the place because he didn't have the time, the skill, or the money it would take. He must have had a change of heart because the living room looked better than it ever had.

Yet something didn't feel right in Dylan's gut. He gripped his hat as he walked past a couple of BPD officers and gave them a nod. He set his hat on the back of the couch and spent the next ten minutes searching the room for something that might confirm what his gut was telling him.

When he didn't find anything, he walked through the house that better reflected Nate's personality. The place was a mess with clothes scattered on the floor, piles of laundry that needed to be washed, junk piled haphazardly, and thick layers of dust on the surface of every piece of furniture.

He opened the door to the room that served as Nate's home office. It was more disorganized than usual, yet still neater than the rest of the house.

Dylan pulled out a pair of surgical gloves. "Now let's have a look and see what we can find. Did you leave anything, buddy?" He didn't have any clue what that something might be, but he needed some way to make sense of this.

As he poked around the office, he had the odd feeling that someone had been here, searching for something.

After looking over the desk, which had a desktop computer, he paused for a moment, wondering where Nate's laptop was. Dylan spent a few moments searching drawers and cabinets, but didn't find anything.

He went to the bookshelf and ran his gloved finger over the titles, mostly classics. Nate had loved to read. Dylan stopped when he came to one book that was sticking out by half an inch past the other books on the shelf. It was a book he recognized at once by the name on the spine, and he felt an odd twist in his gut.

Baseball, An Informal History.

Nate had carried the book around with him in school. It had been the last gift his father had given to him before he'd disappeared with Nate's mother.

Dylan's heart clenched as he carefully withdrew the book from the shelf. The well-worn book jacket was torn in places, exposing the hard cover beneath.

He went to the copyright page and saw that the hardcover was printed in 1969. He continued on through the yellowed pages when something dropped out of the book and hit the floor. He crouched to pick up a postcard of Main Street in Old Bisbee. When he turned it over, he saw his own name and address printed in Nate's handwriting. In the space to the left of the address was a note.

> *Dylan,*
>
> *While you're off on vacation, I'm stuck here in good ol' Bisbee. I want you to promise me something. Remember what you had, buddy. If it happens, second chances only come once. Don't let it pass you by.*
>
> *Hey, remember when I served in Iraq? At the risk*

of sounding like a lovesick teenage girl, I missed your surly ass then, too.

WYB,

Nate

Cold prickles ran up and down Dylan's spine as he stared at the postcard. Not only was he reading something from the dead, but one big detail was wrong with the card. Nate hadn't served in Iraq. He'd served in Afghanistan. He'd received the Purple Heart when he ended up with a leg full of shrapnel, along with an honorable discharge.

Dylan took a plastic evidence bag out of his pocket, dropped the postcard in, then sealed it. He should give the postcard to the BPD, but instead he shoved the bagged card into his back pocket. It couldn't be seen beneath the overshirt that also covered his service weapon, a Browning 9mm semi-automatic pistol. The postcard was between him and Nate, and Dylan didn't intend to leave it for the BPD to take over before he had a chance to study it.

He stood and slid the book back into its place on the bookshelf and then ran his finger along the spine. What the hell had been going through Nate's mind when he'd written that note? He shook his head and turned to leave the room. As he strode through the office doorway and closed the door behind him, Dylan felt as though a physical weight was in his back pocket where he'd slid the card.

Iraq? Maybe Nate had been drinking a bit too much when he'd written that note. Dylan frowned. No, Nate would have to have been beyond plastered to mess up something like that. But why would he purposely make that mistake?

Putting the postcard out of his mind wasn't easy, but Dylan did his best and went into the kitchen where a few dirty dishes were piled in the sink with more stacked on the counters. Takeout and pizza boxes were scattered on the surfaces and the kitchen table, and crammed into a tall garbage container.

He used a dishtowel to open the fridge, keeping his fingerprints off the handle, and looked inside. The only things on the shelves were a range of condiments and more takeout boxes from local restaurants and delis, as well as Bisbee's best-known pizza place, the Puma Den. He studied the kitchen, seeing Nate in everything.

Joe's leash hung from a hook by the refrigerator. Nate had always been good about taking the dog for walks.

When Dylan returned to the living room, he felt a twinge in his gut again.

Something was definitely off.

He looked along the baseboards, which had not been painted like everything else had. Strange. His gaze came to stop on a dark circle, a tiny spatter that he hadn't noticed before. He moved to the baseboard and crouched to study the spatter that was smaller than a dime. It was a dark substance that could have been dried blood.

Detective Jensen walked in the house just as Dylan looked up. Jensen appeared to read Dylan's expression and headed toward him.

She came to a stop beside him. "Surprised you're still here, Agent Curtis."

He stood, towering over the petite detective, and gestured to the spot. "I believe that's a blood spatter." He made a motion to encompass the room and explained about Nate and the conclusion he'd come to. "I've got a feeling the new paint and carpet is a cleanup job." He explained about Nate not planning to make improvements on the house and its general appearance before.

Jensen frowned and then nodded slowly. "We'll take care of it, and I'll give you a call when everything is processed."

"Thank you." He gave her a grim look. "Just to let you know, I'm taking the dog until I can find him a home."

She nodded. "He needs a good home now."

Dylan went to the kitchen and took the leash from its hook. He returned to the living room and picked up his hat from where he'd set it on one corner of the couch.

He settled his Stetson on his head and touched the brim as he inclined his head toward Jensen in a brief nod. His mind continued to work over the death of his friend as he turned to walk out of the house.

Dylan reached the bottom of the stairs and stood in the rain as he looked at Joe sitting in the dog run. A doghouse was at one end, but the shepherd clearly had no interest in it. With the leash in his hand, Dylan walked toward the run.

"Hey, boy." As Dylan let himself into the run, Joe turned his gaze on him. The dog was drenched. "I won't leave you just to see you taken to the pound." Dylan shook his head. "Guess you're coming home with me."

Joe barked in response. Dylan wasn't sure if the shepherd would leave his master's home, but he remained still as Dylan crouched beside him and clipped the leash to the dog's collar.

Dylan stroked the top of Joe's wet head. "I'm sorry about Nate."

Joe barked, as if in response to Dylan's words.

"Wish you could talk." Dylan frowned as he rubbed Joe behind the ears. "You might be able to tell me just what the hell happened here."

Joe whined as if asking the same question. He licked Dylan's fingers.

Dylan got to his feet, opened the gate, and led Joe out of the dog run.

Joe bared his teeth, growled, and jerked against the leash. He was staring at the shed where BPD officers still worked. Joe barked, the sound vicious and filled with fury.

Dylan frowned. Joe had never been a hostile dog, but he had been protective of Nate. What was making the shepherd bare his teeth, snarl, and bark like he was doing now?

For a long moment, Dylan let Joe carry on as he pulled hard against the leash. Finally, Dylan tugged on the leash to get Joe's attention. As well trained as he was, the dog calmed and walked beside Dylan to the truck. Once Joe was settled into the back of the king cab, Dylan climbed into the driver's seat and left the Saginaw section of Bisbee to head to the DHS office near Douglas.

Smells of wet dog and rain filled Dylan's office. Joe sat by the desk, looking like a sphinx as he stared ahead, ever on watch.

No matter what he'd seen in his line of work, the calls Dylan had made were the hardest he'd ever had to make. He gripped the phone as he wrapped up his conversation with Christie Reyes.

She'd broken down, and tears were still in her voice. "I just got a postcard from him yesterday. It didn't feel like a goodbye note."

Dylan went still as he remembered the card in his back pocket. "You received a postcard from Nate? By U.S. Mail?"

"Yes." She said the word in a way that told him she was having a difficult time speaking. "It surprised me. We live in the same town, yet I haven't heard from him in so long."

Dylan wanted to press her, but she sobbed and he made the decision to give her some time to get used to the idea of Nate's death. He needed to read his own postcard again.

She cleared her throat and pulled it together. "I'll make funeral arrangements."

His voice was thick as he replied, "Thank you, Christie."

"The CoS was Nate's only family." She echoed Dylan's words to Jensen before adding, "We take care of our own."

"Call me for anything you need." Dylan tried to swallow. "Anything."

"I will." She sounded beyond sad. "I'll call Belle and let her know."

A rush of relief hit Dylan. He'd been dreading that phone call the most.

His gut tightened. He was such a chicken shit.

He clenched one hand on his desktop as he imagined Nate watching him, his disapproving stare burning into Dylan.

Dylan let out a long breath. "Thanks, Christie, but it's my duty. I'll call her."

Christie hesitated. "Do you need her number?"

"I've got it." He'd kept her number for a long time but had never called it. "Thanks again. I'll talk with you soon."

A sniffle. "Yes, soon."

He touched the disconnect icon on his phone and stared at the mobile device. He'd called Leon, Tom, Marta, and now Christie. No one had taken it well, and Dylan knew they had to be feeling the same shock and ache of loss that he had in his own gut.

The only thing that matched Dylan's pain was what he'd felt at his father's death. Ben Curtis had been murdered when Dylan was in high school and there wasn't a day that went by that he didn't miss his dad. The man had been his hero, and larger than life. If Dylan hadn't been bent on revenge over his father's murder, he probably would have been a rancher just like his dad.

Dylan turned his gaze to his office window and stared out at the dark skies and pouring rain. It hadn't let up since early that morning, as if grieving for his good friend, too. He'd need to call his mother and brother, Aspen, after he called Belle.

His gut churned again as he looked at his phone. It was the right thing for him to be the one to call Belle to let her know about Nate.

But then again, maybe she wouldn't want to hear from him. It would probably be for the best if Christie were the one to call Belle.

Shit. Dylan clenched the phone harder. No, it was *his* job.

Goddamn, but he'd never been so indecisive or been known to shy away from anything.

But this was Belle.

Joe let out a long sigh, drawing Dylan's attention to the dog that had lowered his head to his front paws. Thank God Leon had said he'd take Joe. Leon's three kids were older and would like having a dog around. Leon said he'd come by Dylan's office in a couple of hours to get Joe.

Dylan would have kept the shepherd, but with his job he was rarely at the ranch and Joe deserved better than that. Dylan had a ranch hand who took care of the livestock and kept an eye on things.

A knock came at the door and Dylan looked up to see Trace Davidson with his knuckles against the doorframe. Despite the fact that Trace, also a DHS agent, was a good friend, Dylan didn't feel like talking to anyone at the moment. "You okay?" Trace asked.

"Yeah." Dylan leaned back in his chair. "Fine."

"If that isn't a heaping load of bullshit, I don't know what is." Trace's Texan drawl seemed more pronounced than usual. He stepped into the room and shoved his hands into his front pockets. His overshirt was slightly pushed aside, revealing his service weapon. "Nate was a good man. I'm sorry as hell to hear what happened."

The ache in the pit of Dylan's gut only seemed to grow worse. "That makes two of us."

"I'll let you get back to whatever you were taking care of." Trace pulled his hands out of his pockets. "Just wanted to see how you're doing."

Peachy. Fucking peachy.

"Thanks." Dylan didn't mean to sound as terse as he knew he had.

Trace gave Dylan a long hard look. "Call me if you need anything," Trace said then walked out the door.

Dylan blew out his breath as he turned back to his phone.

He pulled up his contacts and found her name. *Belle Hartford.* As far as he knew, she hadn't married, but there'd been spells where he hadn't checked in on her. For all he knew, she could have married and kept her maiden name. He could have pushed harder, looked deeper into her life, but somehow that hadn't seemed right.

Even though he knew he was stalling the inevitable by not calling Belle immediately, he reached into his back pocket. He grasped the postcard he'd forgotten about in his grief until Christie mentioned her own. It wasn't like him to forget something so important, but today had been like no other.

He pulled the postcard out of its baggie and stared at the picture of Main Street in Old Bisbee, a colorful location filled with history. He flipped the card over and set it on his desk. He stared at his name and the address to his ranch scrawled on the right and then the note on the left. Nate could have sent an email, but he'd handwritten the note.

Once again Dylan read it. Two things stood out. The first was *"Hey, remember when I served in Iraq?"*

The second thing that bothered Dylan was that Nate had signed it *"WYB."*

Dylan narrowed his gaze as he stared at the acronym he and Nate had used in school, back when they'd been young and had passed handwritten notes. *Watch your back.* That was long before the cell phones that kids now used to text each other.

What the hell did it all mean? Again, why would Nate write something so off, and why didn't he just leave a voicemail while Dylan was undercover, or send an email?

Unless Nate was worried someone would overhear the call or read his email.

Why hadn't Nate mailed the postcard? Maybe he hadn't had time. Yet he'd had time to mail Christie one.

Had he sent postcards to everyone in the CoS? Tom, Marta, and Leon hadn't mentioned it if they'd received anything. Of course they might have been too upset. Still, it seemed like an odd thing to not mention.

Dylan leaned back in his chair and stared through the open blinds to the window that looked out at the cubicles where support staff and some of the junior agents worked. The office was busy and it was almost like nothing had changed.

Over a year ago, the Jimenez Cartel had blown part of the DHS's ICE building all to hell. Agents and support staff had been killed in the blast. More agents had been murdered while protecting a witness who had been set to testify against one of the key heads of the cartel.

The Feds had come down hard on the cartel, seizing assets, arresting key individuals, and making their lives a living nightmare. Diego Montego Jimenez, El Demonio, was out of the picture now. The Demon was no more.

Diego's son, Alejandro, was also no longer a problem. Alejandro had been known as El Puño, The Fist, and the world was a better place without either one of them.

The remaining heads of the cartel had retreated, but no one was fooled. The Jimenez Cartel would be back in business, this time with Rodrigo Jimenez, El Verdugo, at the helm. It was only a matter of time before "the Executioner" would drive the cartel forward.

Dylan's gaze returned to the postcard and again he tried to make sense of it. Finally, he put it into the center drawer of his desk and locked it.

He picked up his phone again and held his finger over Belle's number. He pressed it and brought the phone to his ear.

CHAPTER 2

Belle Hartford tried to keep a smile on her face but let out a silent huff as she walked away from the upset patrons at table three. What a crappy day. Normally she didn't believe in dwelling on the negative, but today was an exception.

First her car wouldn't start and she'd had to call AAA. She'd had to buy a new battery, which she barely had the funds for now, without dipping into savings. She'd called the owner, Gerald, to let him know he'd have to open his wine bar/restaurant, D'Vine, himself. As usual, he'd been an ass.

She'd been in such a hurry to get to work that she'd gotten a speeding ticket, which she *really* couldn't afford. Even traffic school would be expensive.

Once she got to D'Vine, she'd learned that a prep cook had called in sick and a server had broken her leg. Belle hadn't been able to find anyone who could come in to take over their shifts.

And now table three. Just one more thing to pile onto all of the other problems that had come up at the restaurant since she'd walked in the door.

Belle's long ponytail tickled her neck as it swished across her back while she strode to the kitchen. She walked through the swinging doors and headed toward the head chef, Gustav. He was a rotund man who was easygoing when *not* in his element, which was lording over the restaurant's kitchen. Here he was hell to work with.

He barked orders to the prep cook then glanced at Belle. He narrowed his bushy brows, most likely reading her expression. "What is wrong?" he growled in a thick German accent.

She wasn't about to let the big man intimidate her. "The guests at table three are complaining that each meal tastes like it was covered with the contents of a bottle of salt."

Gustav flung out several German curse words and then some. Belle had been working with the chef for two months now, and even though she didn't know the language, she had a pretty good idea of what he'd said just from his hand gestures.

She'd had enough today and she didn't need to put up with Gustav's crap. Yet she didn't want him walking out on her either, something she'd had happen in the past. Managing a restaurant this size was like balancing on a high wire.

"Prepare new entrees for our guests." Belle tried not to let her impatience show. She didn't have the time or patience for a kitchen diva. "I don't know what happened or if they're complaining in hopes of a free meal or dessert. Just do it."

Gustav glared at her. "I will see to every step myself." He looked as if he was going to add more obscenities. Instead, he went to the computer and pulled up the meals he'd made for that table so he could prepare them again.

Her phone vibrated in the pocket of her favorite black slacks as she turned away from Gustav. She pulled the phone out and checked the display. It was an unfamiliar number with a southern Arizona area code. For a moment she thought about not answering—what if it was her stepfather? But she pushed that thought aside. He didn't have her number and he hadn't tried to contact her in twenty-three years. Why would he call now? He probably didn't even know she was alive.

Maybe it was someone in the CoS. Marta or Leon or Tom? Nate and Christie she had programmed into her phone. It wouldn't be Dylan. Definitely not Dylan. For all she knew it could be a solicitor or a political call. She'd had several of those from other states.

After the day she'd had so far, it would be nice to talk with one of her old friends, but which one could it be? She talked with Christie regularly and had talked with Nate a couple of times, but that was it.

She walked toward her office in the back as she pressed the answer icon and brought the phone to her ear. "Hello?"

"Hi, Belle." A male said her name and she stilled. The voice was deeper but as familiar to her as her dreams of him. "This is Dylan."

Dylan. It was Dylan. A sharp burst of pain shot through her chest at hearing his voice, and for a moment she couldn't speak. Couldn't think. "How did you get my number?" was the only thing that came to mind.

"I'm calling because I have bad news." He sounded tired.

Her heart started thumping. "What kind of bad news?"

He hesitated. "Nate's dead."

"Oh, God." Belle's skin went cold and all other thoughts left her mind as she tried to register what Dylan had just said. Almost robotically she walked into her office and closed the door behind her. "What happened?"

"He committed suicide this morning."

"Suicide?" The word gripped Belle's heart like a fist of ice. "Nate? I can't believe that."

"I was at the scene myself this morning." Dylan spoke gently. "He hung himself."

Belle leaned her back against the door and her legs didn't want to hold her up any more. She slid down the door until her butt hit the floor, her knees bent. She'd been emotionally off balance when she'd heard Dylan's voice, but now she felt numb to everything.

"Christie is making funeral arrangements and we'll have a memorial," Dylan said. Belle knew Christie always did better when she had a task to keep her busy. "She offered to call you, but Nate would have wanted me to."

A tear rolled down Belle's cheek as Nate's death started to hit her as real. "I'll drive to Bisbee tomorrow. I need to pull a few things together and then I'll hit the road."

"It's a long drive from Houston," Dylan said. "I can pick you up from the airport in Tucson if you'd rather fly."

For a moment she wondered how he knew she was in Houston, but figured Christie had given him the information.

"Finances are tight and I'll need a car to get around anyway." Belle would also need money for a hotel, which meant she would have to take cash out of her savings for that and gas. It was times like this she was grateful to have a hybrid car that got nearly fifty miles to the gallon. She did a quick mental calculation to figure out how many gallons it would take to make a drive that was a thousand miles one-way.

"It'll take me about fourteen or fifteen hours to get to Bisbee," Belle continued, "so I'll probably spend tomorrow night in Las Cruces, rather than driving straight through."

"That's good," Dylan said. "Safer to get a good night's sleep during a trip like that."

She swallowed past the giant lump in her throat that had formed when she'd heard of Nate's death. "Thank you for calling me, Dylan." She was surprised she managed to say his name without falling apart even more than she was already.

"It's good to hear your voice, Belle." The sincerity in his tone only made her ache more. "I wish it was under better circumstances."

"Me, too." She struggled to hold back sobs that she knew she couldn't restrain for much longer. "I'll see you at the funeral."

"See you." And then he was gone, the call disconnected.

Sobs broke free as Belle continued to sit with her back against the door while tears flowed down her cheeks and memories flooded her mind.

Nate had been such a great guy. What had happened to him that would make him want to take his own life?

The CoS had drifted apart over the years. In truth, Belle knew she had broken it irreparably when she'd run away from home. The group had stayed friends, but Christie had told Belle that it had never been the same. Christie had said that Dylan had changed, withdrawing from everyone in the CoS but Nate. According to Christie, Dylan's easy smile had vanished and he'd become more reserved.

What a shock it had been to hear Dylan's voice after all this time.

Belle hadn't forgiven herself for what she'd done to the CoS and Dylan, but she'd *had* to run. At that point in her life, she knew she had no choice. She couldn't take one more day of the abuse she'd faced at the hands of Harvey Driscoll, her stepfather. She was positive that if Dylan had found out, he would have ended up in prison for killing the bastard.

When she'd discovered that her stepfather had been instrumental in the murder of Dylan's father, it had pushed her over the edge. She'd known Dylan would never be able to look at her the same way, and it would have given him another reason to kill Harvey.

So she'd run. And she'd never gone back.

Over the years, as Internet child pornography had grown, she'd worried sometimes that the pictures and videos Harvey had taken of her would someday surface, but if they had, she had no knowledge of it.

With her husband's connections, Christie had tracked Belle down fifteen years ago. It had been a shock to hear from Christie, but she'd been insistent on rebuilding a friendship, and they had become close friends again. Every year Christie came out to Houston to visit Belle, most of the time with Salvatore. Christie's husband doted on his wife and liked to travel with her when business allowed.

An insistent knock came at the office door, startling Belle. She glanced at the time on her cell phone and saw that she'd been in her office a good half hour and it was the restaurant's busiest time of day.

"Just a minute," she called out as she pushed herself to her feet while wiping tears from her cheeks with the back of her hands.

"What the hell is going on, Belle?" Gerald shouted through the door.

Damn. The owner was not an easy man to be around and she did her best to avoid pissing him off.

She pocketed the phone, turned and opened the door, and faced the scowling man who, at five-six, was half an inch shorter than her. He was almost as big around as he was tall.

He glared at her. "Your makeup is a mess and your eyes are red."

She wiped below her eyes with her fingertips in an attempt to wipe away smudges. "I just learned a close friend of mine died."

"Pull yourself together and cry on your own time." He narrowed his gaze. "I have a restaurant to run. Get back to work. Now."

Her skin prickled. She had only worked for him for two months, but she'd grown to find he was a cold man. This, however, was beyond anything she'd expected. She regretted leaving the restaurant she had managed before this one. It had seemed like such a good opportunity at the time.

She straightened. "Give me five minutes to fix my makeup."

"Make it three." He started to turn away when she stopped him.

"I need to take off the rest of this week." She straightened as he slowly looked back at her. "I have to drive to Arizona for the services and the funeral. I'll be gone five days."

"You are needed here." His tone was icy.

"I'm needed there, too." Belle tried to keep her hands from clenching into fists. "I'm leaving tomorrow morning."

He gestured toward her desk. "If you plan on leaving, then you'd better pack up your things now."

She stared at him, unable to believe his ultimatum. "My friend just died."

"Your leaving isn't going to bring your friend back." He snarled the words. "So get your ass to work."

Belle turned and walked to the desk. She reached into the bottom drawer and pulled out her purse. She hadn't worked here long enough to accumulate anything.

She slung the purse over her shoulder and walked back to the shorter man. "You have my address. You can mail my final check directly to me."

His face turned a deep shade of red. "Don't even think about coming back."

She slipped past him and strode out the back door into the parking lot, letting the door slam shut behind her with a final heavy *thud*.

The fury burning through Belle twisted with her need to grieve for Nate. Damn Gerald. Now she was out of a job, and soon she'd be on her way out of town. She liked having a decent savings, but it wasn't going to last long with all that was hitting her at once. Not to mention she had a mortgage and car payment to make.

And then there was Dylan. He had called her himself.

Just the sound of his voice had brought back memories so sweet they were almost too painful to bear. All they had shared, all the plans they'd made…everything turned to dust.

She climbed into her red Prius and slammed that door, too. In moments she was headed to her house, thirty minutes away from the restaurant.

When she finally reached the subdivision, she pulled her car up to the community mailboxes and climbed out. Her box was lucky number thirteen. She jammed her key into the keyhole and opened the small door before digging out junk mail and bills then locking the door again. She flipped through the mail as she walked back to the car and stopped before she reached for the door handle.

A card with no return address was in the pile of mail. It was a postcard from Bisbee, a photo of the Copper Queen Hotel on the front. Her brow furrowed and she climbed into her car and shut the door behind her. She tossed the rest of the mail onto the passenger seat before focusing on the postcard.

She flipped it over. When she saw the untidy penmanship and started to read, she felt blood drain from her face.

> Belle,
>
> You've come a long way from that teenage girl who had to leave. You've done well, and I'm proud of you.
>
> I'll never forget when your big brown dog bit me on the ass. Don't let your past bite yours.
>
> Please be careful.
>
> Love,
>
> Nate

Belle sat and stared at the note, reading it over and over. Nate had written this, but now he was dead. It was like hearing from the beyond.

The odd thing was the incident he mentioned and the fact that he'd gotten it a little wrong. She'd always known Nate to have perfect recall, so this was strange. Her dog had been white, not brown.

Tears filled her eyes, blurring the words. Why would he send this postcard, then kill himself? Had it been his way of saying goodbye?

She set the postcard on the seat next to the pile of junk mail before driving the rest of the way down the street to her house. She pulled her car into her garage, lowered the door, and then grabbed her purse and all the mail before going into her home.

Inside, after she'd tossed aside her purse and discarded the junk mail, she stood in the middle of the kitchen and gripped Nate's postcard. She closed her eyes and took a deep cleansing breath.

Right now nothing mattered but going back to Bisbee and being with her old friends as they said goodbye to Nate.

Her mind jumped to what she had run away from as a teenager and she shuddered and opened her eyes. As far as she knew, Harvey, her abuser, was still in Bisbee.

A weight came crashing down on her. She'd been through years of counseling where she'd learned to accept that the sexual abuse had not been her fault. Her stepfather had shamed her and capitalized on her self-guilt to have her buy into her shame and take it into debasement.

Fear that the abuse would escalate had caused her to run. She swallowed past the painful tightness in her throat. For all she knew the bastard could have ended up killing her.

During her counseling sessions since, she'd been told she needed to face her abuser for closure. Now the perfect opportunity was waiting for her in Bisbee. Her hands shook and her heart palpitated. She didn't think she'd ever be able to face the man without killing him.

Belle guided the car along the highway, glad she was finally closing in on the Texas/New Mexico border. Not much longer and she'd make it to Las Cruces. She was exhausted from driving and very much looking forward to a hotel room with clean linens and hopefully a comfortable bed.

Truth was, she hated to drive, especially across desolate stretches of land, and there was a lot of that through Texas and New Mexico. It wouldn't be so bad once she entered Cochise County in the lower southeast corner of Arizona.

Driving gave her far too much time to think, and dwelling on things she couldn't change wasn't what she'd wanted to do. Thoughts of Nate, her stepfather, and Dylan continued to bombard her.

And Dylan being the one to call her—she hadn't been able to forget the sound of his voice and the way her body had reacted the moment she'd heard it.

She tried to think about good times. Their old hangout had been the Puma Den, a popular pizza joint in San Jose, a subdivision of Bisbee. The pizza place had been named after their high school's mascot, the puma. She smiled to herself as she remembered the seven of them crowded around a table eating garbage pizza, talking about school, sports, band, and anything else that might come up. Nate had always had to have anchovies, which she'd picked off her pieces.

Then there were the plans she and Dylan had made for the future…the things they would do and the places they would travel to. One of their favorite dreams was their honeymoon. They would go someplace with snow and cuddle up in a cabin in front of a fire. Snow was something they got little of in southern Arizona, and it had seemed so romantic when they were young.

Everything had been romantic until her life had fallen apart. Her throat ached. She had to stop thinking of Dylan in that way. It had been over long ago.

Belle checked her speed and saw that it had crept up too high. She put the car on cruise control as her thoughts remained on the Circle of Seven and Dylan.

The CoS had been an odd group, but they'd been together since their elementary days. What they had gone through together when they were young, thanks to Mr. Norton, had created a tight friendship that survived even the social complexities of junior high and high school. The seven of them were like *The Breakfast Club* in some ways.

During fourth grade at Greenway Elementary, Mr. Norton, the evilest of the evil teachers, had always had it in for them for one reason or another. Only God knew why. Mr. Norton had constantly sent the seven of them to the principal, who had been vile, too. Mr. Johnson had pulled down their underpants to expose their bare bottoms before paddling them. Now she knew it had been perverted and child abuse, but that was back when teachers and principals got away with it.

Mr. Johnson had drilled holes into the paddle so it hurt worse when it smacked their skin. After hitting them, he had made them sit together on the steps outside, during recess, their bottoms stinging and their cheeks burning with humiliation. The seven of them hadn't been allowed to move, but they had talked and talked when Mr. Johnson wasn't checking on them.

They began to call themselves the Circle of Seven and had forged a friendship that had withstood so much over time. Over the years, everything they went through individually also continued to strengthen the group.

At Bisbee Middle School the school mascot had been the Cobras, the colors purple and gold. When they'd graduated, they'd gone to Bisbee High and had become the Pumas with red and gray as their school colors.

Belle had been a cheerleader at BMS and BHS. Once she left Bisbee, she'd fallen into the restaurant business. Over the years, she'd worked her way up from bottle washer to making a decent living in restaurant management.

Christie had kept Belle updated on what everyone else was up to. Interestingly enough, only three of the original seven had children.

Tom had excelled in various high school organizations, as well as being class president and the class valedictorian. He'd divorced recently and had transferred from Tucson Medical Center to take a position at Copper Queen Hospital as a physician. He had joint custody of his son, but only had the boy in the summer because his ex still lived in Tucson.

Leon had been a football hero who now had a wife and three children, and they owned a water well drilling business. He lived a little ways from Bisbee, close to Sierra Vista.

Marta had played varsity basketball. These days she lived with her wife, Nancy, and their fraternal twin sons who had been conceived with donor sperm. Marta had been a stay at home mom with their boys.

Christie had played flute in the band, and had been quiet but popular. After marrying Salvatore, she started working in his office. They'd attempted to have children but they had been unable to get pregnant.

Dylan was a cowboy and had worked on his father's ranch when he wasn't at school or spending time with the CoS. Now he was in federal law enforcement, and had never married. She swallowed and had to push thoughts of Dylan away because thinking about him was too painful. No one had ever made her feel the way Dylan had.

Nate had never had a thing for organized activities or labels. He'd driven a hot rod and had been a girl magnet. Even though he'd dated, he hadn't seemed to realize so many girls had a thing for him.

A smile touched Belle's lips as she thought about Nate as he had been then. Despite his outward appearance and the souped-up Charger he drove, he'd been the quietest of the group. He would interject comments and jokes when they were together that would crack up all of them. He might have been the least talkative, but he'd had an awesome sense of humor and he'd been something of a prankster. They'd always been able to count on him for a little levity.

Like the time when they'd seen their English teacher, Mr. Bishop, smoking pot off campus on the last day of school their freshman year. Marta and Christie were so against any kind of drugs that they'd been upset to see their favorite teacher with a joint.

Nate had cracked a joke, which had them all laughing, even Marta and Christie. They'd headed to the Puma Den, determined to put aside what they'd seen. Who were they to judge?

That one memory of Nate and the CoS shifted to a memory she'd hidden deep for so many years. She swallowed hard and gripped the steering wheel tight, unable to stop her mind from going back to that night.

After they'd left the pizza place, Belle and Dylan had taken off in his truck and had driven up to the Divide. It had been the most precious thing in her life, nearly wiping away the pain of the emotional and verbal abuse at the hands of her mother.

She'd lost her virginity to Dylan that night. It had been something beautiful that she'd held onto until she had ended up running away.

When her stepfather had begun to abuse her months later, at least he hadn't been able to take that part of her innocence.

One memory bled into another.

A tear rolled down her cheek as she remembered how her mother, Mary, had died from a drug overdose that summer, leaving Belle alone with her stepfather. One form of abuse had ended with her mother's death. But a far worse abuse had followed when her stepfather had come home drunk and forced himself on her not long after her mother's death.

She had taken her mother's place in her stepfather's bed whenever he dragged her into his bedroom. The shame and guilt had changed her forever. She had dropped out of cheerleading and had been withdrawn with her CoS friends. She had still hung out with them, still dated

Dylan, but she'd had to force herself to participate in conversations and struggled to smile moment by moment.

The emotions crashing down on her were overwhelming. The blare of a horn snapped her back to the present and she realized she'd started to drift into another lane. Heart thudding, she swerved back into the correct lane. She braked and pulled off the freeway, into the emergency lane, and parked on the side of the road.

Her breaths came hard and fast and she realized she was hyperventilating. She pressed the button for her emergency flashers and put her forehead against the steering wheel as she tried to slow her breathing.

When she finally regained her composure, she leaned back in her seat to take a few more moments to make sure she was calm enough to drive. After another five minutes she switched off the flashers, waited for traffic to clear, and pulled back onto the highway.

The one thing she knew was that going back to Bisbee was the second hardest thing she'd ever done. The first had been leaving.

CHAPTER 3

Rain fell from the sky like tears. Dylan slammed his truck door and shoved his hands in the pockets of his leather jacket. Drops hit his Stetson and rolled off the brim as he headed past five other vehicles, toward a small group gathered on a ridge in the Mule Mountains.

The clearing on the ridge had been one of the CoS's favorite places to hang out when they were in high school and needed some kind of escape.

Dylan couldn't help the churning in his mind or his gut as he trod over wet earth and past scraggly bushes and cacti.

Detective Jensen had called Dylan and confirmed his suspicions that the spatter on the baseboard in Nate's living room was blood. Not only was it blood, but according to DNA tests it belonged to Edmund Salcido, a suspected bookkeeper for the Jimenez Cartel. Edmund had been convicted embezzlement in the past, so they were fortunate to have his DNA in the database.

Dylan's boot slipped in mud as he closed in on the five figures. All wore jeans and jackets, a couple with raincoats. This was not a place or a time for formality. He almost smiled but didn't when he thought of how Nate would have laughed if they had dressed formally and in black.

CHEYENNE MCCRAY

His chest tightened when he let himself acknowledge that one of those standing on the ridge had to be Belle.

According to Jensen, the BPD had attempted to find Salcido, but individuals who knew the man hadn't seen him for days. Finding Salcido's blood and evidence of his possible disappearance had changed the game. Because of the man's ties to the cartel, DHS had taken over the case. DHS would still work closely with the BPD until potential ties to the cartel were confirmed.

Because of all of the questions in the air, the DHS had arranged to keep Nate's body. The autopsy showed nothing beyond Nate dying of asphyxiation; however, the police wouldn't release the body until the DHS was positive no foul play had been involved. Dylan's gut told him that holding onto Nate's body had been the right thing to do, even though it meant the funeral itself would be delayed.

DHS agents were currently tearing apart Nate's house, combing through it for clues to a suspected murder. If Dylan's own suspicions were correct, they'd be looking for proof of two murders that would suggest Nate had *not* committed suicide. If it weren't for Nate's memorial, Dylan would be at Nate's house now conducting his own investigation.

Dylan would have bet anything that Nate hadn't taken his own life. Dylan thought once again of the strange note Nate had scribbled to him but hadn't mailed. Maybe he hadn't had time to mail the postcard and had stuck it in the book at the last minute to hide it. But why would he need to hide it?

When Dylan reached the group, everyone faced him. Christie was the closest, so his gaze met hers first. Her eyes were red, mascara smudged beneath her eyes, her freckles bright against her pale skin, her long red hair drenched.

"Hi, Dylan." Her voice trembled as she went to him and slid her arms around his waist.

He hugged her, then went to each of the remaining friends in the broken circle.

Tom's expression was sorrowful as he gave Dylan a quick hug. "Good to see you."

Marta's throat worked when Dylan moved to her. "I'm sorry it's for something like this," she said before she hugged him.

Leon gave Dylan a quick hug and a slap on the back before releasing him. "We should be getting together now *with* Nate, not at his damned memorial."

Dylan stepped back and his gaze finally met Belle's, and it was like a punch to his gut. She was older now and had grown into a mature beauty. Her expression was stricken, her wide violet eyes showing the depth of her grief. She'd pulled her dark hair away from her face and her pale skin glistened in the rain. The urge to hold her, to comfort her was strong, but it felt awkward, like he had no idea what to do.

She held a small bouquet of daisies, which trembled, telling him she was shaking. "Hi, Dylan." Her voice was as low and sweet as it had been on the phone, just as he remembered it being when they were young.

"Hi, Belle." It was all he could think to say in return as he went to her.

She lowered her hands to her sides, holding the daisy stems in one fist. When he brought her into his arms and hugged her, she hugged him in return. A knife of pain cut through his heart. Her scent was so familiar, the feel of her body natural against his. She sobbed close to his ear and he gave her a tight squeeze before releasing her.

It took a moment before he could tear his gaze from hers. He moved aside to look at the ridge in front of them. For a long time they were all quiet, the rain pattering on the wet earth and making plopping sounds when they hit puddles that had formed on the ridge.

"We should each say something." He turned his gaze on Christie, who was now across from him.

She cleared her throat. "One of my favorite memories of Nate was the time he stood up for me in elementary school. Three older boys were bullying me and Nate tore into them. He came out of it with a bloody nose and a black eye, but none of the other boys were standing."

"I remember that." Dylan couldn't help a little smile. "When we heard what happened, it was one of the things that sealed the Circle."

"Nate was always rescuing animals and people." Belle's smile was soft as Dylan looked at her. "He had a good heart."

"G.I. Joe was a rescue." Dylan glanced at Leon. "Thanks for giving him a good home."

"It's only been a couple of days, but Joe is already becoming part of the family." Leon sounded a little choked up. "The kids love him."

Marta brushed a tear from her eyes. "Few people knew he was behind some of the best practical jokes."

The corner of Tom's mouth curved. "Most of the time the only people who knew were the six of us."

Leon cupped his palms in front of his chest in a gesture that indicated extra-large breasts. "How about junior high, when Nate stole Misty Brubaker's bra out of her gym bag when she was showering after pom-pom practice?"

Tom held up his hand as if placing something up high. His medical alert bracelet for his blood disorder glinted as he moved his wrist. "Not only did Nate steal Misty's bra, but he pinned it above Mr. Bishop's chalkboard the next morning."

Belle shook her head. "She was mortified."

"Damn, but that girl had big ones for a thirteen-year-old." Dylan grinned.

Marta rolled her eyes. "Boys."

"Nate had such a crush on Misty." Christie sniffled but smiled. "Even though she was one of the most stuck-up, snotty girls in school."

"He never could settle for one girl, though," Marta said.

"Or one woman." Dylan rocked back on his heels. "Nate didn't have it in him to settle down."

Belle's gaze looked as if she was seeing something no one else could. "Maybe that was for the best."

Christie looked thoughtful. "But it's possible a family would have given him a reason to live."

Dylan wanted to say that he suspected Nate hadn't killed himself, and instead he'd been murdered. But now was not the time to bring that up. Later would be soon enough.

They spent a good thirty minutes reminiscing, breaking into laughter and smiles at the memories.

"Nate would have liked this." The flowers in Belle's hands trembled even as she smiled. Dylan wondered if the rain was chilling her even though he could tell she was wearing the raincoat over another coat and a cowl necked sweater. "As difficult as it is for us," she continued, "Nate would want us to smile."

Everyone nodded.

Belle moved along the line of friends, starting with Christie, handing each one a daisy until there were only two flowers left. When she got to Dylan and he reached out to take the daisy from her, their fingers brushed and their eyes met. It was a blow to his chest and his heart slammed against his ribcage.

She visibly swallowed and retreated back to her spot. A quiet pause filled the stillness for a long moment. The only thing that could be heard was the patter of rain on the ground.

Belle stepped close to the ridge and raised her flower. "I miss you, Nate, and I always will. I'm sorry I didn't keep in touch like I should have." She released the daisy and it dropped over the edge.

She returned to her place and Leon stepped forward. He said a few words before letting go of the flower.

Marta, Tom, and Christie followed, each of them saying his or her own goodbye.

Dylan was last. "I should have been there for you, buddy." He felt an ache behind his eyes. "I should have been there." Lower, so that the others weren't likely to hear, he added, "I'll be there for them. I won't let the circle break."

He let the flower go and watched it disappear.

When he turned back to the group, each of them had their gazes on him, as if waiting for him to tell them what to do next.

"Let's go to the Den." He tugged down the brim of his Stetson. "And have garbage pizza in Nate's honor."

Every one of them smiled, as if in memory of the times they'd gone to the Den as a group.

"Let's get going." Leon put his hand to his stomach. "I'm starving."

Marta shook her head as they all turned back toward the vehicles. "You were always starving."

He grinned. "Playing football was hard work."

She looked amused. "What's your excuse now?"

His grin broadened. "Drilling water wells is hard work."

"Uh-huh." Their shoulders brushed as they neared the cars. "You just like to eat."

Dylan listened to the banter between Marta and Leon, as well as talk between Tom and Christie. Dylan was used to being aware of everything around him, including more than one conversation at a time.

Belle, however, was quiet and clearly doing her best not to meet his gaze.

Seeing her again, holding her again, had thrown him off balance. She was the only female who'd ever tied him in knots. She'd been doing that since she was a girl, and had continued to do so as she matured into a young woman. His throat tightened as he realized it was happening all over again.

He'd thought he'd gotten over her. He'd been so damned wrong.

They each climbed into their separate vehicles, and one-by-one took the winding dirt road down the side of the mountain. Dylan steered his truck over the rocky road as he followed Belle, who drove a red Prius. She went behind Tom, who was in a black Honda CR-V SUV. Dylan wondered if Belle would try to disappear again and never show up at the Den.

An ache gripped his chest as he remembered how they'd waited for her at the pizza place one night and she'd never shown up.

They'd never seen her again.

God, how he'd searched for her. Everyone in the CoS had been devastated by her disappearance.

Her ass of a stepfather had been worthless, but the police had put out alerts and had looked for Belle for weeks. Dylan had been so afraid she'd been kidnapped or murdered.

That was until he'd gone to their place on the Divide. He'd avoided it because he'd felt it would be too painful to go there. When he finally did, he found the letter along with the silver bracelet he'd given her for her sixteenth birthday. They were hidden in a pile of boulders where they used to sit and watch the stars. He'd seen a glint of metal from the bracelet in the moonlight and that was how he had found it and the note.

"I'm so sorry, Dylan," the note had read. *"Please understand I had to leave and don't look for me. Let the CoS know I'm okay, but don't tell anyone else. I will always love you, Belle."*

All hope had left him that night as he'd gripped the note and the bracelet. He'd been grateful that she hadn't been kidnapped, but he'd known his shattered heart could never be put back together again.

Today he didn't intend to let that little red car out of his sight.

The five vehicles were a small funeral procession as they made their way around what had been known to locals as the traffic circle, but signs now referred to it as a roundabout. They continued on until they reached the Puma Den in the San Jose subdivision.

When they'd parked and exited their vehicles, Dylan realized it had stopped raining. He shrugged out of his leather jacket and hung it up in the back of his king cab. His T-shirt, as well as the overshirt he wore to cover his Browning 9mm, were dry, but his jeans were damp from the rain.

Prickles traveled the length of Dylan's spine. He cut his gaze in the direction of the highway. An older white Buick crept along the highway, in front of the pizza place. The car was headed west and Dylan stood on the north side of the road. Past the empty passenger side, he saw the driver, a dark figure hunched in the driver's seat.

The Buick suddenly sped up and shot down the highway. Dylan managed to catch the first three letters of the license plate number from where he was standing.

It might have been nothing, but his spine continued to tingle. He had automatically memorized everything, and he pulled out his phone. He entered the information into the database application and in moments a name and address popped up for a white Buick, along with the rest of the license plate number. Jorge Perez. Dylan didn't recognize the individual's name, but he saved the information for later.

When he finished, he looked to see that the others had shed their coats, too, and waited for Dylan to reach them before they walked into the pizza joint.

The place was formerly a rundown building that had gone through several changes of ownership. It had only recently been remodeled and rechristened the Puma Den, the same name it had been called when they'd been in high school, when it had been the local teenage hangout.

The interior wasn't a lot different. It was still casual with plain white walls, and the menu consisted of one thing: pizza. Just about any traditional topping possible could be ordered. While the others found an empty table with bench seats, Dylan and Tom went to the front to order two pizzas with everything on them. They included anchovies on one-half of one in honor of Nate, who'd loved the small fish on his slices.

Dylan and Tom joined the table where the other four in their group sat. Dylan placed his Stetson beside him on the bench seat. He sat directly across from Belle who was avoiding his gaze.

He looked at her, drinking in the sight of the woman who had grown from the girl he had loved so much that it had been a physical pain in his chest when she'd left. Gut wrenching pain that hadn't gone away for years. Maybe it had never gone away.

While they waited for the pizzas to be made and delivered to their table, they took turns talking about what they'd done since they'd last seen each other. The sadness and pain of Nate's death hung over them, regardless of the fact that they'd discussed how Nate would dislike them dwelling on his death.

The pizzas were delivered in good time, and their conversation continued.

Dylan couldn't stop watching Belle. It was like a magnet kept drawing his gaze to her. He wanted to reach out and touch her. He wanted to take her into his arms and hold her tightly to him.

God, but she was beautiful. She had on little makeup and had pulled her damp hair away from her face into a ponytail. Her cheekbones seemed more pronounced and her eyes somehow bigger. He'd always loved the color of her eyes, a blue that was almost a shade of violet, like Elizabeth Taylor's had been.

When it came down to Dylan's and Belle's turns to talk, they looked at each other at the same time. A world of unspoken communication traveled between them. He could see how much she didn't want to talk about her past, but he wanted to know all of what had happened with her since she'd left.

Her fair cheeks reddened slightly, but she spoke clearly and calmly. "Why don't you go next, Dylan?"

He wanted to tell her no, that he had to hear her story first. Instead, he set his third slice of pizza on the plate in front of him. "After finishing high school I went to Arizona State and got my BS from the School of Criminology and Criminal Justice."

Belle didn't take her gaze from his as he spoke. Despite his training and natural instincts, everything around him seemed to slip away, and it was like he and Belle were the only two sitting at the table.

He pushed his plate away and rested his forearms on the table. "I was recruited by the federal government right out of college, and the next thing I knew I was training at FLETC and have been working in one branch or another ever since."

"Isn't that the Federal Law Enforcement Training Center?" she asked. He nodded, surprised she knew what FLETC was. "Christie said you work for the ICE division of the Department of Homeland Security now."

"I've worked for DHS ever since it was created in response to 9/11." For a long time his own personal vendetta of avenging his father's death had been pushed aside in his fury over the murders of over three thousand innocent Americans by the Islamic terrorist group, al-Qaeda. "I didn't return to this area until 2011, after Osama bin Laden was finally taken out."

"And then what?" Belle looked and spoke in a way that told him she truly wanted to know. Yet at the same time the guilt she still felt in leaving was in her expression.

"I transferred to Douglas's ICE office when a position opened." He'd been after his father's murderers ever since, hitting one dead end after another. All he knew was that Ben Curtis's death was related to the Jimenez Cartel. Now that he was back and had the resources, it had been his mission to do everything he could do to take down the cartel.

Belle seemed to realize he didn't want to go into why he'd come back. No doubt she knew why. "How are Julie and Aspen?" The depth of caring she'd had for his mother and brother was clear in her voice. Belle had been close with his entire family.

Thoughts of those days brought a lump to his throat as more memories poured through him. He could see in her expression that she was experiencing the same thing.

Dylan held Belle's gaze. "Mom remarried a couple of years ago to a rancher named Bill Petersen and they live in the valley. He's a good guy."

"I'm so happy to hear that." Belle's smile was genuine. "And Aspen? Did he stay with Sally?"

"They broke up not long after you left." Just saying the words hurt. *After you left.* He cleared his throat. "Aspen is doing well and works in Southern California for CBP." When she looked like she wasn't sure what CBP was, he added, "U.S. Customs and Border Protection."

Belle tilted her head to the side. "Does he get back to Bisbee often?"

"Every month or two." Dylan's younger brother had graduated with the same degree and had trained at FLETC, too. "He's been talking about transferring back here if something opens up."

Dylan didn't give Belle a chance to ask him another question. Just as her lips parted, he shot her the question he'd wanted to ask for years. "What happened to you, Belle? Why did you leave?"

Chapter 4

Belle's skin prickled as everyone at the table went completely silent and looked at her. She glanced down at the half-eaten slice of pizza on her plate before raising her eyes to meet everyone's gaze.

"I can't tell you why I left." Belle glanced from one friend to the next. "I will tell you that it was bad, but I just can't talk about it."

From Dylan's harsh expression she could see he wanted to shout something like, "Bullshit." She wanted to reach out to him, to hold his hands, to tell him how very sorry she was. She wanted to stroke the line of his jaw and somehow take away the tension.

She pressed on. "I do want to say I'm so sorry for all the worry I caused you all. I never meant to do that. To be honest, it wasn't well-planned, but once I realized I had to go, I had to get out of there."

"Your stepfather." The words shot out of Christie's mouth, startling Belle. "Harvey must have done something. He abused you."

Belle's face heated as she looked away. She knew the moment she did it that it had been a mistake.

"What did that sonofabitch do to you?" The growl in Dylan's voice caused Belle to jump.

She swallowed and looked at the stricken expressions on her friends' faces. For a long time she couldn't speak. Everyone remained quiet until she finally got the words out. "Harvey started physically and sexually abusing me after my mother died. Day by day the abuse escalated."

"Why didn't you say anything?" Christie's eyes were filled with pain for Belle. "We would have done something."

"I would have killed the bastard." Dylan's expression was thunderous. "Hell, he's probably around. I can still do it."

"Don't you see?" Belle gave him a pleading look. "That's why I didn't tell you. I didn't want you to end up in prison. In my mind the only thing I could do was run to escape the abuse." She reached out and put her hand over Dylan's. "Promise me you won't go after him."

A jolt went through her at touching him this way for the first time in so many years. Something strong and tangible, warm and electric traveled between them and she felt the heat of his fury as well as the depth of his caring.

By the flash of recognition in his eyes, she knew he'd felt it, too. She searched his gaze, looking into his familiar eyes. Familiar, yet she could see the changes in him that made his expression harder and tougher than it had been when they were young. Had she done this to him? Or had something else turned him into a hard man?

"I can't promise anything, Belle." Dylan's voice sounded raw with anger, his hand tense beneath hers. "That bastard hurt you in one of the worst ways imaginable. He deserves to pay."

"He does…" Belle shook her head. "But that isn't the way to do it." Trying to get him to understand how deeply she felt about this, she shifted her hand so that she could squeeze his. "Please."

Dylan looked as stubborn as she remembered him to be. He didn't answer. But through the connection of their hands, she felt something stirring between them, like he would take her in his arms and hold her if no one else was around. He gripped her hand tighter and she saw in his eyes the light of recognition of what she was feeling.

Christie slipped off her end of the seat and went to Belle's side and eased onto the bench beside her. Christie rested her head on Belle's shoulder and put her arm around her. "We're all here for you." Christie raised her head. "We always will be."

"Thank you." Belle looked from one friend to the next, her gaze stopping to rest on Dylan's. "All of you."

Needing to change the subject, her mind flitted back to Nate. The thought of the postcard she'd received from him made her furrow her brows as a wave of sadness swept over her.

"What's wrong?" As she hugged Belle, Christie seemed clearly in tune with Belle's emotions.

"Nate sent me a postcard." She looked around the table. "I got it the day he died."

The reaction that went around the table was almost electrified.

Christie's eyes widened. "I received a postcard from him, too."

"Got one yesterday." Leon was frowning. "It was postmarked several days ago but I hadn't gone through my mail for a week."

Marta started digging in her purse. "I picked up my mail from the post office today." She pulled out a colorful postcard of B Mountain—also known as Chihuahua Hill. The mountain's giant letter B was made of painted white rocks. "This is from Nate."

"I got one, too," Tom said. "It had the Bisbee Mining and Historical Museum on the front and an odd message on the back."

Belle's eyes widened as she looked from one friend to another. "We all received postcards?" She looked at Dylan who hadn't said anything. "Did you?"

Dylan nodded slowly. "I found it in his home office when I was conducting a search. He wrote a note but never mailed it."

"Why would he write all of us notes on postcards?" Christie looked puzzled.

Leon's frown deepened. "Unless he was saying goodbye in his own way."

"Mine was a little strange, too." Belle looked at Marta who was staring at her postcard. "It was not like a goodbye note at all."

The others in the group nodded and indicated their cards also had something odd about them.

Marta pushed aside her paper plate, wiped the table with a napkin, then laid the postcard on the tabletop. She read the note aloud.

> *Marta,*
>
> *Been a while since we've had a chance to sit down and talk. Hope your wife is doing well and your kids are keeping out of trouble. Although the CoS never did!*
>
> *Remember Lindy and the chalkboard incident? One of these days I should apologize. You think? Nah. That's one for the memories.*
>
> *Stay strong.*
>
> *Love,*
>
> *Nate*

All six of them looked at each other.

Tom shook his head. "Even I know it was Misty and not Lindy."

Dylan said quietly, "Do each of you have your postcard here?"

Belle shook her head. "I have mine in my hotel room."

Tom's was in his office at the hospital, Leon's was at home, and Christie had left hers in her other purse. Marta was the only one with her postcard from Nate on hand, other than Dylan, who didn't show his.

"I'd like to borrow all of the postcards." Dylan looked to each one of them. "I think he was trying to tell us something, and I'd like to figure out what that something is. I'll return all of the postcards after they've been examined. I'll let you know if I find any insights into whatever pain made Nate kill himself."

Belle narrowed her gaze. "You don't really think his death was a suicide."

Dylan hesitated, wondering if affirming that belief was the right thing to do. Then he shook his head. "Even though it's a presumed suicide, there will still be a thorough investigation, and I'll need to see the postcards."

Tom filled the silence that followed Dylan's statement. "I've thought from the beginning that it just didn't ring true that Nate would kill himself. It went against his survivor's nature. And that's what Nate was. A survivor."

Murmurs of agreement traveled around the table.

"So that's why they postponed releasing his body for the funeral," Leon said.

"In some ways this makes me feel better, that he may not have taken his life." Marta handed her postcard to Dylan. "In other ways it makes me concerned, not to mention angry. Very angry."

Dylan was looking pretty pissed off too, as he took the card with his free hand. "I'd like to meet with each one of you and get your postcards and your thoughts on possible interpretations of what Nate wrote to you."

Everyone agreed, and he made sure he had each person's mobile number in his phone. Dylan thanked them. "I need to get to the office. I've got some things to take care of."

He focused on Belle, his hand still holding hers. As their gazes remained locked, her skin heated. Every time she looked at him she felt so many emotions, from the memory of the love she'd had for him to regret and guilt.

"Can I talk with you for a moment?" His gaze hadn't left hers. "Privately."

She didn't want to be alone with Dylan, too afraid of what he might say to her, or that she might even break down, but she nodded. She owed him that. He squeezed her hand and then released her before they got up from the table.

"I'll be right back," she told the others.

He picked up his Stetson, said his goodbyes, and then she followed him.

They passed through a crowd of noisy teenagers to the front door of the Den. She'd been so preoccupied with everything her friends had been talking about that she hadn't noticed the place filling up. He held open the door and she stepped past him into the coolness of the outdoors.

Heavy dark clouds moved overhead, looking as if they were ready to release more rain at any moment. He settled his hat on his head and she wrapped her arms around herself, the cowl neck sweater not fully protecting her from the cold.

"Let's sit in my truck." Dylan indicated the big black truck he'd driven earlier. "I'll turn on the heater and we can warm up."

She walked at his side to the truck. He unlocked it and helped her into the passenger seat, his touch burning her skin through her sweater. Her teeth chattered and her arms trembled as he went around to the driver's side. She knew her trembling was not entirely from the cold.

After he was inside, his hat set on the back seat and door closed, he started the truck and turned up the heater. She shivered again as he shifted in his seat to face her. She had to force herself to meet his gaze.

He looked so different, yet the boy was behind the tough-looking man he'd become. The stubble on his jaw made him look rugged and she couldn't believe how big and muscular he was now. She had the urge to touch him, to run her hands over his broad shoulders, down to his massive biceps that looked harder than rocks. She wanted to feel the play of muscles beneath her palms as she rested them on his chest, and let her fingers slide down to his abs.

Their gazes met. Maybe she should have been embarrassed for staring at him so blatantly, but at one time they'd been more than intimate and had explored each other's bodies until they had no secrets.

Not until she started to have secrets that she'd had to keep from him.

"I don't like it." He rested his right arm on the steering wheel. "But I can understand why you felt you needed to leave. What I don't understand is why you didn't tell me. I would have made sure you didn't have to run. I would have kept you safe."

She looked at her hands in her lap. The cab was warming and her teeth no longer chattered. When she met his gaze again, she let out her breath. "Please understand. I was a teenager and all I could think about was escaping my stepfather and keeping you out of jail. Tell me you wouldn't have killed him if you knew, Dylan."

He studied her before staring out the front windshield where raindrops started to hit the surface, rolling down and leaving long trails. She studied the profile of the man she'd been in love with so long ago. His features were now somehow harsher. Somewhere beneath that intensity, she knew there was a gentleness that was now hidden from her. She wanted to trail her fingers along his stubbled jaw and force him to look at her. Yes, he'd filled out in his maturity but beneath that was still the boy with the broken heart.

When he looked back to her, the pain in his eyes nearly shattered her heart again. "I don't think you'll ever know how bad things were after you left." His voice was gravelly. "Nothing was ever the same."

"I'm so sorry." She wanted to reach out and hug him to her, but she kept still, her hands in her lap. "I wish I could, but I can't change what happened. It was the choice I had to make and it was a long time ago."

His jaw tightened. "I do need to get back to work, but we have a lot to talk about. Where are you staying?"

She hesitated. "The Copper Queen."

"Promise me you won't leave until we talk." His gaze held her and she couldn't look away. "If you do leave, this time I will come after you, and I won't stop until you talk with me. I promise you that *will* happen."

Her lips parted as a protest rose up inside her, but then she nodded. "You have my number." She let out her breath. "I still need to give you the postcard Nate sent to me that I left in my luggage at the hotel." She felt a different heat shoot through her and her skin burned at the thought that Nate could have been murdered. "Call me when you can."

Before he could get out to go around the truck and open her door, a gentlemanly thing he'd always done, she hurried to open the door herself. She jumped out of the truck, shut the door behind her, and jogged through the gently falling rain to the front door of the Den. She glanced over her shoulder to see him watching her, and then she slipped into the restaurant and let the door close behind her.

After Belle disappeared back into the Den, Dylan stared at the highway. He'd seen the white Buick drive by again, just a few moments ago, but he hadn't wanted to interrupt Belle. He had the car's information and he'd go from there. This time he noticed some damage to the front fender on the driver's side.

He checked his phone. He kept it on vibrate and had ignored the vibrations when he'd been at their private memorial for Nate and while he and the other remaining members of the CoS were together in the Den. Interruptions could wait as far as he was concerned.

When he looked at his phone, he saw on the screen that he'd missed two calls and a text message from Trace. In the message, Trace told Dylan to get his ass down to Nate's home.

Dylan threw his truck into gear, and gravel spun beneath his tires in the parking lot. He drove on Highway 92, through San Jose, and on past Tin Town and Galena before going around the traffic circle to Saginaw.

During the drive from the Den, he couldn't get Belle off his mind. So many emotions went through him that it was like a fist grabbed his heart and squeezed. Seeing her again had brought back memory after memory—his love for her, how he'd been shattered to his core when she'd disappeared, the relief he'd felt to know she was alive, and the pain that had engulfed him when she'd left him.

Learning that her stepfather had sexually abused her had the potential to put Dylan in a killing rage. It was all he could do to stop himself from going to Harvey Driscoll's place this very moment and putting the sonofabitch out of everyone's misery. Dylan knew exactly how to make it look like self-defense or even a random murder. Over the years he'd learned any number of ways to kill someone and get away with it. He never had, but this was one time he wasn't above doing it.

He dragged his hand down his face, trying to regain his self-control. As much as he wanted to face Harvey, he needed to be in on the investigation into Nate's death.

When he reached Nate's house, he parked and exited his vehicle. He headed through the gate and up the sidewalk, but paused as he watched DHS agents walking out of the house, carrying Nate's computer and related electronics.

As much as he hoped there was no evidence that Nate was involved in any illegal activities, Dylan did want something that could tell him why his friend ended up dead. He was certain it hadn't been suicide and he was going to exhaust every possible resource in proving that belief.

What had Nate gotten himself in the middle of?

"Dylan." Trace Davidson's voice drew Dylan's attention to the tall man standing on Nate's front porch. "Don't you answer your damned phone?"

Dylan strode toward Trace. "What have you got?"

Trace adjusted his western hat while he waited until Dylan had climbed the steps. "Your suspicion that this was a cleanup job appears to be right on the mark."

"What did you find?" Dylan walked through the front door. This time he didn't take off his Stetson. It wasn't like he was walking into his friend's home this time. It was a full-out investigation.

Trace stepped into the house behind Dylan. "Whoever did the cleanup must have been in a real hurry and did a piss-poor job of getting everything." Trace gestured to the couch in front of the location where Dylan had found the blood spatter. "Forensics sprayed luminol on the couch, and sure enough they found a spray of blood. Whoever did the cleanup should have taken the couch with them."

Dylan walked up to the piece of furniture. "It's possible they didn't have transportation big enough or the time to do it."

"There's a good chance they planned to come back for it." Trace nodded toward the wall behind the couch. "If there was blood on the wall, they did a pretty good job of cleaning it up with oxygenated bleach before painting it."

"And they replaced the carpet that could have been soaked with blood." Dylan looked down at the cheap carpeting. "Yeah, I'd bet you're right that they were coming back. This carpet needs to be pulled up in case any blood made it through to the padding."

Trace glanced at the forensics team. "That's next, after they finish up with what they're doing now."

Dylan studied the scene. "They probably didn't expect Nate's body to be found so soon." He said it more to himself than to Trace.

Trace cocked his head. "You seem pretty damned certain that Nate's death wasn't a suicide."

Dylan folded his arms across his chest. "I am."

Trace raised an eyebrow. "Do you want to share why you've come to that conclusion?"

Dylan hesitated and shifted his stance. "From elementary to high school, Nate and I hung out with five other kids." Dylan thought about the old friends he'd just left and the one big hole now in the group. "We called ourselves the Circle of Seven. We've drifted apart over the years, but Nate and I stayed tight."

Trace motioned for Dylan to continue.

"Nate wrote each of us postcards before he died." Dylan shook his head. "He apparently mailed them at different times. For some reason mine was never mailed."

Trace frowned, but before he could question him, Dylan continued. "I found my card in his home office the day he died. It was hidden in a book but addressed to me. The card is in my office now."

"All right." Trace hooked his thumbs in the pockets of his Wranglers. "So you took evidence from the scene. What's on the postcards?"

"It wasn't evidence at the time." Dylan knew he was talking semantics. "I've only read two of them—mine and one of the others—and they were both odd." Dylan looked around the room that looked like it had been worked over well by a forensics team. "According to everyone who received a card, the one they got from Nate had something odd about it."

Trace looked thoughtful. "Some kind of code?"

"I don't know." Dylan pushed up the brim of his hat as his mind turned over the problem. "I need to see all of the cards. After I finish up a few things here and at the office, I'm going to gather up the other four and examine them along with the two I have."

"If you need any help, let me know." Trace said in his slow drawl as he eyed Dylan. "And if you feel like you're too close to the case, I can take over the investigation."

"I need to handle this one." A fire burned behind Dylan's words. "I am going to find out what happened and why. And who the hell is responsible for Nate's death." One thought seared his mind that he kept to himself.

And then I'm going to make them pay.

CHAPTER 5

Salvatore Reyes sat at the desk in his home office, going over paperwork and writing in a ledger that he hadn't had a chance to get to until now. He had to finish erasing money trails to accounts he'd set up for the Jimenez Cartel in various tax havens. He would reintegrate the money into the market by buying and selling valuable classic cars and real estate to create legal profits. He was good at it and was paid well.

His cousin, Rodrigo Jimenez, ran the cartel now that Diego was gone. Rodrigo was known as El Verdugo, the Executioner. He was good to his cousins, like Salvatore, but was not someone to fuck with even if you were related to him.

Salvatore spent some time taking care of business until his stomach growled. He glanced at his watch. Yes, it was nearly dinnertime. Christie was good at having dinner on the table in a timely manner, although since the death of her "friend" she hadn't been on schedule as she normally would have been.

The thought sent a twinge of irritation through him, like an annoying itch. He felt it every time the "Circle" was mentioned.

He opened the very expensive and rare cherry wood humidor that sat on his desk. He liked to collect rare and beautiful things. He pushed aside the Cuban cigars and removed a special key that was beneath the pile.

When he had the key, he had to kneel, reach beneath his desk, and run the key along the side of a floorboard that was too small to put a finger in. He found a small switch with the key that he used to press the button, and the hinged door clicked and rose. He took the key and unlocked a square door. The door swung up to reveal a floor safe that Christie was unaware of. No one knew about it with the exception of the contractor, one of his many cousins, who had installed it, among other things, for Salvatore. Not even another cousin, the one who helped manage his offshore accounts, had any knowledge of the safe.

Salvatore's wife was a part of his collection of beauty. Their wedding day had been one of the most satisfying times in his life because it was then that he had collected her. He punched in the numbers for their wedding date on the safe's entry pad. The lock clicked. He opened the safe that was filled with over a million in cash along with several passports with fake identities for both himself and his wife.

Of course Christie knew nothing of the money or the IDs, much less the millions he kept in the offshore accounts. He was primed for any circumstances that might arise. He believed in being fully prepared in all ways.

Salvatore leaned over the safe and put away his paperwork, including the handwritten ledger he'd been making notes in. He tucked it all next to several other notebooks. Not all of the ledgers were his, but every one of them held damning information. He should destroy the ones he'd recently acquired and soon, he just had to do it himself and he hadn't had the time. All was secure here with no chance of anyone finding what he kept safe, so he wasn't too concerned about them.

After everything was where it belonged, he secured the safe, the door, and the hinged floorboards. He got to his feet and paused a moment, thinking of things that still needed to be done as he pushed his chair back in its place at the desk.

He left his office, closed and locked the metal door behind him and then strode through his home in the Terraces that was filled with the finer things in life. If he didn't need to be in Bisbee for his line of work, he would take his wife someplace far more suitable for a man of his means. Eventually he would buy an estate in Mexico, but now he was needed here for business.

Smells of the dinner his wife was cooking warmed him. Some kind of meat and tortillas, he guessed. Long ago he had taught her how to prepare his favorites as his mom had done when he was growing up.

He smiled as he stepped into the doorway of his kitchen and slipped his hands in the pockets of his black slacks. He studied his petite and beautiful wife, who was busy at the stove cooking dinner. He loved seeing Christie so domesticated. He would keep her barefoot and pregnant with a dozen kids if she could have children. Instead, he settled for keeping her busy at his office or with women's work around the home. He rarely let her out of his sight for long.

She didn't notice him as he took in the long ringlets of her red hair that fell down her back but swung forward as she leaned over a pot to stir it. With an annoyed swipe of her hand, she pushed the hair from her face so that it was over her shoulder. A couple of times she had told him she wanted to shorten her hair, but he refused to allow her to do more than have it trimmed. Her hair was far too beautiful to cut. She was a natural redhead, her hair vivid and unique. The smattering of freckles over the bridge of her nose added to her beauty.

The redness in her cheeks from working over the heat of the stove gave her a pretty blush. With her petite stature and delicate bone structure, and the pureness of her fair skin with its few freckles, she looked like a china doll with red hair that was such a unique shade that it was almost difficult to describe. Not a flame red, but not dark, somewhere in between.

When they were young he had coveted her, and then he had cherished her when they were finally together during their senior year in high school. It had taken him some time to win her over, but when he had, he'd made sure he did everything in the world to keep her. She had all she could desire, including a doting husband who continued to romance her, even after twenty years of marriage. He would do something special for her for their next anniversary. Perhaps he would take her to France or Italy, or maybe someplace more tropical such as Aruba or Costa Rica. Not Hawaii—it was too full of tourists.

The feeling of possessiveness within him was so strong his muscles ached with it. Christie was his and always would be. He would put her six feet into the ground before he would ever let her go.

She nibbled on her lower lip and he didn't like the sadness in her expression, but that had certainly been unavoidable. Eventually the emotional pain would pass and she would get over what he'd had to do. Of course she didn't know he was the one responsible, and she never would.

As if sensing his presence, she looked up from the pot and gave him a shadow of a smile. He didn't like that the smile didn't reach her eyes that were an unforgettable shade of blue.

"Dinner will be ready soon." She put the lid back on the pot. "We're having *al carbón*, homemade tortillas, and cilantro-lime rice."

"By the amazing smells, I know it is perfect, *mi mariposa*." His butterfly. He went to her and brought her into the circle of his arms, loving the feel of her warm body.

She rested her head against his shoulder and let out a soft sigh. "I want to have my friends over for dinner."

He stilled then drew away from her. "You know I do not want them here as guests."

"It would mean a lot to me." Tears brimmed in her eyes and a flash of anger made him want to slap her. "They like you."

He nearly sneered but tried to keep his expression free of anger. "Your friends excluded me from your little group. Do not think I have forgotten that." And damned if he'd let a federal agent into his home.

Christie let out her breath. "It wasn't that you or anyone else was excluded, it was just that the seven of us had been together since elementary school. We had a tight bond. Anyone would have felt like an outsider."

"No." Salvatore's voice was sharper than he'd intended. "It wasn't until Belle left that you would even look at me."

"Please." She placed her palm on his chest. "They mean so much to me."

Salvatore caught her hand in his. "When will dinner be ready?" He was making it clear to her that the subject was now closed.

Her lips trembled and she looked away. Again the desire to slap her was strong, but he'd never laid a hand on his wife. Once he started, he was afraid he might not stop, that it would be the first time of many. It was similar to the ways of a man who drank—just one drink led to another and another.

The thought of putting her in her place until her friends were out of her mind was far too tempting. He took in a deep, controlled breath and let it out again.

"I have something to attend to in my office." He had difficulty in keeping the hardness out of his tone. "Dinner will be on the table by the time I return." He glanced at his watch. "Fifteen minutes."

"Yes, Salvatore." She spoke quietly as she lifted the lid on the skillet filled with *al carbón* and didn't look at him.

He wanted to grab her by the shoulders and shake her. Instead, he turned and walked out of the kitchen, toward his home office.

When he reached his private space, he unlocked the metal door before relocking it behind him. He went straight to his desk and opened the cherry wood humidor and retrieved the key from beneath the cigars.

He knelt and opened the floorboard, the door beneath that, and then the safe. He looked down into it, directly at what he'd come for.

As tense and angry as Salvatore was, he needed a fix. Just a small one, but enough to curb his anger. From the corner of his safe, next to his handwritten ledgers, he withdrew the stash of cocaine he kept for trying moments like these. He snorted a couple of lines on top of his desk, breathing in the drug.

As he knelt again and started to put away the coke, he bumped his arm on the desk and spilled a good amount of the drug onto the floor beneath his desk. Irritation made him growl, his muscles tensing. He swept up the cocaine into a small envelope, closed it, and put it away with his supplies before locking everything up again. No sense in discarding perfectly good coke. He might be rich, but he didn't believe in waste.

He stood then put the key back in its place beneath the cigars in the humidor. He closed his eyes and breathed in and out a few moments until he relaxed and his mood improved significantly from the coke. He let the moments of irritation slide from him before unlocking his office door, closing and locking it behind him, and heading back to the kitchen and his beautiful wife.

CHAPTER 6

Belle's purse bumped against her hip as she walked through the glass double doors into Salvatore's office on Main Street in the Copper Queen Plaza in Historic Old Bisbee. Both practical and decorative copper items filled the room, and the furniture and bookcases were all walnut.

A walnut and glass display showcased several gorgeous pieces of famous Bisbee Blue turquoise along with valuable natural stones and crystals. The office exuded the kind of elegance that didn't exactly match the small town charm of the community.

"Hi, Belle." Christie smiled as she looked away from the large computer monitor on her desk.

A lone closed door was a few feet away from her. Behind that heavy walnut door must be Salvatore, where he conducted most of his business. According to Christie, he didn't like doing anything in the office in front of the glass double doors. "He's a very private man," Christie had said many times.

Belle usually liked being around her friend's husband, but it was true that he certainly was a private man.

"Ready for lunch?" Belle asked.

"Absolutely." Christie clicked a couple of keys on her computer before pushing back her chair and glancing at the closed door. "I forgot to tell Salvatore that I'm going out with you for a couple of hours." She worried her bottom lip with her teeth. "He told me he absolutely could not be disturbed, so I don't dare knock on his door."

Belle didn't like the concerned look on Christie's features and for a moment she wondered if the man abused her friend. Belle mentally shook her head—as an abuse survivor, she was fairly confident she knew what to look for. Salvatore had always treated Christie like a princess whenever Belle was around.

But what if there was more to it than that? What if he liked to intimidate Christie? Belle tried not to frown as she considered the fact that Salvatore could be an emotional and verbal abuser. She wasn't so positive she'd be able to read those signs.

"Maybe we should wait or reschedule." The last thing Belle wanted was for her friend to have to face any kind of domestic squabble.

"He'll be fine. I'll leave him a note that we're just going to the café downstairs." Christie leaned over and looked at the computer screen. "There are no appointments for the next two hours on our shared calendar, so he's not expecting anyone. He's a perfectionist when it comes to updating it." She scribbled on a square notepad, retreated from her desk, and pressed the hot pink sticky note against Salvatore's door, where it stayed. "I'll just lock up so no one walks in without me being here. He hates that."

Despite Christie's assurances, she had concern in her eyes and Belle felt uneasy. Belle forced a smile. "Why don't I go to the café and pick something up for all three of us?"

Christie hesitated. She looked at the pink note and back to Belle. "Would you mind?"

Belle kept the smile on her face. "Jot down what you'd like me to get and I'll be right back."

CHEYENNE MCCRAY

Christie's shoulders relaxed. She retrieved the note from the door, crumpled it and tossed it in a copper wastebasket. She grabbed another hot pink note and this time wrote down what she wanted Belle to get.

When she took the note from Christie, she saw "grilled chicken sandwich" and then "turkey club". The club sandwich had a detailed list of what to put on it and what to leave off. Christie pointed to it. "He's very particular about what goes on his sandwich."

Belle couldn't say she was surprised. Salvatore had been very "selective" the two times the three of them had gone out to dinner together in Houston. *Make that picky,* Belle thought. Having been in the restaurant business all of her adult life, picky customers weren't her favorite thing. But Salvatore did tip well.

The thoughts reminded her of her last night at the restaurant before she quit, and table three's complaints. Every trying thing that had happened that day already seemed so long ago. She had a hard time believing that she'd be returning to Houston with no job and only a savings account to live on. At least what money she had should tide her over, hopefully long enough to get a job.

"Don't worry about getting drinks." Christie returned to her seat "We have sodas and water here."

Belle nodded. "I'll be right back."

Christie gave her a little wave and Belle headed out the glass doors and downstairs to the Bisbee Coffee Company. The café was also in the Copper Queen Plaza but on the opposite side of the large building from Salvatore's office. She didn't rush, not in a big hurry to get back.

She passed other glass-walled businesses with a variety of arts and crafts displayed for purchase and promised herself she would spend some time going through the shops just to enjoy looking at all of the things she could look at but didn't dare buy on her budget.

The café was at the corner of the plaza. It smelled of coffee and warm quiche. She placed Christie's and Salvatore's orders, along with a chicken salad sandwich for herself. While she waited for their lunches to be prepared, she walked out on the patio.

Her cream crew neck sweater, black blazer, and jeans were just enough to keep out the early November chill. She breathed in the cool air as she looked up at the overcast sky. It hadn't rained since yesterday, but it still smelled of rain.

She let the clean air and the relaxed environment calm her nerves that had been on edge for the past several days. She wondered where Dylan was and what he was doing with the investigation. Could Nate have been murdered? It was hard to believe, yet not. It was harder to believe that he would take his own life.

But murder? She rubbed her arms with her palms and stared out at the street. A white car was illegally parked in front of the Bisbee Mining and Historical Museum across the street from the Copper Queen Plaza. What caught her attention was not the car, but the man leaning with his backside up against the vehicle. He had his hands in his pockets and he was staring right at her.

What had been a chill on her skin now felt like ice. She turned and dodged back into the café. Her order was ready and as she grabbed her wallet out of her purse, her hands shook a little. She didn't know why the man had unnerved her, but he had. The car had seemed familiar, too, and she wondered if she'd seen it someplace before.

After she paid, she thanked the employee who had assisted her, left a tip in a small silver bucket by the register, and headed back to Salvatore's office.

By the time she'd pushed open the office's glass doors, she'd shaken off the creepy feeling the man across the street had given her.

She walked in, returned Christie's smile, and held up the bag. "Lunch is served."

"I am starving." Christie pushed aside papers on her desktop and pointed to a chair in front of the desk. "If you don't mind, we can eat here."

"Perfect." Belle peeked into the bag and pulled out one package labeled "grilled chicken", along with the one printed with "chicken salad" and two small bags of BBQ chips. She left the club sandwich in the bag.

After they spread out their meals, and Christie had grabbed a couple of Cokes from a small fridge cleverly disguised as a cabinet, they started to eat.

Christie brought up the topic of the small memorial they'd had for Nate in the mountains and the subject weighed heavily on Belle's heart.

"It was beautiful." Christie sighed. "It almost felt like Nate was there, you know?"

"Yes." Belle pictured the white daisy she had dropped over the ridge and how it had floated down. "I wish I had stayed in touch with him more than the couple of times we spoke." She thought about the conversation at the Den and learning what everyone was up to. "I wish I would have kept up with everyone." Yet that would have meant Dylan, too, and she wouldn't have been able to handle that.

"Heck, Belle." Christie brushed strands of long red hair from her face. "I *live* in Bisbee, and I didn't keep up with everyone. If anyone feels guilty for not keeping in touch, it's me."

Belle shook her head. "Don't think that way."

Christie tilted her head to the side. "Only if you don't."

"I guess regrets don't really serve a purpose." Belle let out her breath. "All we can do is change what we do from this point on."

"Agreed." Christie washed down a bite of her food with Coke.

They ate their sandwiches in silence for a few moments as Belle turned everything over in her mind from the call to the memorial, to the gathering and Dylan's statement that he didn't believe Nate committed suicide. Belle figured that Christie was also thinking about Nate and the CoS.

Christie took another sip of her Coke then placed the can back on her desk. "You started a new job, didn't you?"

Belle set her sandwich on its wrapper. "I had to quit." She explained her boss's refusal to let her take time off for Nate.

Christie scowled. "What an ass."

"Christie…" A warning tone came from behind her and she and Belle looked up to see that Salvatore had walked out of his office. "Language like that is unbecoming of you."

Belle's first instinct was to narrow her eyes, but she worked to keep her expression placid.

Christie winced and looked at Salvatore. "Sorry, baby. I was just a little upset for Belle."

"Regardless, you should keep yourself above foul language, *mi mariposa*." Salvatore placed his hands on Christie's shoulders from behind and leaned down and kissed her on the top of her head.

Still gripping Christie's shoulders Salvatore raised his head and looked at Belle. "What happened?"

Belle shrugged. She didn't want to explain again, but it would have seemed rude not to. "I don't have a job now. My boss wouldn't let me take off time for Nate's funeral, so I quit."

"That's a shame." Something flickered in Salvatore's eyes, but he moved to the desk and reached into the café bag. "Mine?"

"Just the way Christie ordered it for you." Belle picked up the remaining half of her own sandwich.

For the first time, Belle wished the man would leave, but he seemed intent on hanging around. Maybe it was because she wanted Christie to herself for a while.

Christie looked at her husband. "Dylan doesn't think Nate's death was a suicide."

Salvatore stilled. In a casual movement, he looked at his wife. "Oh?"

She nodded. "Nate sent all of us postcards and Dylan doesn't think Nate would have sent them if he had intended to kill himself."

A sinking feeling weighted Belle's stomach. She didn't like that Christie had brought up anything about the CoS to her husband. It was personal, especially the postcards.

"Nate sent cards to all of you?" Salvatore leaned his hip against Christie's desk. "Including you, Christie?"

"I'm sorry." Christie looked apologetic. "I was so upset about Nate's death that I forgot to tell you." She leaned down and opened a large drawer in the lower left side of her desk. She brought out a purse and pulled out a postcard of Bisbee's Mule Pass Tunnel.

She turned over the card when the glass doors to the office opened.

They all looked in that direction and Belle's heart made a strange swooping sensation.

Dylan.

He looked so damned good. He wore a blue overshirt with a black T-shirt beneath. His worn Wranglers fit him well and hugged his hips and athletic thighs perfectly.

The crazy urge to go to him, press her body against his, and wrap her arms around his neck to kiss him, almost made her dizzy with need. She wanted to slide her hands down his chest, feeling the hard muscles beneath her palms. And my God, she'd never seen biceps as powerful as his. Her body reacted just to the sight of him, her nipples hardening beneath her sweater and an ache developing between her thighs.

If he was surprised to see Belle, he didn't show it. He took off his Stetson and nodded in Salvatore's direction. "Salvatore." In turn he said, "Hi, Christie. Belle."

"Hi, Dylan," Christie said. "I have the postcard right here." She flipped it over. Something's off about it, like the others' postcards." She read it aloud,

Christie,

I hope life and all that goes into it is treating you well. Time has flown by and it's been much too long.

One of these days we'll have to go out for ice cream. I'll always remember how much you love strawberry dipped cones. You know how chocolate is my favorite flavor and I'm ready to hit the Dairy Queen again.

Watch your step.

Love,

Nate

"Nate *hated* chocolate." Christie shook her head. "He was a vanilla man all the way. What do you think he was trying to say to us?"

Dylan extended his hand and Christie gave him the postcard. He tucked the card into the pocket of his overshirt.

Salvatore looked mildly curious. "Each of your friends in the CoS received notes like this?"

Christie nodded. "And everyone says there is something off about their note."

Salvatore folded his arms across his chest and leaned his hip against Christie's desk as he looked at Dylan. "My wife said you believe Nate's death wasn't suicide."

"It's possible." Dylan gave a casual shrug. "Our investigation is standard procedure." He turned to Belle. "Mind if I walk with you to your hotel?"

Considering her hotel was across the street, she didn't really need to be escorted. But then she thought about the man standing in front of the museum, which was right before her hotel, and a shiver traveled her spine. She'd pick a few uncomfortable moments with Dylan over a creep.

"I don't mind at all." She wrapped up the rest of the sandwich and stuffed it into the now empty bag. "My postcard is in my room at the hotel, so it'll be a good opportunity to give it to you."

Christie wore a disappointed expression. "You're leaving already?"

Belle smiled at Christie. "I'll call you and we'll get together."

Dylan put on his western hat and touched the brim as he nodded to Christie before looking at Salvatore. "Have a good one."

Belle gave Christie a hug, smiled and said goodbye to Salvatore, and went with Dylan out the glass doors of the office.

Dylan and Belle walked in silence through the plaza. Voices of shoppers echoed through the large building that decades ago had housed Phelps Dodge Mercantile.

When they walked outside, Belle looked across the street and was relieved that the man who'd been there earlier was nowhere in sight.

Belle's arms prickled with goose bumps and she rubbed them with both hands.

Dylan studied her. "Is something wrong?"

"Not really, I guess." Belle met his gaze. "It's just that earlier, when I was getting lunch from the café, I saw a man standing in front of a white car right over there." She gestured to the museum across the street. "I could swear he was staring at me. It gave me the creeps."

Dylan narrowed his brows. "What was the make and model of the car? Do you remember anything about it, like markings or damage?"

"The front fender was a little banged up." Belle shrugged. "I don't know about the make and model. Why?"

He didn't answer her question, just asked one of his own. "What did the man look like?"

"Hispanic." Her forehead wrinkled in thought. "Five-nine or five-ten, round face, black hair and clean-shaven. He was thickset with big arms." She shook her head. "That's all I can remember."

"You must have gotten a pretty good look at him." Dylan had his phone out again and was typing notes onto the device. "What was he wearing?"

She didn't hesitate. "Beige slacks and a white button-up shirt. I didn't notice his shoes, but I think he was wearing a gold watch."

"Anything else?" He looked up from the screen.

She shook her head. "That's all I can remember."

"Let me know if you see him hanging around again." Dylan holstered his phone, frowning. "Stay away from him if he does come near you."

"Okay." Her skin tingled as Dylan put his hand at the small of her back and looked both ways before guiding her to the crosswalk.

They reached the black iron fence in front of the red brick museum. On the other side of the fence, in front of the museum, was old mining equipment used in the late 1800s in Bisbee's copper mines.

She put her hand on one of the fence's black railings and turned to Dylan. "Why would anyone be watching me?"

Dylan shook his head. "I don't know that anyone is watching you." She released the rail and he guided her down the sidewalk that went around the museum. "But I may have seen a vehicle matching that description hanging around. I'd prefer to err on the side of caution."

Belle and Dylan walked to the back of the museum to a steep street. A little jog to the right was the infamous Brewery Gulch and straight ahead was a Mexican restaurant. They crossed the street and walked uphill to the entrance of the Copper Queen Hotel, which was built in 1902.

They walked up the stairs and he pushed open a pair of wood and glass doors that led into the lobby. Once the largest city between St. Louis and San Francisco, Bisbee had seen its fair share of well-known individuals. Some of the many famous guests who had stayed in the Copper Queen over its historic past included John Wayne and President Teddy Roosevelt, Stephen King, and J.A. Jance.

The hotel was also considered by many to be haunted, but Belle hadn't experienced any activities related to local spirits.

She and Dylan walked up the stairs and she dug the big brass key out of her purse. The hotel still used real keys for its rooms. He took the key from her and opened the door that swung open to reveal the room she was staying in.

Belle had one of the hotel's smaller rooms filled with antique furniture, including a full-sized bed and a writing desk. Simple nightstands with small, pretty tiffany lamps were on either side of the bed. The walls were papered with roses, and drapes covered the windows. The TV seemed out of place in the old-fashioned room that also had Internet, which seemed odd in a room that took one back over a hundred years.

She set her purse on a quaint wooden armchair. She slipped out of the blazer she wore and hung it on the back of the chair in front of the writing desk. When she turned to face Dylan, he had closed the door behind him and locked it.

The air in the room suddenly seemed too thin to breathe as they stared at each other. He was so tall and virile, a dominant man in every way. He looked rough and untamed.

She knew how gentle he could be. She'd never forget the way he'd touched her and loved her in the sweetest ways.

Time flew backward and she remembered when she'd looked at him for what she knew would be the last time, and how hard it had been to keep him from seeing it in her gaze.

An ache started at the backs of her eyes, and pain welled up inside her. Old memories, old wounds that had never healed. And secrets. Secrets too great to bear.

A tear rolled down her cheek and she wiped it away with her fingertips, wishing she could take it back.

He looked at her almost helplessly, but caring so deep in his gaze that it made her want to crumble.

More tears flooded her cheeks.

"Oh, sweetheart." He crossed the few paces between them and took her in his arms. He held her to him, his big body seeming to swallow her with comfort. "Shhh." He gripped her so tightly that she felt more secure and cared for than she could remember—since leaving him all those years ago.

She cried harder, trying to hold back sobs, but failing.

He held her and held her.

CHAPTER 7

It was like the years slid backward, to another place and time, as Dylan held Belle in his arms again. He pressed his face against her dark hair, breathing in her feminine scent as he did his best to comfort her. She felt sweet and soft and perfect in his embrace.

He rubbed her back, feeling the tension in her muscles and wanting to ease it. He moved his hands in circles, her face against his chest, her tears soaking through his cotton T-shirt.

"I'm sorry." She sniffed and drew back. "I don't know why I broke down like that."

"Nate's death was a big blow." He held her by the shoulders. "I have a feeling you also have a few things you need to work through and get off your chest."

"It's been a hell of a week." She searched his gaze. "I think one of the hardest things is seeing you again."

He brushed his knuckles along her cheekbone. "Why is that?"

"You should know." She sighed. "I left you without an explanation. I just ran, and I know I hurt you." She held her hand to her heart. "I didn't want to leave. If I thought there was any other way, I never would have. And I never would have hurt you."

He tucked hair behind her ear. "I would have done anything for you." He still would, but he wasn't sure that was something he should say aloud.

"Like I said before, that's one of the reasons I left." She looked down, staring at his chest before she looked up at him again. "Promise me you won't go to see my stepfather."

Dylan said nothing as anger burned in his chest. He couldn't make that kind of promise.

"Dylan?" She searched his gaze. "Please."

A stirring of longing took hold of him. He cupped her face in his palms. "God, how I missed you."

She gripped his T-shirt in her fists and raised her tear-stained face to his.

He couldn't help himself. He lowered his head, slowly, giving her a chance to say no, to push him away.

She did neither. Instead, she rose on her toes, her fists still gripping his T-shirt, and brushed his lips with hers.

The groan that rose inside him came from missing her for what seemed like a lifetime. He took her mouth, kissing her with an intensity that he'd never felt before. Her lips were so soft, and when he slid his tongue into her mouth and tasted her, it was like going back all of those years and tasting her again for the first time.

The intensity of her kiss matched his own and a low groan escaped him. She was so soft in his arms, a memory come to life. He wanted to take her to bed and make up for all of the loving they had missed.

He struggled to think clearly as need and desire burned bright. She moved her palms up his T-shirt to his shoulders and slid her fingers into his hair, knocking off his Stetson. It hit the floor with a soft thump.

Each movement she made seemed as urgent as his, if not more so. It was as if she'd been craving this ever since she'd left and she wanted to make up for lost time. Just like he did.

Her low purr vibrated through him. He remembered her making that sound every time they'd made love and he almost followed through with his desire to sweep her into his arms, lay her on the bed, and cover her body with his.

She had filled out, and no longer had a girlish figure but the real curves of a grown woman. He wanted to explore those curves with his hands, his mouth, his tongue. He wanted to taste her again, to hold her, to make love to her.

It might have been the hardest thing he'd ever done, but he took her by the shoulders and put just enough space between them so that their bodies weren't plastered together. But he continued to keep a grip on her, their gaze holding and not breaking.

God, she was beautiful. He'd always thought she was the most beautiful thing he'd ever known. From childhood through high school he'd been in love with everything about her. He didn't think she'd known it until their freshman year in high school, when he'd taken her for a walk under the bleachers at a football game.

Her chest rose and fell, clearly breathing as hard as he was. She swallowed. "That was probably not a good idea."

He studied her for a long moment. "You're going through a lot. I can see it in your eyes."

She looked down before meeting his gaze again. "Thank you."

Despite the fact that he wouldn't take advantage of her when she was so vulnerable, he couldn't help the disappointment that swelled within him when she'd agreed. He moved his thumb to her cheek. "I missed you."

Her eyes glittered and he thought for a moment that she would cry again. "I missed you, too."

He pressed a kiss to her forehead. He had to change the subject or he'd take her in his arms again and this time he wouldn't let go. "Why don't you show me that postcard?"

"Oh." She went to the antique writing desk and picked up a bag on the desk chair. She dug inside and drew out a postcard. She looked a little teary and choked up as she did.

When she handed it to him, he read it through. "It's similar to the others."

Belle seemed to compose herself and her voice was steady. "The part that was off on mine was about my dog biting him."

Dylan stared at the card. "Your dog was pure white and he refers to it as brown."

She nodded. "Yes."

He read it a second time. "He was trying to tell us something."

"I agree." She smoothed her hair away from her face. "The sooner you get all of the postcards, the better."

"Yes." Dylan looked up from the note. "You and I have a lot to talk about that has nothing to do with Nate."

She let out her breath. It was clear that she wanted to avoid any discussions, but she said, "I know you're right. It will just be…difficult."

"I need to drive to Sierra Vista to stop by Leon's office and pick up his card." Dylan slid Christie's and Belle's cards into his shirt pocket. "Why don't you come with me? His kids are older than Marta's and a couple of them work for him. They might be there."

A touch of surprise flickered over her features. She paused, as if not sure what she should do, then nodded. "I'd like to see him again and perhaps meet his family."

Dylan scooped up his hat that had fallen to the floor and waited for her to slip on her black blazer. The blazer covered the cream sweater that hugged the soft curves of her breasts, and he loved the gentle way her waist flared out to her hips. She lifted her dark hair, pulling it from where it had caught in the collar of her blazer, and then picked up her purse.

He opened the door for her and followed before using the big brass key to lock the door behind them. He handed the key to her and she dropped it into her purse before swinging the strap over her shoulder. Finding any excuse possible to touch her, he put his fingers to her lower back as he escorted her out of the hotel. Even through the blazer, he felt a shiver go through her.

They walked across the street to the plaza, then headed to the parking lot behind the building. When they reached his truck, he unlocked it and helped her into the passenger seat before climbing into the driver's side and starting the vehicle.

His cell rang and he left the truck in park as he un-holstered his phone and saw from the screen that it was Trace.

Dylan answered the call. "What's up?"

"Edmund's Salcido's blood at Nate's place, along with his disappearance, got us the warrant to search Salcido's home," Trace said. "We're on our way now."

"Text me the address." Dylan glanced at Belle. "I'll be right there."

"You've got it." Trace disconnected the call.

"I need to make a detour that's part of the investigation related to Nate's death." Dylan considered dropping Belle off back at her hotel, but decided he'd prefer to keep her close. "Mind tagging along? You'll need to stay in the truck, but I don't know how long it will take. I could be in and out or it could be an hour."

Belle appeared to be considering his question. "I don't have anything else to do, and I want to see you get to the bottom of what happened to Nate."

His phone vibrated and he looked down at the screen to see the address Trace had texted. He started to have second thoughts when he saw where the home was located, and he looked at Belle. "The house is in Galena."

Her face paled. The Galena subdivision was where her stepfather lived, and where she had lived before she ran. "What's the address?" she asked quietly.

Dylan gave it to her and she visibly relaxed. "That's on the opposite side of the subdivision."

"You don't have to go." He studied her. "I can take you back to the Copper Queen."

She shook her head. "I'll be fine."

Despite his growing misgivings, he put the truck into gear and headed away from Old Bisbee, on the road that hugged the fenced-in pit mines, on around the traffic circle, and then to Galena.

During the drive, he was incredibly aware of her sitting next to him, a familiar sense that he'd missed all these years. When he glanced at her, he saw her watching him and wondered if she was feeling the same kind of connection.

It didn't take long to reach Salcido's home. A number of law enforcement vehicles filled the street in front of the house as agents performed their duties.

Over the years the neighborhood had fallen mostly into disrepair. Dylan pulled up behind a black DHS SUV in front of the home. The house was one of the few that were in good shape. It had a white exterior and green shutters that looked recently painted.

A Hispanic woman stood on the porch next to a swing, talking with Trace. She looked furious and was making angry gestures with her hands as DHS agents went in and out of the home.

"Hang tight." Dylan looked at Belle as he opened the door of his truck, letting in the sound of voices. "Hopefully this won't take too long."

"No worries." Belle pulled a flat device out of her purse and held it up. "I have my e-reader. I'll just continue where I left off in this mystery I'm reading."

"Lock your door." Dylan gave her a quick kiss and squeezed her arm. "You have my number in your phone from yesterday. Call me if you need me," he added before he climbed out of the truck, shutting the door firmly behind him. He waited for her to lock her door before turning away.

He strode past agents carrying boxes of paperwork and computer equipment out of the house. When he reached the top of the stairs, the woman was still yelling at Trace, rattling off her anger in Spanish.

Trace put his hands up in a "slow down" gesture. "Mrs. Salcido, we have a warrant." Trace spoke in fluent Spanish. "As I explained, we need to find out what happened to your husband."

"Why are you taking my husband's belongings?" Her Spanish was rapid, almost hard to keep up with. "You are destroying my home."

She started to go into the house, but Trace stepped in her way. He continued speaking in Spanish. "You cannot go in. You must wait out here." He gestured to Jennie Ortega, a young DHS agent. "This is Agent Ortega. She will stay with you, Mrs. Salcido."

Mrs. Salcido swung around to face Jennie and started in on her. Jennie was tough and never put up with anyone's B.S. She, too, spoke in Spanish. "If you do not calm down, I will put you in the back of one of our vehicles and you will wait there."

At that point Mrs. Salcido burst into tears and dropped onto the porch swing.

"I've got this." Jennie spoke to Trace as she switched to English and gestured to the front door. "Go do your thing."

Trace gave Jennie a nod. "Thanks." He and Dylan walked into the house.

Dylan wasn't surprised that Mrs. Salcido was upset. Agents were going through the house, leaving no stone unturned. He walked with Trace through the house, passing agents who were busy combing the place. "Hopefully we'll find some answers here."

"What we're finding are more questions." Trace led Dylan to a closet, its door ajar. An open safe was in one corner on the floor. "The safe wasn't locked, and inside we found a slip of paper and approximately ten thousand in one hundred dollar bills. Presumably for Mrs. Salcido. According to her, she never messed with the safe and didn't think to look to see if it was unlocked."

"Ten thousand. That's some stash for an accountant to leave behind." Dylan looked from the safe to Trace. "What did the note say?"

"*Lo siento.*" Trace shook his head. "That's it."

"Who is he saying 'I'm sorry' to?" Dylan stared at the safe again before answering his own question. "Likely to his wife."

"Probably." Trace looked around them. "Ten grand and a house. Guess he figured that was enough to take care of Mrs. Salcido."

Trace and Dylan walked out of the office and to the living room as Dylan added, "If he intentionally left on his own and wasn't forced."

"That's the million dollar question." Trace reached the front door and looked out, Dylan following.

Through the front windshield of the truck, Belle could be seen staring at her e-reader.

Trace nodded toward the truck. "You brought company."

Dylan started down the porch stairs while Trace remained on the top step. "If you've got everything under control, I have someplace to be."

"I can handle it." Trace made a gesture with his hand. "Take care of what you need to."

Dylan turned back to the truck and headed across the street. Belle glanced up as he opened the truck door, climbed in, and shut it behind him.

He looked at her. "Good book?"

"It's twisted but compelling." She shrugged. "And it's better than facing what's going on now. I don't like our real life mystery."

"I couldn't agree more." Dylan threw the truck into gear.

She tilted her head to the side. "Did you find anything that could help shed light on Nate's death?"

"Not yet." He shook his head as he backed up the truck. "But I'm hopeful we'll find something."

"I hope so, too." She turned to glance out the window, clearly lost in her thoughts.

The drive to where Leon lived outside of Sierra Vista was a good half hour from Bisbee. Belle continued to stare out the window as he drove, as if hoping Dylan wouldn't want to talk. He did want to ask her more questions about the past, but he figured he'd stick with the present.

He steered the truck down the empty highway. No one ahead and no one following. "Christie mentioned you've been in the restaurant business for some time."

Belle turned her gaze from the window and looked at him. "I started from the bottom up. I began as a dishwasher and moved on to bussing tables, then hostessing, waitressing, and on from there. Over the years, I transitioned my way to restaurant manager."

He felt a knot in his chest when he thought about her having to wash dishes just to survive after running away. "You manage a restaurant now?"

"I did." She let out a long sigh. She explained the circumstances leading up to walking out on her job.

"What kind of ass—" Dylan let out his breath, "—*idiot* would refuse to let an employee leave for the death of a friend?"

"Now I have job hunting in my future when I return to Houston." She looked tense as she shifted in her seat. "But I'll be fine." He wasn't sure if she added the last words to reassure herself or him.

He didn't like the way it made him feel to think about her leaving and returning to Houston. A very big part of him wanted to claim her and tell her he was never letting her out of his sight again. He'd loved her with everything he had then, and now his heart wanted her back.

What the hell was he thinking? She left once. What was to stop her from running again?

But that had been because of her stepfather. She was an adult now and the bastard couldn't hurt her.

Dylan ground his teeth. It was taking every ounce of restraint he had not to drive straight to Harvey Driscoll's home and beat the shit out of the sonofabitch. Dylan had always had a temper and it was only hard won control that kept him from acting on it.

It took effort, but Dylan turned his thoughts to the present and the fact that they'd arrived.

Leon Petroski's business was located on a property near his house, which was one of the nicer homes in the area. Dylan pulled his truck up to a huge workshop where Leon was talking with a couple of men. They wore shirts with logos on the back that read *Leon's Pump and Well Service.*

Leon said something to the men who nodded, and walked to a truck bearing the same logo on the doors as they had on their shirts. The men were driving away by the time Dylan and Belle parked in front of Leon and his shop. The place was filled with heavy equipment, drilling and pump supplies.

After Dylan helped Belle out of the truck, she hugged Leon and Dylan clapped his hand on his friend's shoulder.

"Thanks for stopping by." Leon, who was tall and lean, adjusted a ball cap, pulling it down on his sandy blond hair. "It's been crazy around here, and getting back to Bisbee over the next couple of days to give you the postcard would be difficult."

"Not a problem," Dylan said.

"G.I. Joe is up at the house." Leon nodded in the direction of his home. "He seems to be settling in well."

Dylan nodded. "I appreciate you taking him in." He looked over the shop and at the office building attached to the much larger workshop. "Some setup you have here."

"We keep busy." Leon nodded in the direction of the office building. "I'll introduce you to my wife and get you that card."

"Does your wife work with you?" Belle walked on the opposite side of Leon from Dylan.

Leon shook his head. "Jane owns a clothing boutique in Sierra Vista. She took the afternoon off."

He led them into the attached office building and wiped his work boots on a mat before stepping inside.

A tall woman with short spiky hair glanced up from a paper she had been poring over as she sat behind a desk. She looked from Dylan to Belle and smiled as she stood.

Leon made introductions. Jane had a firm grip as she greeted both Belle and Dylan. "Leon has mentioned your Circle a few times over the years." Jane glanced at the postcard on the desk before picking it up. "I understand this was from one of your group."

Dylan reached out and took the card from her. On the front of the postcard was a picture of Bisbee's Brewery Gulch. His gaze slid over the words as Belle peeked over his shoulder.

Leon,

Hear you've got quite an operation going over in Sierra Vista and that you have a beautiful wife, a daughter, and two sons who keep you busy. I'm happy life is treating you well.

I'll never forget that Hail Mary pass you caught to win the game over Douglas. You were one hell of a receiver.

Take care of you and yours,

Nate

Dylan frowned. "*You* were the quarterback and you *threw* that Hail Mary pass to win the game."

"Exactly." Leon braced one hand on a file cabinet. "That's some mistake."

"Leon said you all received a postcard and each one is odd." Jane tilted her head to the side. "What do you think that's all about?"

Dylan shook his head. "Not sure."

Jane gestured to the postcard. "We've made a copy, so you can take the original."

"Thank you." Dylan tucked the postcard into his shirt pocket with the two others.

Jane turned to Belle. "Leon mentioned you left while still in high school." Jane seemed to be the type who said whatever was on her mind.

Belle shifted her stance and looked uncomfortable with Jane's forward statement. "That's true," Belle said quietly.

Leon came to Belle's rescue. "Anyone like a beer or a soda? We can head on over to the house."

"I'm on the job, so no beer for me." Dylan figured they should probably spend a few moments with Leon and his wife.

Belle nodded her agreement. "Soda is fine for me."

They drove to the house and then spent the next hour talking with Leon about his business and his kids. His wife was pleasant but continued to be very direct, and her questions often seemed to throw Belle off balance.

Belle also got to meet Joe, and she spent some time caressing and talking to him. The German shepherd was friendly to everyone there, but to Dylan he seemed to be a little less enthusiastic than he usually was. No doubt the dog missed Nate.

When Dylan thought he and Belle had stayed long enough, he thanked the Petroskis for their hospitality and Belle echoed his thank you. Dylan handed Leon his business card, which included his personal cell number. Dylan patted Joe one last time before following Leon to the front door.

"You don't think Nate was just messing with you all?" Jane said as Leon reached for the doorknob. "It might have been his way of saying 'Let's talk.'"

"Could be." Dylan gave a slow nod. "One way or another, we'll figure this out. You can count on it."

Chapter 8

Afternoon sunlight faded as they drove from Leon's home to Bisbee. It had been a long day, but Belle found herself not wanting it to end. She knew she shouldn't stay close to Dylan, not with the secret she still kept, but she couldn't tear herself away from him. The energy between them was electric, but familiar and comfortable.

She watched him as he drove, studying his strong features and the dark stubble on his jaw that hadn't been there when he was a teenager. He'd been a clean-cut country boy, not nearly as rough and toughened as he looked now. She wondered what he'd been through all these years, what had given him the hardness she sensed in him. It almost surprised her that he was gentle with her the few times they'd been around each other. And that kiss…it had been so sensual, almost as if he'd been communicating something through it. Yet he didn't appear like a man who was gentle for anyone.

She knew she had to tell him the truth, the whole truth, but she was afraid of what he might do when he found out her stepfather was partially responsible for Dylan's father's murder. He'd also be angry she hadn't told him sooner. Should she wait for the right time? Would there ever be a right time?

"Tom is working until eight tonight." Dylan shoved his phone into its holster as he glanced from the road to Belle. "He'll be home by eight-thirty and he's going to text me his address when he's there."

She reached into her purse and glanced at the time on her phone. "That's another three hours from now."

Dylan met her gaze. "Tired?"

"A little." Her stomach growled. "But mostly hungry."

He glanced back to the road. "Do you want to go out to eat?"

She sighed. "I don't feel like going to a restaurant. Maybe I should order room service at the hotel."

"Let's get takeout." He pulled his phone out of its holster again. "I know the perfect place we can go to enjoy it."

Her belly flipped at the way he looked at her and she thought about their moment alone in the hotel room. She almost suggested they go back there but managed to bite back the words.

He called a small dive they used to go to in Old Bisbee and placed an order for two of the place's popular enormous hamburgers. Her mouth watered at the memory of them. They had always been the best she'd ever remembered tasting. And the place had made the most amazing milkshakes.

After he placed the phone order, she asked. "So where are we going?"

He gave her a look with the slightest of smiles that made her stomach do funny things. "Do you have to ask?"

With that comment, she knew exactly where he was taking her. "I guess not." More flips in her belly. "Do you think that's a good idea?"

He glanced at her. "You can't beat the view."

"I can't argue with that." She did want to argue that it was the last place on earth that she wanted to go. But that wasn't true, so she didn't say anything more.

He stopped at the Arctic Circle, which Dylan told her had been open and closed numerous times over the years. New owners had remodeled and painted it, and just being at the place reminded her of long ago times. Mostly good times, and that's what she held onto.

Dylan paid for their order and then they were headed up Tombstone Canyon, and sure enough, rather than going through the tunnel, he took a detour and went up the Old Divide Road, on top of Mule Pass Tunnel. He didn't stop there, a place where teenagers had always stopped to party. He continued on up Juniper Road, all the way to the towers. He parked there so that the rear of the truck was facing the view of the town, like he used to the times they'd come up here to make out.

The thought of those old days brought back good memories, yet they were so good that they were almost too painful to bear.

He went to her side of the truck and helped her out, then grabbed the bags of burgers and fries, along with a blanket from the back of the cab and two jackets. While she got the milkshakes, he put down the tailgate of his truck and spread the blanket on the cold metal.

"Do you need a jacket?" He held them up as he set the fast food bags aside.

"Not yet." She touched the lapel of her blazer. "This is warm enough for now."

Before she could climb up, he grasped her by her waist and set her on the tailgate. He didn't let go. He held onto her while she gripped the large Styrofoam cups so tightly she thought her fingers would go right through them.

She held her breath, her heart pounding, half afraid he would kiss her and half afraid he wouldn't. After a long moment he released her and she let out her breath as he scooted onto the tailgate beside her. He was so close that his big arm brushed hers as he moved, and his leg pressed against her thigh. Her skin tingled wherever his body touched hers.

He grabbed a burger out of the bag that was wrapped in the old-fashioned way, with the plain white paper the place had always used. He handed the burger to her when he'd partially unwrapped it.

She breathed in the warm, delicious smell. "It smells as good as I remember."

He unwrapped his own. "The new owners have done a good job of staying true to the original menu and way of making everything."

She bit into it and closed her eyes and chewed. When she opened her eyes again, Dylan was watching her.

"It's amazing." She had to tear her gaze from his and focused instead on the view.

The sun was sinking behind them, but there was enough daylight left for one of the best views she could remember. The mountains, the high desert vegetation, and the houses built on the side of the hills in the canyon.

Lights began flickering on in the town as the sun went down and it seemed almost surreal, like fairy lights appearing in the hills.

They ate in comfortable silence, but it allowed her to think too much about secrets and lost years. She knew she should tell him, but the words wouldn't come.

The burger was so huge that she handed him the rest after she'd eaten half, just like she used to when they were dating. It came naturally, as if they'd still been doing it for years.

He'd already downed his burger and all of his fries. He took the rest of hers and ate it as she picked at her fries. The sunset faded away as they finished eating.

When they were done, he crumpled the wrappers and used napkins, and then stuffed them into one of the empty bags, which he set behind him in the truck bed. He gripped his milkshake cup as he studied her.

She took a sip of her chocolate milkshake, lowered it, and looked at him. He was much taller than her and even sitting on the truck bed she had to tilt her head a little to meet his gaze. It was nearly dark now, but she could still make out his features.

"You were about six-feet-tall when I left." She let her gaze drift over him. "You're around six-three now?"

"On the money." He set his milkshake on the truck bed, reached up, and took several strands of her hair, letting them run through his fingers. The way he did it, so sensually, so familiar, caused her to tremble inside. "I want to know everything that's happened since you've been gone."

She looked down at the cup that she still gripped. He hooked a finger beneath her chin and raised her face so she was looking at him. A lump grew in her throat. "There's not a lot to tell."

"To me it's everything." He spoke quietly. "Please tell me."

"Okay. You deserve to know." She sighed and he released her chin. She looked away for a moment before turning her gaze back on him. "When I made the decision to leave, I only took a backpack, two changes of clothing and a few other items, basic toiletries, and cash. I'd managed to accumulate over a thousand dollars from years of babysitting, and I'd kept it hidden beneath a floorboard so that my mother and stepfather would never find it. They would have used it for drugs."

His brows narrowed slightly. "You'd planned that long to leave?"

"No." She cleared her throat. "At the time I was just saving it for something special someday." Like a ring for Dylan, if he proposed to her when they were out of high school. She wasn't about to tell him that. "But things got worse and worse at home after my mother died, and one night I decided I had to leave."

Tears bit at the backs of her eyes as she continued. "I would have told you everything, Dylan. Honestly. But I didn't want anything to happen to you."

The full moon peeked through dark clouds and she could see his anger in the tightness of his jaw. "What did your stepfather do to you, Belle?"

She bit her lower lip. What hadn't Harvey done? Telling Dylan wouldn't change it or take the pain away. "It doesn't matter now."

"Like hell it doesn't." If it were possible, flames would have lit Dylan's eyes, he looked so furious.

She blew out her breath. "He sexually abused me. Took pictures and videos, too."

The rage on Dylan's face had her hurrying to speak.

"After I left, I hitchhiked my way to Albuquerque." She kept talking as anger grew in his gaze. "I only rode with women. I also cut off my hair until it was spiky and dyed it white-blonde so that no one would think twice about me looking like the girl on the news. I even wore glasses with plastic lenses, made to look like they were prescription." She thought of those days when she'd been running scared, afraid the authorities would find her and take her back to her stepfather. "I saw my face on newspapers once. Back then there weren't Amber alerts, so it was a little different."

The way the moonlight hit his face let her see his intense expression. "Why didn't you at least tell the authorities if you wouldn't tell me?"

"I didn't want to be put in foster care, and ultimately it would have come back to you." She pleaded with him with her gaze.

She set the milkshake cup aside and folded her arms across her chest as she shivered, the cold getting to her now. He retrieved his jackets and helped her put on one of them. It was lined and comfortable although so huge she was practically lost in it. Dylan slipped on the other jacket and then looked at her again as he stuffed the two empty milkshake cups into the remaining empty bag from the hamburger place.

"It wasn't easy but I managed to get a job with a woman in Albuquerque." Belle hugged herself tighter. "Marybeth let me sleep in her backroom and wash dishes to earn money. I saved everything."

Dylan's frown deepened. "Why didn't she turn you in as a runaway?"

"She was going to, but I told her my story and begged her not to send me back to that monster." Sadness for the woman gripped Belle's heart.

His expression was so intense. "I'll bet Marybeth had a story similar to yours."

At first Belle was surprised, but then realized in his line of work he was trained to listen and pick out details.

"Yes." She nodded. "Marybeth was abused by her uncle and she ran away at a young age, like me. So even though I was over forty years younger than her, we were kindred spirits in our own way. I started off with menial jobs and worked my way up to waitressing over the two years I spent working for her."

A tear rolled down Belle's cheek. "One night Marybeth was killed in a car accident by a drunk driver. I was homeless again and my closest friend was dead."

He put his arm around her shoulders and drew her close to him until her head rested on his chest. "What happened then?" His voice rumbled against her ear.

It felt so natural, so comfortable having him hold her. "I'd saved almost everything I earned, so I moved on, got an apartment, and found another waitressing job. It took a long time, but I made my way up to restaurant management."

He squeezed her tighter to him and just held her for a moment.

She tilted her head up. "What about you?"

"Pretty much what I told you and the others at the Den." He played with the ends of her hair like he used to. It was a natural, comforting movement. "I've worked in Washington, D.C., California, Phoenix, and then transferred here when a position opened up."

She wanted to know more, like what kind of relationships he'd had, if there had been a special woman in his life. But then she wasn't sure she wanted to know. Her heart ached at the thought of him being with someone else. Even after all these years, she still felt more for him than she should.

"Did you ever marry?" His question startled her out of her thoughts. "Is there someone back in Houston waiting for you?"

"No." She shook her head, her hair sliding over his shirt beneath his open jacket. "And no."

"Why not?" His question was simple but it caused heat to flush over her skin.

"I've just never met the right man." *Since you,* she thought. *No one ever measured up to my memories of you.* She dove in despite her earlier thoughts. "What about you?"

She felt him shrug his big shoulders. "Nope, never married." He squeezed her tightly to him. "I wouldn't have kissed you if there was someone I cared about." He caught her face in his hand and tilted her face up so that she met his eyes. "And I'm sure you wouldn't have kissed me back if you had someone back in Houston. So I asked a dumb question."

"What if I'd been lost in the moment?" she whispered as she looked at his moonlit features.

He shook his head. "You wouldn't have done it."

Her lips parted and the stirrings in her belly grew more intense. Her breasts felt heavy and she ached between her thighs, a need so great for him that she wanted to beg him to kiss her again. And more. So much more.

He lowered his head and slowly brought his mouth closer to hers. "I've missed you so damned much."

His kiss was slow and gentle, his lips moving over hers. He nipped at her lower lip, causing her to gasp. She remembered him being a good kisser, but now he kissed like a man with more experience, a man who took what he wanted.

A spike of jealousy shot through her at the thought of him being with other women. It was an irrational thought, but she felt it just the same. Even though she didn't deserve it, she still wanted to be the only woman he'd ever loved, just like he was the only man she'd ever loved. Every man she'd dated over the years had paled in comparison to her memories of this man, even back when he was so much younger.

She slid her fingers over his cheek and moaned against his lips as he slipped his tongue into her mouth. He tasted so good, of the milkshake he'd been drinking and of the flavor that was uniquely Dylan.

His scent was so familiar, filling her like nothing ever had before. He smelled earthy and masculine, and she hadn't realized how much she'd missed him until now. No, the truth was she hadn't let herself think about how much she'd missed him, but her heart and soul always had.

A groan of need swelled inside her. She felt the dampness between her thighs, the ache growing ever more powerful.

He shifted, picking her up and settling her on his lap as he continued to kiss her. He slid his hand into her hair and pulled back so that he could kiss her neck. She gasped at the dominant move that was unfamiliar, but felt so right with him. It was like he was claiming her all over again.

Her chest rose and fell, and small sounds of need escaped her as he moved his mouth to her ear. He rubbed his stubble along her soft skin as he slid his lips to her throat and kissed his way to the hollow.

She inched her hands up his chest and wrapped her arms around his neck as she tilted her head back, finding it harder and harder to breathe.

His hand eased beneath the jacket, pushing aside her blazer, and then cupping her breast. She squirmed on his lap, tingles running from her belly straight between her thighs as she felt the length and hardness of his erection. His cock seemed even bigger than she'd remembered it.

He circled her nipple with his finger through the soft material, and she grew wetter, wanting so badly to have him inside her.

The thought of sliding his cock into her mouth, licking him, tasting him, sucking him, was overwhelming. She slid off his lap and off the tailgate so that her feet hit the ground, and moved between his thighs.

He grasped her ass and pulled her close for another kiss. She leaned into him, sighing and sliding her hands to his huge biceps before skimming her fingers over his pectorals and then down the hard plane of his abs.

She liked the way he had filled out over the years, and loved touching him again. She moved her hands further down to his lap. A shiver of desire ran through her as she traced the outline of his erection before finding his belt buckle.

He captured her hands so quickly in his that he caught her off guard. He broke the kiss and braced his forehead against hers. "Don't play with fire, sweetheart."

She swallowed. "What if I want to?"

"No." He said the word firmly. "When I take you, it's not going to be out in the open at a teenage make out location. You deserved better than that."

A warm flush traveled through her at his words, *"When I take you."* But she'd wanted to give him something before telling him her secret. Once she told him, there no doubt wouldn't be a next time.

With a sigh she broke free of his grip and wrapped her arms around his neck. "You always were the gentleman."

He snorted. "Your memory is a little faulty. I seem to remember quite a few times when we went farther than we should have right here."

She couldn't help a laugh, but then she sobered. It was time—it wasn't right to hold back any longer. He might not forgive her for hiding what she'd learned, but somehow she would convince him not to go after Harvey and kill him in retribution for his part in Dylan's father's death.

"I—I have something I need to tell you." She bit her lower lip. "You are going to be so angry with me that you probably won't want to see me ever again."

His brow furrowed as he studied her. "You can't imagine all of the things I've seen and heard, and even done over the years. I doubt you could say anything that would make me that upset with you."

"You'll change your mind." She took a deep breath, trying to fight back tears that suddenly burned at the backs of her eyes. "My—"

An explosion rocked the night.

The ground trembled as a brilliant orange glow split the darkness.

Belle whirled around as a fireball reached for the sky.

CHAPTER 9

An electric charge swept over Dylan and he cut his gaze to Belle. "Get in the truck."

He grabbed the blanket as Belle snatched the two bags of garbage, and then he slammed the tailgate shut. He rushed with Belle to the passenger side, helped her up into the truck, then ran to the driver's side. In moments they were tearing down Juniper Road and on down, off of the Divide and onto the road that went through Tombstone Canyon.

When they got closer, he saw that it was a house on the hillside that had gone up in flames. Bisbee No. 2 Fire Station was five minutes from the home and he heard the sound of sirens even as he drove toward the explosion.

He spotted the road that led up the side of the canyon to the house and swerved onto it. Behind him came the flashing lights of a fire truck, the siren growing louder. Bisbee fire trucks were specially made to order to navigate the narrow one-lane streets to reach homes on the sides of the canyon.

Dylan stepped on the gas pedal, putting distance between his vehicle and the fire truck. When they reached the fiery home, he parked far enough to be out of the way. He backed into his parking space so that he was facing downhill and wouldn't have to maneuver the truck to drive away from the area, if for some reason he was in a hurry to leave.

He left the truck running, the heater on. "Stay here," he ordered Belle before he jumped out of the truck and ran toward the home.

Before he even got to it, he knew if anyone had been inside, they wouldn't have survived. Nothing could be done for the house that was not much more than flaming rubble. The danger now was to the homes on either side of the one aflame—the firefighters would concentrate on saving those houses.

The heat was tremendous, flames still licking the sky. The fire crackled, hissed, and popped, and smoke roiled and rose. What had happened? A gas leak?

Neighbors were out of their homes and staring at the fire. Dylan started to go to the next door neighbor's house to make sure everyone was out, when he saw a newer model black Honda CR-V SUV in front of the destroyed home.

His gut clenched. Tom Zumsteg had been driving the same model when they'd left the memorial for Nate. Was his home the one that had been blown to hell?

He didn't have time to think about that as the fire truck cut its sirens. It pulled up in front of the closest fire hydrant, blue and red strobes flashing over the scene. Firefighters jumped off the truck in full bunker gear and proceeded to hook up a pressurized hose to the hydrant. The crowd was ordered back, but they didn't move as far as they should have.

Dylan hurried to speak with people in front of the neighboring home on the left and asked if everyone was out of the house. When he was reassured they were, he ordered everyone to back up farther away from the fire.

As he did, he looked over the crowd, checking to see if someone was watching the fire with a different kind of interest than the neighbors, who would look horrified or in shock. An arsonist often liked to see his own handiwork—if this was arson. Dylan scanned the crowd twice, but no one in particular stood out from the rest.

He also searched those surrounding the house for Tom, hoping he would be one of the onlookers and not a victim.

Two police cruisers, lights flashing, pulled up behind the fire truck. Soon they had the area cordoned off as the firefighters did their job. Officers spoke to people in the crowd, asking for questions, looking for witnesses.

Dylan spotted Lieutenant Marks of the BPD and went up to him. "What can I do to help?" Dylan asked.

Marks looked mildly surprised. "You just happen to be in the neighborhood?"

"Yes." Dylan gave a single nod. "Do you know whose home that was?"

Marks blew out his breath "According to the address, it belongs to Dr. Zumsteg."

Dylan's heart hit the pit of his stomach. "That's his vehicle out front. I'm certain of it."

"Damn." Marks' features tightened. "The doc is a damned fine man. I hope to hell he wasn't inside that home."

"That makes two of us." Dylan stared grimly at the fire that was dying down, as did Marks. The firefighters had managed to save the houses on either side of the decimated home. "Tom's been a friend of mine since childhood." Dylan looked at Marks. "Tom was also a close friend of Nate O'Malley."

Marks cut his gaze from the fire to Dylan. "That's a big coincidence."

"Yeah, it is." Dylan shook his head, an ache deep in his gut. If Tom had been in that house when it exploded, another member of the CoS was gone.

By the time the fire was out, and the neighbors had been interviewed, Dylan was exhausted. He'd kept himself busy enough that he hadn't allowed himself to believe that Tom could really be dead.

Dylan heard voices and cut his attention to firefighters who were carrying a charred body out of the wreckage. He didn't want to get any closer, afraid of somehow recognizing Tom in what would be a horror to look at.

Forcing back the fear that it was another one of his friends, Dylan strode toward the firefighters and police officers attending to the body. His stomach churned when he looked at the sickening remains and caught the smell of burned flesh. It would take a DNA test or dental records to confirm the victim's identity.

Dylan started to turn away when he saw a metal bracelet burned into remaining flesh on the wrist of the body. Dylan crouched next to Lieutenant Marks and pointed to the soot-covered metal.

"Dr. Zumsteg wore a medical ID bracelet for a blood disorder." Dylan thought he might heave. This wasn't just another body. Now he believed it was his friend. "I think that's what's on the victim's wrist."

"Shit." Marks shook his head. "If this is Zumsteg, you've lost two close friends in the span of less than two weeks. What are the odds of that?"

Dylan considered Marks' words and the postcard Dylan didn't have a chance to get from Tom. Could it be possible that the deaths were somehow related?

He thought about the rest of the CoS. Belle, Marta, Leon, Christie, and himself. Was it a stretch to think that each one of them could be in danger? Tom's would have been the last postcard and now it was a puzzle piece likely missing forever. He'd planned on giving Dylan the note tonight, so he'd probably had it on him.

The adrenaline rush from all that had happened started to fade. Now his skin prickled. Was he reading into this something that just wasn't there? Pulling at straws.

"Lieutenant." One of the firefighters caught Marks' and Dylan's attention. "We found what I believe to be the cause of the explosion."

Marks made a quick introduction. To Dylan he said, "This is Lieutenant Lee Hansen, BFD's arson investigator. Lee, this is Special Agent Dylan Curtis with DHS."

After Dylan shook hands with the arson investigator, Hansen continued. "A Molotov cocktail was thrown into the house, likely through a window."

"So someone just blew this house to shit." Dylan ground his teeth. "It definitely wasn't an accident."

"That's what my preliminary investigation suggests," Hansen said.

The investigator studied Dylan, as if reading him. "Once we've conducted a thorough investigation, we will get with BPD and DHS."

"This is too much of a coincidence." Marks's forehead creased as he frowned. "Both Nate O'Malley and Dr. Zumsteg dead? A little unbelievable that they would be unrelated if you ask me."

"I'm going to call in a team," Dylan said. "I believe this relates to an ongoing investigation."

His skin grew cold as he realized Belle had been alone the whole time he'd been helping with the fire and the investigation. He'd thought she was safe out in his truck, but that was before he'd discovered this explosion had been a deliberate act. Murder.

He turned to Marks and Hansen. "I've got to check on something."

Dylan didn't wait for a response as he made his way through the rubble and back out into the street that was crowded and still surrounded by neighbors who looked on with worried expressions. Dylan's heart pounded and his blood raced through his veins as he hurried to check on Belle. He ran to where his truck was parked. The lights were off and the engine was no longer running.

He jerked open the passenger door.

His heart nearly stopped and a wash of cold swept him from head to toe.

Belle was gone.

For a moment he stood there, his gaze sweeping the cold truck cab. His heart jackhammered. His keys were no longer in the ignition. Her purse was where she left it on the passenger floor. The jacket he'd given her to wear wasn't there, so she was probably wearing it. But she was gone.

He whirled and slammed the door shut, trying to think. Had the person or persons responsible for killing Tom have taken Belle?

Almost crazy with the need to find her, he whirled to go back to the thinning crowd and locate Marks. They had to find Belle.

Just as he turned, he saw her walking toward him, away from the crowd. He braced his hand on the truck, afraid his legs wouldn't hold him up. He'd been so afraid she'd been taken and worse—the possibility that she'd been murdered, too.

She had her arms folded, hugging the jacket around her as she neared him. Blue and red lights flashed, illuminating her face.

"I told you to stay in the truck." He didn't mean the sharp bite in his tone.

She didn't seem to notice. "Is it true that was Tom's home?" Her lower lip trembled. "Was that his body they brought out of the house?"

Dylan took her and held her close. So damned glad she was alive and in his arms, he squeezed her even tighter to him. He knew the only thing he could do was tell her the truth and let her know that her life could be in danger. All of their lives could be.

"I believe it was." He pressed his lips to the top of her head, his hand cupping the back of her head as she buried her face against his chest. He wasn't sure how he could comfort her. "I'm so damned sorry."

Her shoulders trembled with the force of her sobs.

Hair on the back of his neck prickled. "I think I should get you out of here."

"I just want to go back to my hotel room." Her voice sounded small as she spoke.

103

He worked through everything in his mind. If he was right, and someone had been watching them, they might know where Belle was staying. They'd also probably know where his ranch was, and that he was a part of the CoS.

"We need to go somewhere else." He drew away and took her by the shoulders. "I know a little bed and breakfast. I'll take you there. Okay?"

She nodded, tears running down her cheeks and a fearful expression on her features. "What about the others?"

He opened the passenger side door for her. "While I'm driving, you call Leon, Marta, and Christie."

She stepped up into the chilly cab and dug his keys out of the jacket pocket. "Sorry for scaring you. It was just that you'd taken so long and I wanted to know what was going on."

"It's all fine." He took the keys she handed to him. "As long as I know you're safe."

Once he'd climbed in, started the truck, and heat was blowing from the vents, they headed away from the horrific scene and back down the hill.

After Dylan gave her instructions as he drove, Belle started to make the calls. Her hands shook as she found Leon's name in her contacts and pressed "Call". Everything felt so surreal. Each member of the CoS might be targeted? Why? Nothing was computing in her brain for it to make sense.

It was after midnight and Leon sounded sleepy but concerned as he answered the phone, and clearly saw her name come up on his caller ID. "Belle?"

"Leon, I'm still with Dylan." She took a deep breath, trying to keep from sobbing. "Tom's dead."

"What?" Leon sounded fully awake now. "Tom?"

"Dylan thinks someone might be targeting the CoS, and the remaining five of us are in danger." The words didn't seem real as she spoke them. "He believes it might have something to do with the postcards."

"You're sure?" Leon's voice held disbelief. "How did Tom die?"

She explained about the explosion and that Dylan thought it wasn't an accident.

"You need to get yourself and your family to safety." She swallowed and proceeded to give Leon the instructions Dylan had spelled out to her. "Dylan said to go to a small hotel in Sierra Vista where you can go under an assumed name without showing ID. Some kind of crappy no-tell motel."

"Shit." Leon bit out the word. In the background, Belle heard Leon's wife's voice, asking what was going on. Leon's words were a little muffled as he must have pulled the phone away from his ear. "Babe, get the kids together. I'll explain in a minute." His voice was clear again. "Okay, we'll go."

"Tell Leon to call me in the morning," Dylan said.

She repeated the instruction.

"I still have Dylan's card." Leon sounded agitated. "I'll get a hold of him. Both of you be careful."

"Just get going." The urgency within Belle made her jittery. "I'm going to get a hold of Marta and Christie."

Streetlights flashed by as Dylan drove. She disconnected with Leon and pulled up Christie's number. The call went straight to voice mail. Feeling almost frantic, she pressed redial and again she heard Christie's voice, telling the caller to leave a message.

"Christie." Belle tried not to rush her words. *Call me. I need to talk with you. It's urgent."

When Belle disconnected, she looked at Dylan. "What if something has happened to her?"

"We'll go to their house." Dylan's expression was grim. "See if you can get a hold of Marta."

Belle nodded and got Marta's number. The call was answered after two rings.

"Hello?" The voice was not Marta's and it was far from calm. "Who is this?"

"This is Belle Hartford." A sick feeling gripped Belle's stomach. "I'm trying to reach Marta."

"This is Marta's wife, Nancy." The woman sounded like she was crying. "We're at the hospital."

"Oh, Nancy. What happened?" Horror rose up inside Belle, clawing its way through her chest as her gaze met Dylan's. "Is Marta okay?"

"She's in serious condition." Nancy's voice was tight. "Someone hit her over the head. When I found her there was blood everywhere."

"Oh, my God." Belle put her hand over her mouth then lowered it to speak. "Are you at the Copper Queen Hospital?"

"Yes." Nancy sobbed. "The force of the blow caused swelling to her brain and the doctors induced a coma. They said it was to protect her brain from being damaged by the swelling and pressure."

"We'll be there." Belle's heart thudded. "We just have to check on Christie."

Nancy was apparently too distraught to question why Belle had called at this hour and why she was checking on a friend this late at night.

"Ask her if there are police officers at the hospital," Dylan said.

Belle asked Nancy the question.

"Yes." Nancy's voice cracked. "Why?"

Dylan took the phone from Belle. "Tell one of the officers to stay close, that Agent Curtis with DHS believes it might be an attempt on her life. I'm going to call BPD to make sure an officer is posted."

Belle could hear the woman's frantic questions. Dylan said, "We'll be there as soon as we can to explain."

After he ended the call, he handed the phone back to Belle. "Try Christie again."

Belle's mind was spinning as she brought up Christie's number. When it went to voicemail for the third time, she wanted to scream.

While she tried to call Christie, Dylan spoke on his phone and she heard him address someone as Lieutenant Marks before giving a quick rundown and asking for an officer to be posted by Marta's hospital room.

Dylan made a second call as Belle left Christie another message. She heard him explain the situation in more detail to whoever was on the other end of the line.

She realized they were almost to Warren, where Christie lived. Dylan shoved his phone back into its holster and guided the truck to one of the terraces where some of the nicer homes were located.

Belle gripped her phone so tightly that it dug into her hand and her fingers ached. When they pulled into Christie and Salvatore's driveway, Belle was opening her door before Dylan had brought the truck to a full stop.

He grabbed her arm as he put the vehicle into park. "Stay here." His expression was hard as he looked at her. "Lock the doors when I get out. I need to make sure it's safe."

The look on his face told her she shouldn't argue because she wouldn't win even though she wanted to see for herself that Christie was okay.

But what if Christie wasn't all right?

Dylan climbed out and waited for her to lock the doors before he strode to the wrought iron security door at the entrance.

CHAPTER 10

Salvatore held his phone to his ear and listened to Ryan Davies. Salvatore stood in front of the special bookcase he'd had installed when his contractor cousin had put in the safe. Just one flick of a switch and the bookcase would swing open to a set of stairs that led to two rooms beneath the house.

In those rooms, he had enough supplies for himself and Christie to survive for well past a month. And beyond that...freedom. If anything ever went down where he needed an out, they would be gone once things had cooled.

He listened to Davies, a mercenary for hire that Salvatore had retained through his most powerful cousin, El Verdugo. Dr. Tom Zumsteg was no more. And thanks to a bug Davies had planted in the doctor's phone at the hospital, Salvatore knew that Zumsteg hadn't had time to give his postcard to Dylan Curtis.

Salvatore gave a triumphant smile as he ended the call with Davies. Now Salvatore needed to get rid of the rest of the circle to make sure they didn't figure out the meaning of the cards. Once Salvatore had gotten more out of Christie, after hearing what had been on her own card, he'd known that those notes were meant to point back to him.

It was too bad Rodrigo required the services of Davies now, so the mercenary wasn't available to wipe everyone out who needed to be eliminated. Salvatore would have to rely on others to rid him of those he despised…every single member of the circle.

He couldn't allow them to figure out what Nate O'Malley had been trying to tell them.

Salvatore's phone rang and he looked at the screen. Oscar Garcia, a nurse at the Copper Queen Hospital, with more good news, he had no doubt.

"Is she dead?" Salvatore asked instead of giving a greeting.

Oscar cleared his throat. "No."

Sudden fury burned in Salvatore's chest like heated metal as he held the phone to his ear and said the words slowly. "Marta De La Paz is not dead?"

Oscar was clearly trying to sound confident as he spoke. "The doctors do not know if she will recover."

"You will make sure she dies." Salvatore clenched and unclenched his free hand as he stopped and stared at the closed door. The office was soundproofed and his wife would not hear even if he shouted. He managed to maintain control. "You are a fucking nurse. You can go into her room when there is an opportunity. Smother her with a pillow. Anything."

Oscar let out an audible breath. "The authorities have posted a guard at her door. A policeman."

Salvatore's body went rigid. Law enforcement had already figured out that the precious circle was being targeted? Had Dylan Curtis figured it out so soon? He had to be behind it.

Trying to relax his muscles, Salvatore forced himself to take a deep breath. He should not be surprised since Curtis was a federal agent. With the attack on Marta and the explosion happening at the same time, however, Salvatore had hoped Curtis wouldn't have time to catch on until tomorrow when it was too late and the rest of the circle would be dead.

"Find a way," Salvatore said in a fierce growl to Oscar. "Kill her."

"Yes, sir." Oscar had barely spoken the words when Salvatore disconnected the call.

If only they had known where Curtis was tonight, they would have taken care of the one man who could have put everything together so quickly.

Salvatore made another call, to his most trusted man, Paco Esperanza. He'd have Paco keep an eye on Oscar and make sure he did the job.

With a growl, Salvatore started to reach for his humidor to get the key to the door above the safe. He hadn't indulged in a few days, but right now he wanted to snort a line of coke more than he cared to admit.

A knock at the office door jerked his attention from his thoughts and his hand from the humidor. Why would Christie bother him this late at night? He frowned and strode toward the door, unlocked it, and yanked it open to see his wife standing in front of him, a robe wrapped around her slender form, her red hair tousled.

"Someone is at the front door." Christie furrowed her delicate brows. "The doorbell has been ringing. I thought you might not want me to open it myself this late at night."

The doorbell rang insistently through the house as she finished speaking. He hadn't heard it before, thanks to the soundproofing in his office.

Without answering her, he headed down the hallway to the front door that was heavy and solid behind the security door.

He peeked out the peephole and saw that Dylan Curtis was on his doorstep.

For one moment Salvatore wondered if Curtis had guessed who had ordered the murders of the circle members. He mentally shook his head. No doubt Curtis was here for a more noble cause—to inform and warn them.

Salvatore opened the door. The irritation that was likely on his features would be excused as being interrupted at such a late hour.

"What's going on?" Salvatore tried not to snap as he spoke through the screen of the security door.

"Dylan." Christie moved beside Salvatore and he wished he'd sent her to bed. "Has something happened?"

"Do you mind opening up?" Curtis gestured to security door.

"Of course not." Christie bit her lip as she looked up at Salvatore.

He clenched his jaw tight, unlocked the door, and pushed it open, but did not invite Curtis in.

Curtis looked from Salvatore to Christie. "There's no easy way to say this. Tom is dead."

Christie's eyes widened and she clapped her hand over her mouth as if to hold in a scream.

Salvatore tried to look appropriately shocked. "What happened?"

"An explosion at his home." Curtis moved his gaze to Salvatore. "It was a bomb."

"My God." Salvatore looked at his wife and put an arm around her shoulders as shock and disbelief crossed her features.

"That's not all." Curtis turned back to Christie. "Marta's in the hospital."

Christie's fear filled eyes widened. "Is she going to be okay?"

"The doctors don't know." Curtis looked at Salvatore. "I don't have time to explain anymore. I believe we need to get everyone in the circle to safety. I think we're all being targeted."

"Of course." Salvatore held Christie closer. "I won't take any chances with my wife's safety."

"Where is everyone?" Christie looked terrified.

Curtis shook his head. "We don't have time to discuss it. You should leave your house now. For all we know, a bomb could be set to blow in your house."

"I have my keys." Salvatore reached into his pocket.

Dylan shook his head. "We know my truck is secure. Come with us."

Salvatore's mind worked through this unexpected problem. He hadn't planned on being expected to go into hiding. Perhaps he should have.

Everything incriminating he owned was tucked in the safe, all of it handwritten. He kept nothing that would be of use to the police computerized. Nate, however, had put much on his own laptop. Fortunately, Salvatore had "acquired" the laptop and he had destroyed the hard drive himself in one of the two rooms beneath the house that he accessed via the bookcase.

Even an explosion wouldn't open that safe. He had no reason to be concerned.

As far as going with Curtis, this might be a very good thing. He would be able to keep tabs on the rest of the circle and in the loop about what progress was being made on the five remaining postcards.

Christie looked up at Salvatore and he gave her a nod. "We will go with him."

She wrapped her robe more tightly around her as they stepped over the threshold and Salvatore locked both the front and security doors behind them.

When they reached the truck, he saw that Belle was sitting in the front passenger seat. He heard the locks click as Dylan gave her an obvious signal to unlock the doors.

"Oh, thank God," Belle said as Christie climbed into the back seat.

The two women hugged, tears rolling down both their faces. Salvatore found it difficult to wear a concerned expression when all he wanted to do was take a gun with a silencer and shoot all three of them in the head right now. He could picture the blood spatters and imagined himself calling the cleanup crew to get rid of the bodies and the truck.

As Christie put her seatbelt on after she sat behind Belle, Salvatore eased into the seat behind Curtis.

Yes, he would have to kill Christie. It might put suspicion on him if she were the only one who did not die, and he couldn't take that chance.

If he had his handgun with him, he could pull it out and shoot the fucking federal agent in the back of the head then kill the other two bitches before they knew what was happening.

Even though he'd loved his wife since high school, he had never been able to forgive her for not bearing him sons. It was time to take care of her, along with the rest of the circle, and move on.

CHAPTER 11

Belle had a hard time pulling herself together, but she felt she needed to for Christie's sake. They got out of the truck after Dylan parked in the hospital parking lot. Christie still looked pale and shaken, and kept her bathrobe and one of Dylan's jackets tightly around her. Belle hugged her friend with one arm as they headed to the front doors of the hospital.

Salvatore walked behind them with Dylan, who was answering most of Salvatore's questions but dodging others. Some information Dylan seemed to be holding back, and she assumed it was because of the investigation.

The glass doors slid open and they walked into the lobby. The hospital had been remodeled and smelled like new carpet and paint. Belle waited with Christie as Dylan showed his credentials at the information desk and asked where Marta's room was. He was given directions and then they headed that way.

When they reached the nurse's station, Salvatore, Christie, and Belle were told they would have to take a seat in a small waiting area. Dylan had once again shown his badge and he went down the hall and out of sight.

Belle and Christie sat next to each other as Salvatore paced the room. Christie rested her head against Belle, who still had her arm around her friend's shoulders.

The horror of the day weighed on Belle. They'd just had Nate's memorial, and now Tom was dead and Marta was clinging to life.

"What's happening?" Christie's voice was thick from crying. "What's in those postcards that makes us all targets?"

"I don't know." Belle swallowed back the fear enhanced by Christie's words. "Whatever it is, it has to be bad."

"It's a nightmare." Christie was dry eyed now as she raised her head and looked at Belle. "How can any of this really be happening? I feel like I'm going to wake up and find out it was all a bad dream."

"I wish it was a nightmare." Belle stared at her lap. "Because then none of this would be real."

She fingered the hem of her sweater, feeling its softness between her fingers. That small movement helped to ground her in a strange way, like a touch of what was real when everything around her was so unreal.

What was going on? Why were they being targeted? What was in those damned postcards?

She knew Nate would never intentionally put them in danger. He must have thought that he could give them clues to something big, knowing that they would all discuss the cards if something happened to him. He must have been certain that he wasn't going to survive whatever trouble he'd gotten himself into.

Nate, she thought, her chest hurting with the pain of all that had happened, *what did you get us all into?*

Dylan strode down the hallway to Marta's room. He didn't recognize the BPD officer at the doorway, but his name patch said Hathaway. Dylan showed his creds.

"Lieutenant Marks said to expect you." Hathaway opened the door to the room and let Dylan in.

His gut sank at the sight of Marta amongst all of the tubes, along with a horrifying-looking instrument inserted into her skull. Marta was not a small woman but with the way she was hooked up on a life support system, the bed seemed to swallow her. Seeing his friend like that sent a sharp pain through his gut.

A blonde woman sat in a chair beside the bed, holding Marta's hand in hers. The woman's blue eyes were red and it looked like she was holding onto her composure by a thread.

She met Dylan's gaze as he stopped directly in front of her. "I'm Special Agent Dylan Curtis with DHS. I'm also a friend of Marta's."

"I'm Nancy." The woman looked at Marta and back to Dylan. "I'm Marta's wife."

"Marta spoke of you with love and pride." Dylan studied the pretty woman's face. "I'm sorry meeting you wasn't under better circumstances."

Nancy looked at Marta. "She's talked about you and your Circle of Seven many times over the years." A tear squeezed from one of Nancy's eyes. "She commented on how she'd wished you all had done a better job of staying in touch."

"I agree." Feelings of regret ran deep, burning Dylan's soul like a white-hot river of lava. Nate, Tom, Marta. People he'd loved but hadn't taken the time to keep up with. Even with Nate, Dylan felt he should have been there for his friend far more than he had.

He took the only other empty chair in the room and sat close to Marta. "What can you tell me about what happened tonight?"

It looked as though Nancy was struggling to speak. "I had a late shift." She brushed hair from her eyes. "When I got home, I checked on the kids and both were sound asleep. Sometimes Marta waits up for me, sometimes she's asleep. I didn't see her in bed, so I went into the bathroom."

Nancy's eyes welled with tears and her voice was thick when she continued. "Marta was on the floor by the toilet, blood in a pool by her head."

Dylan's gut tensed as he leaned forward in his chair and braced his forearms on his thighs. "Take your time."

She took a deep breath then let it out again. "I called 9-1-1. While I was waiting for them, Marta stopped breathing. I tried mouth to mouth, but couldn't get her to breathe." Tears rolled down Nancy's cheeks. "The paramedics made it just in time. They were able to resuscitate her and brought her to the hospital where they induced the coma."

Dylan waited for her to go on.

Nancy wiped tears from her face with the back of her hand. "Why would someone do this to her?"

Dylan studied Nancy. "Did you see anyone around when you got home?"

She shook her head. "No."

"Where are your children?"

"With my mom." Nancy looked back to Marta. "She lives close to us."

Dylan pulled his phone out of its holster. "I want you to call your mother and tell her a law enforcement officer will be coming to take her and the kids somewhere safe."

Nancy's eyes widened and she put her hand over her mouth before lowering it. "You think our sons and my mom might be in danger?"

Dylan hesitated. "It's a precaution. We don't know what we're dealing with yet."

Nancy released Marta's hand and reached for a purse on the floor by the bedside table. She pulled out a cell phone and pressed a couple of icons.

By the time Nancy had her phone to her ear, Dylan was already speaking with Sofia Aguilar, the Resident Agent in Charge, and explaining the situation. Sofia was at her home, but took calls all hours of the night when it came to something as important as this.

His RAC didn't drill him about the cards, but he knew she would later. She focused on the problem at hand. "Give me the address and we'll get the kids and grandmother to a safe house. I'll get a couple of agents to the hospital for security. I'll also see to safe houses for Salvatore and Christie Reyes as well as Belle Hartford."

Dylan caught Nancy's attention from her phone call and got the grandmother's address before relaying it to Sofia.

"I will call you back with information." Sofia's voice was a little harder. "You and I also have a few things to discuss."

"Yes, Ma'am." Dylan blew out his breath as she disconnected.

Nancy set her phone on the bedside table. He could see her hands were shaking.

She turned back to him, fear in her eyes. "Are the kids going to be all right? Can you keep them safe?"

"We will." Dylan took her hands in his and squeezed. "Stay with Marta. I'll have someone bring you a tray at mealtime. I don't want you going anywhere without an escort." As the fear in Nancy's gaze magnified, he added, "Just as a precaution."

"Whatever you can do, do it." Her expression turned hard. "And find whoever did this to my wife." She took Marta's hand in hers again and gripped it. "So help me, if Marta doesn't pull through, *I'm* going to find the one who did this and kill them myself."

"We'll find him." Dylan stood. He placed a hand on Nancy's shoulder and squeezed. "You can count on it."

She looked at him for a long moment then nodded and turned back to Marta. He went to the opposite side of the bed and took Marta's other hand in his. Her fingers were warm but her body so still, so lifeless. A lump rose in his throat as memories of times long ago scrambled in his brain. So many memories of all of them and he hadn't bothered to make new memories with his oldest friends. Now they were being taken away from him one by one.

"I'll see you soon, Marta." Dylan squeezed her hand one last time before he turned away and walked to the door. When he opened it, he stepped back into the hallway and closed the door behind him.

He stopped in front of Officer Hathaway. "DHS agents will be here to relieve you within the hour."

The officer acknowledged Dylan, who turned and walked to the nurse's station where two nurses were talking. The nurses were red-eyed and he could tell they'd been crying. He overheard one of them say, "Dr. Zumsteg was a wonderful man." Her voice cracked.

The other nurse looked up and saw Dylan. She'd been the nurse he'd shown his credentials to earlier.

The curly-haired brunette nurse stood and approached the divider. Her badge had her picture and her name was Carrie Prince. "What can I do for you, Agent Curtis?"

"I'd like to talk with to Ms. De La Paz's physician." He looked from Carrie to the other nurse. "And I'd also like to speak to you a moment about Dr. Zumsteg." More DHS agents would be asking questions, so he intended to keep his questioning brief.

Carrie nodded. "I'll see if I can reach Dr. Miller."

While they waited for the doctor, Dylan asked the two nurses if they worked closely with Dr. Zumsteg and they both had.

"I can't believe his house just exploded." The other nurse, Jan Wickenburg, blew her nose with a Kleenex, then lowered the tissue. "How could that have happened?"

"Rest assured it's being fully investigated." Dylan looked at both nurses. "Did anything seem different about Dr. Zumsteg tonight, out of the ordinary?"

Carrie frowned and shook her head. "Not that I noticed. I was just coming in as he was leaving. He nodded to me and told me to have a good night, but that was it. Although he did seem a little more subdued."

"My shift started about an hour before Dr. Zumsteg left." Jan tilted her head. "He seemed preoccupied. He is normally a little more talkative. Not a lot since he's so busy, but today he was quieter."

A woman in a white coat approached, stethoscope around her neck. As he turned to her, Dylan saw by her badge that her name was Dr. Emma Miller. She was gorgeous, her blonde hair pulled back with a clip, and a no-nonsense look about her. Dark circles were under her eyes, but that didn't detract from her beauty. He wondered if the darkness was caused by exhaustion or the death of Tom. Or both. When he looked into her gaze and saw the depth of pain within them, he knew.

"Dr. Miller, I'm Special Agent Curtis with DHS." Dylan held out his hand. She shifted the chart she was carrying to her left arm then took his hand. Her grip was firm.

She held his gaze as they released hands. "What can I do for you, Agent Curtis?"

Dylan nodded to the empty corridor. "Mind if we speak in private?"

"Not at all." She fell into step with him.

He came to a stop, out of earshot. "I have a few questions to ask you."

She didn't smile and he was certain why there was such pain in her gaze. "I'll answer whatever I can."

First things first. "Please tell me about Marta De La Paz's condition."

"Certainly." Dr. Miller explained what Nancy had already told him, about the blow and having to induce the coma. "We're doing everything we can for her."

He asked her a few more questions before he said, "How well did you know Dr. Zumsteg?"

The pain was back in her eyes. "I knew Tom well."

He dove in. "You were seeing Dr. Zumsteg outside of work."

Her eyes widened slightly. It took only a flash for her to compose herself. "Yes, but we were discreet about it. How did you know?"

"I'm adept at reading people." Dylan studied her. "You're doing a good job at holding yourself together, but I have a feeling when you go home you're going to fall apart."

She cleared her throat. "So you need to question me?"

"Yes." Dylan took in the magnified pain in her eyes. "I'm sorry, but I won't be the last."

"I understand." She visibly swallowed.

"I need to know if you noticed anything different about Tom earlier today." Dylan watched her expression intently. "Did he mention anything unusual?"

A look of recognition dawned on her features. "You're the agent he spoke about, a good friend of his. He was supposed to meet you tonight."

Dylan did his best to not look surprised. "What did he say about that meeting?"

"Not much." She gripped the medical chart with both arms, hugging it to her. "He told me he had a postcard to give you that an old friend sent him. The friend that committed suicide."

"You two were close." A sharp pain tore his gut at the mention of Nate. "Did anyone else know about your relationship?"

She shook her head. "We made sure that no one did."

"Did you go out in public together?"

"No." She looked at him curiously. "Why?"

"Your home or his?" Dylan asked.

She looked as though she was starting to get perturbed. "Why does that matter?"

"It will help." He spoke in a low voice as a nurse passed by. "Trust me."

"I went to his house." She looked like she was forcing herself to relax and she shifted the chart to one arm. "I have a fifteen-year-old daughter and I never know if she might come home at a time I expect her to be gone."

"Why don't you take the day off?" Dylan said gently. "Is there anyone on call who can cover for you?"

"I am the on call physician." The beautiful doctor looked as if she was hanging on to her emotions by a thread. "I'm replacing one of our staff members who came down ill with strep."

The last thing Dylan wanted to do at that moment was contribute to the doctor losing her cool when she needed to maintain calm professionalism for her patients.

He dug his card out of the pocket of his overshirt and extended it. "This has my office number and my cell. Contact me if you think of anything that might have seemed odd or out of place. Perhaps a person you didn't know that you saw around more than once."

She took the card with an amazingly steady hand. A doctor's hand. "You think someone might have been following him?"

"Just looking at all angles, Dr. Miller." He stepped back.

"Thank you, Agent Curtis." She tucked the card into a pocket of her white coat and turned away.

Dylan headed for the waiting room. Before he reached it, his phone vibrated in its holster. When he withdrew it, he saw that it was his RAC.

When he answered, Sofia didn't waste time. "Everything has been arranged. Trace will be in contact with you."

"Thank you," Dylan said.

"You have some explaining to do." Her tone was hard. "Why the hell didn't you bring those postcards in?"

Dylan stayed outside the waiting room where he couldn't be heard. "This was personal. The cards were addressed to members of the Circle."

"Personal, my ass." She maintained an even tone but it had a harsh edge to it. "If it's so damned personal, you should be taken off the case."

"No." Dylan spoke sharper than he'd intended to. "These cards have very individualized messages to them, and I believe they have clues that only we can decipher."

He could picture Sofia pacing her home. "I don't give one shit about what you think. Get those cards to the office. You can make copies but the originals are to be on my desk when I get in. I'll be there at eight-thirty."

"I'll get them to you." He wanted to keep the originals, but he did need to allow them to be examined. Not to mention they could be evidence to more than one murder case. He glanced out a nearby window and saw that the sun was rising. It had been one hell of a long night. "I'm keeping Belle with me. We'll get her to the safe house later."

A couple of seconds passed, as if Sofia was deciding whether or not to tell him otherwise. "Once the agents arrive for Salvatore and Christie Reyes, and take them into protective custody, get your ass to the office."

"Yes, Ma'am." Dylan holstered his phone as soon as Sofia disconnected the call.

He walked into the waiting room, where he saw Salvatore staring out a window. Christie had her head against Belle's shoulder and both women appeared rumpled and exhausted. They had discarded the jackets on one chair.

Christie's bathrobe had slipped off one shoulder, and beneath it she wore a silky nightgown in a peach shade. Her dark red hair was tumbled around her face and she looked younger than she was.

Belle's cream-colored sweater was smudged with a black streak, probably from the scene of the fire when she'd left the truck. Despite her exhausted appearance, she was even more beautiful to him than ever.

Salvatore whirled from the window to face Dylan. "How is Marta?" It felt as though a touch of insincerity was in Salvatore's tone, and Dylan had to work to keep from frowning at the man.

Both Belle and Christie glanced up, apparently not having noticed Dylan in the room until Salvatore had spoken.

"She's still in a coma." Dylan cut his gaze from Salvatore to the women. "The doctor won't state whether or not Marta will make a full recovery."

Tears rolled down Christie's cheeks as she looked at Dylan.

Belle appeared even paler than she had a moment before. "Why would someone do that to her?"

Salvatore cursed under his breath. "Marta was a good woman."

"She *is* a good woman." Belle's voice rose and she glared at Salvatore. "She is *not* going to die. She *is* going to come out of this."

"Of course she is going to survive." Salvatore put his hands on his hips. "I am sorry. I am very angry at whoever is responsible."

"We all are upset." Christie sat up and wrapped her bathrobe more tightly around her. Her blue eyes pleaded with Dylan. "Find them. Make them pay."

He nodded slowly and gave them the same promise he'd given Nancy. "Trust me. I will."

Salvatore looked as if a thought had just occurred to him. "What about Leon Petroski and his family? Where are they?"

"Somewhere safe." Dylan wasn't sure where Leon and his wife and children were, but he would find out and get them to a safe house. But he wasn't about to discuss it with anyone.

"Where will we be going?" Salvatore went to his wife's side and rested his hand on her shoulder. "You and Belle will be going with us, of course."

Dylan dragged his hand down his face, feeling so damned tired. "You and Christie will be going to a different safe house than Belle will be at."

"I'm going to a safe house alone?" Belle frowned.

"It's safer keeping you all separated." Dylan met her eyes. "It's not good for you all to be at the same location."

"I guess that makes sense." Belle was still frowning. "What about you?"

"I have work to do to get this solved." Dylan looked from Belle to Christie. "I'm going to need to talk with everyone separately to determine what Nate was trying to tell us."

Belle said quietly, "With Tom dead, that's going to be a lot harder."

"Yes, it is." Dylan clenched his jaw before forcing himself to relax. "But I will figure this out, one way or another."

"*We* will figure this out." Belle's eyes had the same determined look in them that he remembered from when they were younger. "We're all in this together."

CHAPTER 12

Belle stood in the hospital lobby and worried the inside of her lower lip with her teeth. Her insides hurt, a gut wrenching pain that felt as if it might tear her apart.

She watched Salvatore and Christie being swept away by two agents in a black SUV. They were on their way to the safe house they'd be staying in, wherever that might be. Dylan had told her it could be anywhere in the county—Sierra Vista, Wilcox, Benson, or right here in Bisbee. No one would know but the agents.

When they were gone, Dylan walked with Belle out to his truck. He'd given the keys to two other agents who had pulled the truck up to the hospital doors so they wouldn't have to walk across the parking lot, leaving them wide open. The agents stayed with them until they were safely inside.

The agents had swept the vehicle for tracking devices and explosives, just in case someone had gotten to the truck while Dylan was in the hospital. When they left the parking lot, the two agents followed them in another black SUV.

Instead of taking Belle immediately to a safe house, he brought her with him to his office just outside of Douglas. A tall chain-link fence with barbed wire surrounded the buildings. He mentioned the office had been remodeled a year ago, and the fence added after an incident, but he didn't go into detail. She didn't press him because it didn't seem to be something he wanted to talk about, or maybe it was because he couldn't.

When they arrived at the DHS office, Dylan unlocked the glove compartment and pulled out the familiar postcards.

Once they were out of the truck, the agents accompanied them inside the office. It was just before eight AM and Belle was dead on her feet. She hadn't felt this tired since the old days when she'd worked two jobs at a time, each one a busy diner, just to get by.

Dylan took her into a large conference room. A big rectangular table was at the center of the room with padded office chairs surrounding it, slate gray industrial carpet, and a bank of monitors on the wall. He had her sit in one of the chairs.

After she was seated, he brought out the postcards. He spread the five out on the conference table, side-by-side, print side up.

They remained silent for a long moment as they studied the cards.

Belle broke the silence. "Why did Nate mail them on different days?" She looked at Dylan. "Maybe we're meant to read them in the order they're postmarked."

"Good idea." He arranged them by postmarked date.

They studied the cards a little longer.

Belle gestured to her own card from Nate. "What is he trying to say when he wrote *I'll never forget when your big brown dog bit me on the ass*?" She looked at Dylan. "I didn't have Flipper for long, but Nate would have remembered he was white."

Dylan's brow furrowed as he looked at her. "That's right. After Flipper bit Nate, your stepfather made you get rid of him."

Belle's expression clouded. "That was just an excuse because Flipper didn't even hurt Nate. It was a play bite. Harvey just never wanted me to have a dog and Mom was too wrapped up in getting his approval for everything that she caved in to him on that."

"Maybe that's it." Dylan ran his gaze over her postcard. "There are clues in the *wrong* details."

Belle thought about it. "You could be right. Everyone said his or her card had something wrong on it, but we didn't talk about what that was." She looked from the cards to Dylan. "We never had a chance to discuss them."

"On my card, he refers to his Army days." Dylan looked away, like his mind was searching through option after option. "He served in Afghanistan and received a purple heart and an honorable discharge when he was injured. But he referred to it on the card as Iraq. He didn't serve in Iraq. It didn't make sense to me why he would do that, but there's got to be something to this."

Belle shook her head. "What in the world was Nate up to?"

After Dylan had copied the fronts and backs of the postcards, he left the originals on Sofia's desk in individual evidence bags. He knew that it would take the CoS to figure out the meaning of the cards, but his RAC wouldn't understand that until she had a chance to look at them herself.

His cell phone rang and he pulled it out of its holster. He didn't recognize the number on the screen.

He connected the call and brought the phone to his ear. "Curtis here."

"It's Leon." He had a roughness to his voice that indicated a lack of sleep. "We are probably in the crappiest motel in Sierra Vista." A dog barked in the background. "G.I. Joe likes it here about as much as we do."

"The Oasis?" Dylan gave the name of what he knew was the crappiest motel in Sierra Vista.

"Yes, that's the one. Room twelve." Leon sounded disgusted. "We should have brought a black light to check for bodily fluids. Or maybe it was better not to know. None of us slept. We didn't want to touch anything."

"A team and I will meet you there, and we'll get you to someplace decent to stay." Dylan looked out the window at the chain-link fence that had been added after a bomb attack from the Jimenez cartel over a year ago. "I'll pick up Joe and we can board him at the vet's until this is over with."

"Good idea," Leon said. "Safer for him and easier for us to get around."

Dylan arranged for DHS agents to accompany him and Belle to Sierra Vista. The drive was longer this time as they were traveling from the Douglas area, near the Mexico border. As they drove, Dylan made sure they weren't being followed, and he knew the agents in the SUV behind him were doing the same.

Belle fell asleep on the way, her head resting on the window her chest rising and falling, her breathing slow and even. They'd been running on close to thirty hours with no sleep and he was going to have to get them both someplace safe. He needed sleep, too, if he was going to be worth a shit.

When they reached the motel, Dylan found a parking space near room twelve. Belle blinked, looking disoriented for a moment before straightening in her seat. She shoved her hair out of her face, her cheek red from having been pressed against the window.

"Lock the doors." He gestured to the black SUV that had pulled up beside them. "They'll stay on watch."

She nodded.

He left the truck running and heard the locks click as he ran to the door and knocked at the door with the brass 12 on the door. The curtains at the window beside the door moved slightly, as if someone was peering out. A chain rattled and then the bolt lock shot back before the door was opened.

Leon stood in the doorway looking as haggard as Dylan felt. G.I. Joe moved to Leon's side, looked at Dylan, and wagged his tail. He looked warily at the two agents near the SUV.

"Agents Johnson and Ortega will accompany you to a safe house." He gestured to the agents. "Let's get you and your family out of here."

The two sons and one daughter went first, and then his wife, Jane, followed. Dylan stopped Leon before he climbed in. "I'll be by to go over your card with you."

Leon nodded. "I'll see you then."

The agents in the SUV waited for Belle to unlock the truck's doors and for Joe to jump in. Dylan followed and slammed the driver's side door closed before he signaled to the agents and both vehicles left the motel.

Dylan took circuitous routes to ensure they weren't being followed as he made his way to a nearby veterinary clinic they'd looked up on Belle's phone. She called ahead and made sure the clinic also boarded dogs.

When they arrived, Dylan made sure all was clear around them and together he and Belle took Joe into the clinic. Thankfully the clinic was empty of furry patients and their owners when they arrived.

After Dylan checked in with the receptionist, a male tech with a nametag that read Rod Cornwell came out and greeted Joe as well as Dylan and Belle.

Rod crouched in front of Joe and let the dog get to know him before petting him. "Joe will have to be examined by the vet before we can take him back with the other animals we're boarding. But first we'll need some information from you."

Dylan told Rod what he could and explained that Joe had belonged to a war veteran who had recently passed away. They also did not know his shot records, but he did have a current rabies tag. According to the tech, Dylan would have to stay with Joe while the veterinarian performed the examination.

Joe was weighed on a large scale and then they were all shown to a small room before the door was closed behind them. The room had a long examination table along with two blue plastic chairs with wisps of white cat hair clinging to the backs and seat.

Belle sat but Dylan remained standing as they waited. The tech returned and used an anal thermometer to check Joe's temperature. The well-trained German shepherd did not move as the tech performed his duty.

When the vet came into the room, she introduced herself as Dr. Nicholson. The vet's focus went immediately to Joe and she greeted him. "Such a beautiful boy."

Joe jumped onto the table when instructed to, and the vet started her examination.

Halfway through, she hesitated. She frowned and went over a spot on Joe's thigh with her fingers. She parted the hair at the location she was touching.

She looked at Dylan. "A small rectangular object, about an inch long, has been inserted beneath Joe's skin."

Dylan's heart picked up a beat and he walked up to the vet and Joe.

She showed him the part in the hair where there was a small scar that had not yet healed. She met Dylan's gaze. "The incision is recent and you can see there's something beneath it."

"I need that X-rayed, Dr. Nicholson." Dylan studied the location and saw the slight bulge beneath the skin. "I need to know what it is as soon as possible."

She tilted her head. "Can you explain what is going on?"

Dylan hadn't planned on showing his credentials, just needing to get Joe examined and boarded. But things had changed.

He pulled out his creds and showed them to the vet. "I'm Special Agent Dylan Curtis with DHS, and this dog just became part of an investigation."

Dr. Nicholson didn't press him. "We'll take care of it right away."

"I can't let Joe out of my sight." His jaw tightened. "I need to see for myself." The vet hesitated and looked at Belle. "She stays with me." Dylan added, "And everything will have to be performed by you and Rod. No one else is to be involved."

The vet clearly grasped the gravity of the situation. "Right this way." Joe went with the vet and the tech through a door in the back of the room, Dylan and Belle following.

Belle looked a little more alert now. "What was that all about?" She spoke in a low whisper. "Do you think there's some kind of information inside whatever was inserted beneath the skin on Joe's thigh?"

"It's a possibility." Dylan didn't elaborate as they came to a stop in front of an X-ray machine.

The machine was large enough to get a full side view of Joe. Rod was thorough, making sure all angles were covered.

It didn't take long for the X-rays to be developed and the vet took them into a private room to examine them. She clipped the X-rays to a light board.

"There are two foreign objects, one of which is his microchip." She pointed to a tiny rectangular chip. "It appears to be perfectly normal with his registration number on it."

She then gestured to a square that looked to be an inch in width and length. "I'm not sure what that is."

Dylan's blood seemed to flow faster through his veins. He looked from the X-rays to the vet. "I need that removed now."

Dr. Nicholson frowned. "I have a surgery to perform in fifteen minutes, Agent Curtis."

"This is important." Dylan eyed the vet squarely. "It's a matter of national security." He didn't know if it was, but he had to know what that implant was.

Dr. Nicholson studied Dylan, as if determining if he was being honest. She gave a slight nod to the tech. "Go ahead and prep him." The vet looked back to Dylan. "If you'll just take a seat in the waiting room—"

Dylan shook his head. "As I told you before, Joe doesn't leave my sight."

"Very well." She inclined her head toward a door down the hall. "We will perform the surgery to remove the implant now."

Within fifteen minutes, everything was prepared. The German shepherd lay quietly on the surgery table. He was a highly trained animal that did as he was instructed and didn't move. Belle stood beside Dylan as they watched.

After a small area around the scar was shaved, Dr. Nicholson applied a local anesthetic to Joe's thigh. The vet waited for the anesthetic to do its job before beginning.

The surgery took moments. The vet made the incision in the skin and withdrew a small, coated device with a pair of forceps. She set the blood-covered item on the metal tray beside the surgery table. She examined it, turning it over with the forceps, before looking at Dylan.

"It's in a silicone sleeve, likely to keep any sharp edges from irritating Joe's skin." The vet frowned as she looked back to the incision. "This was done much like individuals who are into body modification, of course in their cases for decorative purposes."

Belle frowned. "Body modification for decorative purposes?"

The vet nodded. "The implants can be subdermal or transdermal and can be quite large beneath the skin without harming the individual." She looked at Joe. "Of course that's not likely to be what's going on here. But the silicone should have protected Joe from sharp edges." The doctor examined the wound that remained. "Thankfully, there is no sign of infection."

The tech cleansed and sterilized the wound before stitching it up. Joe remained still.

Dylan nodded toward the thing that had been removed from Joe's thigh. "Let's see what's in there."

Dr. Nicholson used surgical tools to carefully remove the silicone sleeve from the device. When the bloody coating was removed, a small high tech device that looked similar to an SD card was left. It was slender and less than an inch long and an inch wide.

"I need to bag and tag these." Dylan gestured to the device and the sleeve. "What do you have that I can use?"

The vet reached into a drawer and brought out two small clear bags, two labels, and a pen.

Dylan scrawled the information on the labels before putting them on the bags. He used a clean pair of forceps to deposit the device into one bag then sealed it. He again used the forceps, this time to pick up the silicone and drop it into the other bag before making sure it too was sealed.

"No one is to know about this." Dylan looked from the vet to the tech. "Make sure your staff is clear on that."

"Of course. Only Rod has been privy to this." Dr. Nicholson glanced at Rod, who nodded.

Dylan gave his card with his contact information to the vet after she took off her surgical gloves. "I am the only one who should be in contact with you about Joe if necessary. If *anyone* else attempts to ask questions, call me immediately."

She nodded. "I will."

Dylan looked at Joe, who was still lying on the table. "I'll be keeping him with me after all. This changes everything."

Once Joe was ready and they had bought multiple cans of dog food before they checked out, they headed out of the clinic, into the chilly air, and to Dylan's truck. Joe didn't limp even though the wound might have been irritating him. Dylan helped Belle into the truck then instructed Joe to jump into the back of the king cab. The dog did so and sat on his haunches on the back seat.

Dylan climbed into the driver's seat, wishing he had his laptop so he could check out the contents of the SD card now. Just as he started to call his RAC, his phone vibrated. When he un-holstered the cell, the screen showed Sofia's number.

He started the truck to get warm air blowing. "Dylan here."

As usual, Sofia started without bothering with a greeting. "You need to find a secure location to take Ms. Hartford. A rash of witnesses from various agencies needed to be taken to local safe houses, so none are available."

"Damn." Dylan blew out his breath, then thought about a place he'd considered taking Belle to last night. "I know somewhere I can hide her that will be safe."

"Good. Any new developments?" she asked.

"Possibly something important, but I won't know for sure until it's checked out." He explained about what had looked to be an SD card, only more high-tech.

"Trace is in Bisbee right now," she said. "Call him and set up a secure location to meet."

When Sofia disconnected, Dylan called Trace. They arranged to meet at a feed and tack store in Palominas, between Sierra Vista and Bisbee. It wasn't likely they'd be seen in a rural location, behind a mountain of alfalfa hay bales.

They reached the store two minutes ahead of Trace, who drove up in his Ford Explorer. Trace and Dylan parked their vehicles in the back near the feed loading area. Belle stayed in the truck with Joe but raised her hand in a "hello" gesture to Trace. He raised his hand in response.

Dylan walked up to Trace and greeted him as he handed him the bags. "Get these back right away. We need to know what's on it."

"Screw waiting. Why don't we take a look now?" Trace took the two bags as he spoke in his drawl. "I've got my laptop. It'll be interesting to see what's on this SD card."

Dylan grinned. "It pays to know the right people."

Trace opened the front passenger door of his SUV and pulled a laptop from beneath the seat. He set it on the seat and lifted the lid. While the machine booted up, he grabbed a surgical glove from a compartment, removed the card from its bag, and inserted it into a port.

Dylan caught himself holding his breath as Trace pulled up the screen that showed six folders. "This isn't your standard SD card," Trace said.

"No kidding." Dylan shook his head.

"There's a hell of a lot of information on here that would never fit on a standard SD card." Each folder that had appeared was labeled with a number from one to six. Trace tried to open the first folder and a box requesting a password popped up.

"Shit." Trace tried the other five folders with the same result. "I think the passwords are encrypted."

Frustration in Dylan mounted. "Let's get the card to our lead tech guy. Hope to hell George can find out what is on it."

Trace nodded. "Will do."

Dylan braced one hand on the Explorer. "Got a favor to ask."

Trace closed the laptop and put the SD card back into its bag and sealed it. "Shoot."

"I need to swap vehicles with you." He jerked his thumb toward his truck. "I think whoever's behind this knows what my truck looks like. But that means you'll have to watch your back."

"No problem." Trace picked up the laptop. The keys were in the ignition, the SUV still running, air coming through the vents to keep the vehicle warm.

Trace greeted Belle as they changed vehicles, before she and Joe climbed into the Explorer.

"How are you holding up?" he asked.

She shook her head. "I don't know. Everything is too surreal."

Trace touched her forearm and squeezed. "Take care."

Dylan grabbed what he needed out of this truck and transferred it into the SUV. Trace moved away from Belle and did the same with his belongings.

Trace left and pulled onto the two-lane highway, headed back toward Bisbee.

Dylan glanced at Belle. She looked exhausted. He needed to get her to their destination where she could get some rest. He could use some sleep himself.

"What was on that card?" she asked once they were on the road. "Did it have anything important on it?"

"I don't know." He shook his head. "All of the folders are password protected."

She let out a deep sigh. "I was so hoping that there would be something on that card that would end all of this."

He took his gaze from the road to glance at her. "You and me both."

Dylan had decided on a little known, secluded bed and breakfast in Bisbee. Before going to the place, he picked an isolated area in Palominas to change into other clothing from a duffel bag he'd transferred from his truck. He traded his Stetson for a ball cap, his boots for a pair of running shoes, and a Diamondbacks baseball jacket that hid his weapons.

Belle tucked her hair beneath one of his ball caps, slipped back into his leather jacket, and wore an extra pair of his sunglasses. When they'd done their best to alter their appearances, they headed to the small, new and barely known B & B. He made sure it wasn't yet on the town's website of local accommodations before he called to make a reservation. The only room they had available was an upstairs suite that was nearly twice the cost of their normal rooms. He took it and gave the credit card number for one of his numerous undercover aliases.

The place was up in Tombstone Canyon, not too far from Main Street in Old Bisbee. It had once been one of the nicer, older homes that had been recently remodeled and turned into a quaint place to stay. Parking wasn't great in that area, but Dylan found a space on a street with a fairly steep incline.

Before walking into the B & B, Dylan pulled his ball cap low. Inside, with Joe sitting on the floor beside her, Belle perched on the edge of a chair in the entryway. A fit man in his early sixties sat at a small table that served as a registration desk. Dylan introduced himself under his alias.

"I'm Mitch Maddox and I'm the owner." The man appeared tense as he gestured to Joe. "I'm sorry, but no pets allowed."

Dylan shook his head. "He's a mental health service dog for my wife."

Mitch's body language changed and he looked more relaxed. "In that case, come on over here."

The man showed Dylan the old-fashioned guest book and he signed in under the name of the alias he was using. This persona said he was from Phoenix and he played it up. "We're here to get away from city life for some R & R."

"Used to live there myself. Twenty-six years." Mitch's expression screwed up with distaste. "Can't say that I blame you for wanting to get away from that rat race, even if it's a short vacation."

Mitch handed Dylan a couple of brass keys. Dylan thanked the owner and he, Belle, and Joe started up the stairs.

Whoever was looking for them wouldn't expect a dog, and both Belle and Dylan had changed their appearances. He hoped to hell that would be enough to keep them from being recognized from photos or by description, if anyone stopped by looking for them.

CHAPTER 13

When Belle had first curled up on a bed in the suite in the B & B, she thought she'd sleep for a week. Instead, her mind worked overtime, and the longer it whirled through everything that had happened over the last thirty-six hours, the more wound up she got.

Fear that she'd managed to push aside now made her tremble, and despite the blanket covering her, she grew cold.

The blackout shades had been drawn, keeping the late afternoon sun out. Soon it would be nightfall.

They'd eaten takeout earlier. One of the agents Dylan worked with had picked up Italian, including ziti, spaghetti, and garlic breadsticks. They'd fed G.I. Joe one of the cans of food they'd purchased from the clinic.

Belle hadn't expected to be able to eat, but after everything, she'd been hungry and had devoured the ziti and breadsticks. She'd taken a shower and had practically fallen into bed.

Yet she couldn't sleep. She shifted in the bed, pulling the covers more firmly about her as she thought about everything. So much had happened, it nearly made her head spin.

When Dylan had referred to her as his wife earlier, it had caused her belly to loop despite her exhaustion. What would it be like to be his wife? She could picture waking up with him, making breakfast together, and kissing him goodbye when he went to work. Just the thought of doing little domestic things together made her chest feel warm.

The warmth faded. He'd just been making sure Joe could stay with them when he'd referred to her as his wife. She was so exhausted she probably looked like she needed the assistance of a mental health service animal.

Footsteps came to the doorway of the suite's bedroom, startling her, and she opened her eyes. The room was dim but the light from the hallway illuminated Dylan's big frame. She couldn't make out his features with the light behind him.

"Are you all right?" He spoke softly.

"Yes." She swallowed then shook her head. "No."

He moved closer and the mattress dipped as he sat on the edge of the bed. He reached out and brushed hair from her eyes. His callused fingers were warm and gentle against her skin.

"Will you lie down with me?" She hated how weak she sounded. "I—I need you."

He looked at her for a long moment. "If it will help you get to sleep."

"It will." She nodded, her hair sliding into her eyes again. "Where's Joe?"

"He's resting in the living room, near the front door." Dylan shook his head. "I think he's on guard, prepared to protect us."

"I get that feeling from him, too." She pushed the hair back out of her eyes. "The pain meds the vet gave him seem to be working and he doesn't appear to be interested in chewing the stitches."

He turned on the bedside light before he removed his weapon and laid it on the nightstand, and then shrugged out of his shoulder holster. He unclipped his phone holster and set it next to the gun, then pulled out his creds and placed the wallet on the nightstand, too. He toed off his shoes, pulled off his socks, and then slid under the covers with her.

She had taken a shower and wore only the robe she'd found hanging on a hook in the bathroom. He had taken a shower, too, but had dressed before making business calls in the other room in the suite.

Now he faced her, and she was grateful he'd turned on the bedside lamp so she could see his rough features as he reached out to run his knuckles along the line of her jaw.

"I've missed you." The words came out before she could stop them.

He hesitated, and then trailed his fingers over her face, exploring it with his touch as if trying to memorize her features. "I've missed you more than you'd ever believe."

His words both sent warmth and sadness through her. Even though she'd left him, he'd still missed her. But the sadness came from the secret she'd kept so very long.

He brushed the side of her face with his fingers and ran his thumb over her lips. She shuddered with pleasure at the intimate contact. Every stroke of his fingers, every touch of his hand sent spirals of desire through her.

She didn't feel tired any longer. All she felt was the need to be in his arms and to have him inside her again.

He slid his fingers into her hair and cupped the back of her head. "I should leave. I can sleep on the couch." His voice was hoarse, as if he was forcing out the words.

"Please stay." She gripped the front of his T-shirt in her fists as she brought her mouth close to his. "Don't leave."

"Belle." The way he said her name so tenderly, a sigh of surrender in his voice, made her feel somehow powerful and strong.

She pressed her lips to his and he groaned. He moved his lips over hers, sliding to the corner of her mouth. He kissed her, nipping at her lower lip and causing a moan to rise up inside her. He drew her into his embrace, his body so hard and solid against hers. Her breasts ached, her nipples tight, and she was so very wet.

All her previous thoughts and jealousy over past lovers that he'd surely had fled in that moment. What mattered was that she was in his arms now. It was just the two of them existing on this plane in this world. Just the two of them together in a place and time where they belonged.

She moaned, wanting him with a frenzy that his slow kisses didn't allow. She pressed her body more fully against his, feeling his jeans through her robe and the erection that the tough denim barely contained.

Her need was so great that she squirmed against him, reached for the bottom of his T-shirt, and pulled it out of his jeans.

In a surprise movement, he took her wrists in his hands as he rolled her onto her back. The robe parted as he slid between her thighs. He grasped both her wrists in one of his big hands and pinned her arms over her head.

"Not so fast." He pressed his lips to her forehead. "I've dreamed about this moment since you left, and I'm going to treasure every moment I have with you."

His words sent thrills tingling in her belly and warmth sliding through her heart and soul. She no longer felt the frantic urgency, now she reveled in the moment.

He moved his mouth to hers and kissed her slowly, taking his time. She savored his taste and sighed from his gentle touch. He was such a big man now, but the way he moved his hands over her body was like a sculptor putting the finely crafted last touches to his work.

She widened her thighs so he was seated more firmly against her as the bottom of her robe fell completely to the sides. His erection was huge as it pressed against the center of her bare folds.

"You are the most precious thing to have ever happened in my life." He kept her arms over her head as he pressed gentle kisses to first one eyelid then the other, then each cheek, and the tip of her nose. "I've missed you so damn much."

Her heart pounded faster at his words that echoed what she felt, too.

His mouth found hers again and she felt the tightly reined desire within him. But he refused to set it free, insistent on taking his time with her.

"Let me touch you." Her words didn't come easy, she was breathing so hard. "I need to touch you."

"As long as you promise not to try to rip my clothes off again." He gave her a smile that did amazing things to her belly. "Can't have you taking advantage of me."

She couldn't help but smile in return. "I don't promise anything of the sort."

He released her wrists and she slid her hands into his short hair, wanting to clench her fingers in the strands and guide him to her breast so he could suck her nipple. But she let him go at his own pace, sighing and moaning with every kiss, every touch.

She moved her hands to his shoulders, feeling the power rippling through him as he shifted between her thighs. She moved her hands down until she grasped his massive biceps that bulged as he held his bodyweight off her, his hands braced to either side of her shoulders. His biceps hadn't been nearly as big when she'd known him before and she liked how he'd filled out over the years. Liked it a lot. Maturity did something to a man that made him so much more desirable.

He slid his lips along the column of her throat until he reached the hollow at the base. When he placed a soft kiss there, she shuddered from the growing need within. He moved so that he had one hand on the mattress while he used his other to trail his fingers down to the V of the robe.

She bit her lower lip, barely holding herself back from begging him to hurry. Begging him to take her now.

He took his time, skimming his knuckles over her skin, down to the valley between her breasts. He pushed aside her robe, exposing one breast. The areola puckered, her nipple tightening beneath his gaze. He circled the darker skin around her nipple with his finger before moving his hand to the other side of the robe. He undid the simple knot on her robe and slid the material aside, fully releasing both breasts and leaving her completely bare. They felt full and ripe, her nipples so ready for his mouth and his tongue.

When they'd been teenagers, making love had been wonderful and special. But he had never made love so reverently to her as he was now.

"Your breasts are as beautiful as I remember them." He lowered his head and slipped her nipple into his warm mouth.

She gripped his biceps as she gasped and arched her back, barely realizing she was doing it. He circled her nipple with his tongue then sucked it again. He spent time licking and teasing her, drawing out her arousal.

He moved his lips to her other breast and drew her nipple into his mouth and sucked. She was so aroused that tears burned at the corners of her eyes. Tears of want, of need, of desire. He took his time, sucking her nipple then trailing his tongue around the areola.

Her hands slid down his biceps to his forearms as he rose and settled on his haunches between her thighs.

The dark look of need in his eyes made her breath catch. The movement of his Adam's apple as he swallowed was the only sign that he was barely holding on to his control.

He helped her maneuver her arms out of the robe, then slipped it out from beneath her and tossed it onto the floor.

"Let me see you." Her voice trembled, afraid he would deny her. "Please."

He crooked his finger. "Come here."

She got to her knees in front of him and reached for his T-shirt as he raised his arms. He helped her pull the T-shirt over his head and he dropped it to the floor.

A sigh of pleasure escaped her as she looked at the sheer male beauty of him. She skimmed her fingers over his broad shoulders, down his muscular torso, and over his flat nipples.

She frowned when she saw scars and wounds that had not been there before. One looked like an old bullet wound, another a thick scar from what had probably been a serrated blade.

"You've been injured." She traced her fingers over another scar on his chest.

He caught her hand in his and held it to his heart. "Hazard of the job."

She bit her lip and continued over his rippled abs, and on to his belt buckle.

He moved back and eased off the bed to his feet, and he started to unbuckle his belt.

"Let me." She followed him until she was standing in front of him, and then reached for him.

Dylan sucked in his breath as the warmth of Belle's fingers skimmed the waistband of his jeans. She seemed intent on opening him like a Christmas package without tearing the wrapping. He wanted her to just rip it all off him.

He did his best to relax. He wanted to take his time with her and he should allow her to do the same with him.

She unfastened his belt buckle before reaching for the button to his jeans. Her hands were steady as she pushed the button through its hole and then pulled down the zipper.

He let out his breath when the jeans no longer strangled his raging erection. His need for her was so great, however, that he felt only minimal relief. She pushed the jeans down his hips to the floor and she crouched as he stepped out of them and she threw the jeans on top of his T-shirt. She peeled off his boxer briefs, freeing his cock, and got rid of his underwear with the rest of his clothing.

As she sat on her haunches, she stroked his skin with butterfly touches. Her touch drove him nearly out of his mind as she moved her fingers from his hips and down past his groin. She seemed so focused on touching all of him. She avoided his cock as she continued to run her palms along his thighs to his knees and then calves.

"You're so muscular now." She said the words with a sigh. "So big. I loved your body before, but I love the man you've become."

He wanted to say something, but words stuck in his throat as she rose to her knees, her mouth close to his erection.

"And this." She smiled as she traced her finger from the head of his cock to his balls. "I've missed this."

His heart pounded in a way it never had when he'd been with other women. Every woman he'd ever been with had been nothing more than a lay to ease an ache that had never left him when Belle ran from him. He had chosen older women who loved sex and he'd hoped each woman hadn't expected more from him than that.

He tended to chase women away with his gruffness and he'd been told his arrogance had sent many in the opposite direction, too. He hadn't minded that. It kept women from getting attached to him. He hadn't wanted any attachments over the years. Maybe he'd been afraid to lose a woman like he'd lost Belle.

Or maybe he'd been waiting for her to come back. Praying for her to come back.

She lightly held his cock as she ran her tongue from the base to the tip. She circled the head in a way that caused him to clench his fists at his sides. A burst of jealousy shot through him as she fondled his balls and continued to lick his erection up and down before circling the head again with her tongue. Where had she learned that? From some other man?

He shook off the thoughts and focused on Belle. Beautiful, precious Belle.

He wanted her mouth over his cock, wanted to feel the wet warmth. Instead, she went for his balls, lightly running her fingers over them before bringing her lips close, darting her tongue out to lick them. She slid one of his balls into her mouth and lightly sucked.

It was one of the most erotic sensations he'd ever experienced. He slipped his fingers into her hair as he watched her. The silkiness of her hair in his hands added to the feel of her paying such close attention to his balls.

She licked a path from his balls to the base of his erection. She continued up to the head of his erection, then looked up at him as she slipped his cock into her mouth.

Her gaze held his as she took him deep into her mouth. Mesmerized, he couldn't take his eyes off her as she swirled her tongue at the same time she moved her head up and down. He felt the power of an orgasm building in his groin, heat from that one location threatening to explode.

She let him slide out of her mouth and licked her lips as he watched, his cock almost at the bursting point. "Can you still come more than once?" Her words sounded like a purr.

He gritted his teeth and had to nod before he could get anything out. "Yes, baby."

"Perfect." She gave him a sultry smile. "I want to swallow every drop."

Hell yes. He wanted to come in her mouth almost as much as he wanted to climax in her pussy.

She wrapped her fingers around the girth of his erection and lowered her head. She worked her hand up and down the base of his cock as she slid her mouth over the length of him, taking him all the way to the back of her throat.

"God, that feels good, Belle." He liked saying her name. It made him feel even closer to orgasm.

She swirled her tongue as she moved him in and out and then she made a low purring sound again. This time the vibrations went straight through his cock.

He bit back a shout as his orgasm erupted within him. His come shot into Belle's mouth as she continued to suck him. He shuddered from the power of the climax, feeling it through his whole body.

For a moment it left him feeling weak, almost as if he might not be able to remain standing much longer. Had it been anyone else, he could have controlled it, but seeing her on her knees before him, giving him pleasure like that, he just hadn't been able to hold off.

He caught her by the shoulders and brought her to her feet. She was licking her lips as she smiled at him. "That was so good."

"You're telling me," he managed to get out, and she gave him a naughty grin.

He scooped her up in his arms. "You know what they say about paybacks."

She laughed as she clung to him. God, how she'd loved taking him in her mouth and giving him pleasure. And his taste had been incredible.

He laid her down on the center of the bed and moved so that he was over her. His cock was hard again and she marveled at his stamina.

His eyes seemed to burn hot as he looked down at her. "Roll onto your belly."

She gave him a sexy smile. "You want to take me from behind?"

He slid off the bed. "Roll over. I'll be right back."

She did as he instructed her to and rested her head on her hands. She watched his back, enjoying the sight of his muscular ass and his muscles flexing as he walked across the room and came back with something in his hand.

When he reached her, she saw that he'd grabbed the complimentary lotion the B & B had provided and a condom packet.

"Close your eyes." The command was gentle but firm.

She did as he told her, then shivered as he squeezed lotion down the length of her spine. She caught the scent of oranges. The bottle made a small *thunking* sound as he set it on the nightstand.

The bed dipped with his weight as he straddled her buttocks and started massaging the lotion into her skin. "You need this." He worked his hands over her shoulders. "You're even more tense than I realized."

She sighed with pleasure as his powerful hands worked out the kinks in her muscles. "I wonder why." She said it lightly, not wanting to take away from the moment.

"No telling." He massaged the base of her neck, and she was glad he played along with her.

For those moments it was almost easy to forget all that had happened. To feel like they were the only two in the world and they had come together by the forces of fate and evil.

Which they had. Only it might kill them all.

It had already taken Nate and Tom, and possibly Marta.

"You tensed again." Dylan's voice interrupted her thoughts, and she was glad for it. "Put everything out of your mind and relax."

She sighed as she fell into the massage, letting herself live in the moment and forget everything else. This time she was more focused on his touch, the way his callused hands felt on her skin, the weight of him as he partially rested on her buttocks, and the way his cock lay hard and erect against her ass.

The movement of his hands and the magic touch of his fingers lulled her into a state of relaxation. But as he eased down her body, her arousal grew.

He eased his hands to her ass cheeks as he scooted down. He squeezed more lotion onto her skin and worked the back of her thigh. His fingers brushed her folds and an involuntary gasp escaped her. The flood of moisture between her thighs was instantaneous.

She tried to made herself relax again as he continued to her calf, then her ankle, and her foot. Moved to her opposite foot and began to work his way up from her ankle to her calf. When he reached her thigh, he once again brushed the lips of her pussy.

Just as she thought he was going to pass it by again, he slid two fingers into her slick channel. She made a surprised sound that turned into a moan as he moved his fingers in and out.

"You're so damned wet." His words came out in a hoarse murmur. "I can't wait to be inside you."

Again. He didn't say the word, but it hung between them as if she could grab it and hold it close to her chest.

He removed his fingers from within her. "Turn onto your back."

She rolled over and reached for him.

He shook his head. "I'm not finished yet."

A moan rose up inside her. "I can't wait any longer. I *need* you inside me."

The lotion bottle was only half full as he squirted more onto his palm. "Oh, you can wait."

She whimpered then sighed as he massaged more lotion into her arms and legs, completely bypassing her torso. She was so wet for him, her nipples so hard, that she had a difficult time continuing to relax.

He moved over her again so that he was straddling her hips. She looked into his eyes, blue eyes that she had never forgotten. Some had called them icy blue, but they'd never been anything close to icy to her.

She thought of them more like the blue of a summer's day, when the sky was almost too beautiful to bear.

She reached up and ran her fingers along his jaw. The growth of his beard felt coarse beneath her fingertips as she traced his rough features. What had life been like for him over the years? Someday he would tell her. Someday she would have the answers to all her questions.

He gave her no more time to think as he massaged lotion on her breasts. He lightly rolled her nipples between his thumbs and forefingers. He watched her, never taking his eyes from hers. It was like he wanted to see every play of emotion across her face.

His fingers continued to work their magic as he eased down her body, rubbing lotion on her belly. When he reached the trimmed hair on her mound, he paused to run his fingers over the short hair.

He tossed aside the empty lotion bottle and it made a hollow sound as it hit the floor. He shifted and pushed apart her thighs with his palms and lowered his body.

Her belly flipped and anticipation caused her entire body to tingle.

He moved his head so his face was close to her folds and audibly inhaled. "God, I love your scent." He swiped his tongue along her folds and watched her as he did it. "Your taste..." He growled and dove back in.

She whimpered for more and he slid two fingers inside her again as he licked her folds and sucked her clit. She thought she'd go wild with all of the sensations that were burning her up, making her wriggle in his grasp without intending to.

His rough stubble abraded the insides of her thighs, an erotic sensation that made her feel even more sensitive.

He lifted her legs over his shoulders as he growled and his attention to her became even more intense. Her thighs trembled with the force of her oncoming orgasm. She could feel it rising inside her, growing stronger and stronger. Her body heated and perspiration broke out on her skin.

His fingers were so big it was almost like a cock was pumping in and out of her core while he licked her, sucked her, and took her higher.

It was there. So close. She was on the edge, just waiting to tip over.

He growled against her pussy and that was all it took.

She cried out, her eyes going wide as waves of pleasure took over. She barely had the presence of mind not to scream. She gripped the bed covers in her fists, her body bucking against his face as she came hard.

Her mind whirled, yet she could think of nothing but the sheer pleasure of the orgasm. He didn't slow until she was thrashing, tears rolling from the corners of her eyes.

When he finally stopped, her core continued to clench around his fingers. He withdrew them and she gave a sigh of relief.

"That was amazing." She kept trying to catch her breath. "It was so intense I'm not sure I could survive another one like it."

He grinned. "That's just the beginning. There are plenty more where that came from."

She couldn't help a smile, but it only lasted a moment. His words made it sound as if this would continue, as if they had a future together. But that would never happen.

He rose up so that he was over her and he searched her gaze. "What's wrong?"

"I just want you inside me." She was usually good at hiding her real emotions. She reached for his cock and guided it to the entrance of her core. She gave him a teasing look. "You're just taking too damned long."

"We'll just have to change that." He lowered his head and kissed her.

It was a long, sensual kiss, matching the pace of the night. He'd been serious when he'd said he was taking it slow with her. She'd found every moment of it so special that she knew she'd never ever experience anything like it again.

When he'd taken her breath completely away with his kiss, he quickly donned the condom and he started to slide into her wet core. "Damn, you feel so good." He slid in farther. "Wet and tight."

She gave a gasp and a cry as he filled her. Her eyes widened as she felt him stretch her and press hard inside her.

His pace was slow and even, his eyes never leaving hers. His cock rubbed against her G-spot and she found it hard to breathe. He appeared to have a difficult time breathing too, and beads of perspiration dotted his forehead and one trickled down the side of his face.

She raised her hips to meet his every thrust. His biceps bulged as he held his weight partially off her. The solidness of his body made her feel warm and secure. And his rock-hard body against her soft flesh didn't hurt anything, either.

He increased his pace, almost as if he couldn't help himself. He moved harder and faster and she watched as his jaw grew tight and his eyes darkened.

"Let go." She dug her nails into his back. "You've shown me how amazing you are. Now break free and take me hard and fast."

He kissed her hard this time, a kiss of fire and unrelenting passion. He grunted and raised his head, and then drove in and out, as hard and fast as she wanted.

Another orgasm spiraled inside her, growing and growing. This one was different, intense in a different way, and she cried out with every thrust of his cock. Her eyes nearly rolled back from the exquisite sensations and she had a hard time keeping her gaze focused on him. But somehow he managed to hold on, not letting her break eye contact.

Where the last orgasm had pushed her over a peak, this one slammed into her like a freight train. She shook her head from side to side, thrashing as her climax sent her mind tumbling so that she couldn't begin to think clearly.

She was barely aware of Dylan throwing his head back and shouting with his orgasm. His cock throbbed inside her as her core clenched around him, gripping him like a fist.

Several more strokes and then he collapsed on her, still managing to keep from crushing her.

"You are so amazing, Belle." He was breathing hard. "It is so good to be with you again."

She smiled as she came back to earth and kissed his forehead as he slid to one side and brought her close.

"For me, too," she said softly.

He tucked her in his arms and held her like he was never letting go.

CHAPTER 14

It was all Salvatore could do to keep from tearing into Christie and the two DHS agents protecting them. He wanted to break their necks, all three of them.

Maybe he should—although that would mean he'd have to abandon everything, and he enjoyed his life and his wealth too much. One day, when he'd accumulated millions, he would go to Mexico and live in a fine mansion. For now he had a good life.

As long as a dead man didn't fuck it up.

He'd had to give up his cell phone due to the DHS's fucking standard procedures, but what they didn't know was that he had a second cell for what he considered to be his "real" business. The one they had taken had been for personal calls and the "legitimate" business he ran.

They'd had no reason to search him as he had been placed into protective custody with his wife and wasn't a suspect.

The agents had taken them to some shithole place in Bisbee. Of course he hadn't been blindfolded, so he knew where he was. All he had to do now was get the information to his men.

Somehow he had to learn where the three others were being hidden. He had men all over the county and the Jimenez Cartel spread throughout the state. He knew the make and model of Dylan Curtis's truck and he had memorized the license plate number. He needed to get that information out to El Verdugo's men.

A cold sweat broke out on Salvatore's skin. If the new head of the Jimenez Cartel knew just how much of the cartel's empire could be exposed by Nate O'Malley's knowledge, Salvatore's own life would be in danger. There was a reason the head of the cartel was known as the Executioner. Even though they were distant cousins, Rodrigo wouldn't let that stop him from eliminating Salvatore.

All Rodrigo knew was that sensitive information in Salvatore's business could be exposed. Salvatore was a valued asset to Rodrigo, and the capo of the Jimenez Cartel had been willing to help.

Christie was deep asleep in the bedroom they'd been assigned, exhaustion and emotions finally overcoming her. Both agents were in the living room watching TV. Salvatore slipped into the bathroom, locked the door, and pulled his phone from his pants pocket. The phone was a slim model that he could make secure calls from.

He pulled up Oscar's number. The moment the man answered, Salvatore said, "Is she dead?"

A hesitation then, "I am sorry, señor. I have not been able to get to her. Law enforcement has been guarding her closely."

Salvatore would have exploded with fury if he didn't have to be concerned about the agents overhearing him. "I want you to kill that woman. Marta De La Paz must die. If you have to sacrifice your own life, so be it."

"My life?" Oscar's voice trembled. "But, señor, I have a family who needs me. Who will pay for their food and clothing and education if I am dead?"

"I will provide for them." Salvatore spoke calmly now. "I will make sure they want for nothing."

"I do not wish to die." Tears were in Oscar's voice now. "Please, señor."

"Do it or your family dies in your stead." Salvatore injected ice into his tone. "Either Marta dies today or I will have your wife and children slaughtered. Do you understand?"

"Yes, señor." Oscar was clearly crying. "I will make sure her life ends today."

"Your family's lives depend on it." Salvatore ended the call.

The next call he placed was to Carl Joplin, who had handled jobs for Salvatore in the past.

"Joplin here," came the voice.

"I require your services." Salvatore shoved one hand in his pocket as he spoke. "I am at a safe house, and I need you to take care of a problem I have as soon as possible. As usual you will be paid well."

"I'll take care of whatever it is." Car; didn't even have to know what the job was as long as there was good money in it.

Salvatore gave Carl the information on his location and those guarding the house. "Wait for a call before coming," Salvatore said. "I am requesting additional men from El Verdugo."

"Yes, sir," Carl said.

"My wife is with me. Do not touch her," Salvatore added.

"I'll be there as soon as everything is coordinated."

Salvatore drew in his breath and let it out. Now that he knew Marta would be dead before sunset, and that he would be rescued from this shithole, he had to make the harder call.

It angered him that his hands shook a little when he keyed in the numbers for his cousin, El Verdugo's, private phone.

"What?" The man's voice was like a bark when he answered in Spanish. "I am busy."

Probably busy with some young woman sucking his cock, Salvatore thought. Rodrigo was known for conducting business while forcing women to perform sexual acts. He'd done so on more than one occasion when Salvatore had been on business trips to Mexico to meet with the man. It had been clear that it excited Rodrigo to have other men watch but not participate. Not that Salvatore would have wanted to.

"I require assistance." Salvatore took a breath to continue, but was interrupted.

"Have I not given you enough?" Rodrigo spat the words. "I have problems of my own to deal with." In the background was a woman's muffled sound, as if she had something big in her mouth, confirming Salvatore's thoughts.

"I would not ask if it was not important." Salvatore began to feel a sense of panic that he was unaccustomed to. "The deaths of these people are key to protecting my business." *And yours.*

Rodrigo gave a grunt. "Wait while I attend to something."

The phone clattered and then Salvatore heard Rodrigo's shout of triumph, something Salvatore had heard Rodrigo do when he climaxed in front of others. A woman's cry followed. Rodrigo had probably backhanded her. He liked to get physical with the women when he was finished with them.

He shouted in Spanish, "Leave me, woman."

Salvatore gritted his teeth. It was one thing to kill a woman if it was necessary, another to treat innocent women the way Rodrigo did.

When Rodrigo got back on the phone, he sounded more relaxed. "Explain, Salvatore."

Salvatore told Rodrigo all that had happened, leaving out only the part that the Jimenez Cartel's operation was compromised as well. Salvatore spelled out what he needed and gave Rodrigo the contact information for Carl. Rodrigo agreed that his men would coordinate with Carl.

When Rodrigo disconnected the call, Salvatore gripped the phone and clenched his jaw. He looked around the bare bathroom. He wanted to slam his fist into the mirror, take a shard, and use it cut Christie's throat and the throats of the agents. Breaking their necks wouldn't be nearly as satisfying as seeing their blood spray across the room and watching them bleed out.

Instead of allowing himself to lose control, he reined in his emotions. He had to use them to find Leon, Belle, and Dylan. Marta would be taken care of, and soon Christie would, too.

There would be no mercy for anyone who got in Salvatore's way. Including—no, especially—his wife.

As rage poured through him, he pocketed the phone, jerked open the bathroom door.

Christie stood there, her eyes wide, her hand covering her mouth.

And Salvatore knew—she'd heard the conversation. Maybe all the conversations.

Fury burned through him like a raging fire. He glanced down the hallway and saw no one. Christie started to take a step back and lower her hand as if to scream. He clamped one hand over her mouth as he grabbed her, whirled her so that he wrapped his other arm around her throat.

She struggled. Kicked him. Clawed at his hands. Made muffled screams behind his hand.

He dragged her to the room they shared. He closed the door behind him and said in a low voice that he put all the menace in that he felt, "Do not scream, Christie. Or I will snap your neck."

She went limp in his arms and he threw her on the bed. He unzipped his pants. She looked at him in horror as he grabbed her foot and dragged her to the edge of the bed.

For the first time since he'd known Christie, he slapped her. He'd never gotten physical with her, and had been an attentive lover. She stared at him in shock.

When she tried to scramble back, he slapped her again. "Shut up," he said coldly.

He flipped her onto her belly. She struggled as he shoved her nightgown over her hips, tore off her panties, and took her without mercy.

CHAPTER 15

The light that came through the open bedroom door of the suite was enough for Dylan to see Belle's features. He studied her, looking at her lovely face as she slept, her eyelids closed, her lashes dark against her fair skin.

A little smile touched her lips and he wondered what she was dreaming about. In all the horror happening around them, somehow she had found a moment of peace.

So many feelings for Belle wound through him. He felt anger for what her stepfather had done to her, fear for her safety, the desire to protect her from anything that could ever hurt her… And a depth of caring that filled his chest with warmth, yet pain at the same time. He thought about the pain. It came now from knowing what she went through as a teen, her leaving, and all the years they'd missed together.

God, they'd missed so much. It occurred to him that part of what Nate had written on the postcard had everything to do with Belle:

"I want you to promise me something. Remember what you had, buddy. If it happens, second chances only come once. Don't let it pass you by."

Dylan's heart skipped a beat. This was a second chance with Belle and he couldn't let it pass him by. He *wouldn't* let it.

Images of Belle slipped through his mind, images of their youth and the love they'd shared. Even now it didn't feel like it was some silly teenage love. It had been real and deep...and special. And after all these years, it hadn't waned. He'd never been able to love another woman after losing the one woman who had made his world make sense.

When she'd left, that had all crumbled and he'd barely made it from one day to the next for so long. Eventually he'd moved on, but he'd never gotten over her.

But she was back now, and he had another chance.

A smile touched his own lips. Maybe she was dreaming the same thing he was thinking.

The blackout shades made it impossible to tell what time it was, but his internal clock told him it had to be around six-thirty in the morning. He hadn't intended to fall asleep as early as he had, but apparently he'd needed it. Belle certainly had.

He wanted to touch her, to brush hair from her cheek and kiss her forehead. He did none of those things, not wanting to wake her.

It was hard turning his mind back to work. For the time being, everyone should be safe at their respective safe houses. He could concentrate on the problems at hand.

He thought about the SD card that had been implanted beneath Joe's skin. Six folders, all password protected...

He nearly bolted upright in bed. Six passwords, six postcards from Nate. The cards could provide the password or passwords to open the folders. Why hadn't he thought of that before? Probably because it had been a long couple of days.

Careful not to disturb Belle, he slipped his arm from where he'd settled it on her hip. When he turned over and looked at the clock on the nightstand, he saw that it was six thirty-five.

He slid out of bed and gathered his discarded clothing. After tugging on his jeans, he strode barefoot into the front room of the suite. From off a small writing desk he picked up a pen and a pad of paper with the B & B's name and logo. He grabbed his duffel bag and retrieved a folder with copies of the five postcards he'd gathered. At the office he'd scanned everything electronically and it was all on his tablet, but he'd had a feeling that he needed hard copies to spread out like he and Belle had at the office.

He crouched on one knee and set each copy of the postcards on the coffee table, in order by postmark date. Each paper had a copy of the picture on the front of the postcard and a copy of the back with the message.

He took the notepad and made three columns, then crossed the vertical lines with six horizontal lines. He looked over the cards, each with a different postmark date. Leon's was dated first, and Dylan picked out the incorrect sentence.

"*You were one hell of a receiver.*"

On the top line of the chart went *Leon* in the first column, *receiver* in the second, and then *quarterback* in the third.

Marta's card was second: "*Remember Lindy and the chalkboard incident?*"

Down went *Marta*, then *Lindy*, and lastly *Misty*.

He studied Christie's card next. "*You know how chocolate is my favorite flavor and I'm ready to hit the Dairy Queen again.*"

On the grid he wrote her name, *chocolate*, and *vanilla*.

His gut clenched and he paused for a moment when a date skipped. Following the logic, if Nate had mailed one postcard every day, Tom's would have been on the fourth day. He wrote *Tom* and left the next two spots empty.

Belle's card had been fifth—she'd received hers the day that Nate had died. "*I'll never forget when your big brown dog bit me on the ass.*"

On the fifth row he wrote her name followed by *brown* in the second column and in the last, *white*.

His card had been last, since it had never been mailed. He studied the one sentence that was off. "*Hey, remember when I served in Iraq?*"

In column one, on the sixth row, he wrote *Dylan*, then *Iraq*, followed by *Afghanistan*.

He frowned. How could they figure out what the missing words were without Tom's card? And what the hell were they supposed to do with the words? It could be any number of things.

Something as simple as the right or wrong word being a password, but he doubted Nate would do anything so obvious. They could be meant to use the first letter of the wrong words, or the first letter of all of the right words, or even a twelve-letter password using the first letter of the right *and* the wrong words, and that would have to be done a few different ways.

Or hell, it might not even have anything to do with the password or passwords for the folders on that SD card.

He blew out his breath as he stared at the table he'd written. "Nate, what the hell did you get us into? What were *you* into?"

Tom was dead, probably thanks to these damn cards. Dylan knew Nate would never have intentionally put them in danger, but the anger flowing through him burned in his gut. His muscles tensed and he clenched his jaw.

"*Goddamnit.*" He flung the notepad with the chart across the room and it hit the door with a *thunk* and dropped to the floor.

"Is everything all right?" Belle's concerned voice came from the bedroom doorway.

Dylan got to his feet from his crouched position and faced her. She was so beautiful wrapped in the robe she'd been wearing last night, her hair tousled, and still looking a little sleepy. And here he was, temper flaring, acting like a frustrated jerk.

"Sorry about that." He did his best to relax his tense muscles. "Hope I didn't wake you."

"I was already awake." She walked over to him and laid her hand on his arm. The heat traveling through him from her touch went straight to his heart. "Tell me what's wrong."

Dylan couldn't help himself. He brought her into his embrace and held her. He rested his chin on the top of her head and stroked her hair. "Just a little frustrated with Nate and his postcards."

She leaned back and looked up at him, and met his gaze. "You know Nate never would have done anything to put us in harm's way, if he'd thought there was the slightest chance any of us would get hurt."

"Yeah, I know." The protectiveness he felt for her welled up inside him, nearly overcoming him. He kissed her forehead. "I need to call in to work."

She stepped back when he released her. "It's just after seven. You must get to work early."

"Some of us do." He pulled his phone out of its holster. "The guy who's handling that memory card always comes in early."

He found George's direct number and pressed the connect button. When the tech guy answered, Dylan said, "What have you got for me on that memory card?"

"Nothing yet." George sounded slightly irritated. "This is high tech and slightly unusual. The passwords are encrypted and breaking them is going to be a bitch."

"I have something that might help." Dylan stared at the notepad, where it had landed near the door. "It's not much, but it can't hurt to look at it."

"I'm open to whatever you've got."

"I'll send you a copy. Hold on." Dylan retrieved the pad and took a picture of the pad and sent it to George's email. "Get it?"

"What the hell is it?" George asked.

Dylan explained the chart. "It's missing information." He put his fingers to his forehead. "Think you can get anywhere with what I sent?"

"It's something to go on," George said. "I'm going to do my damnedest to get you answers."

"Thanks, George," Dylan said before he disconnected the call.

For a few seconds he stood there, his thoughts returning to the cards. If only there was a copy of Tom's, like Leon had made—

Blood pumped faster through Dylan's veins. God, he was mentally running on empty with everything that had happened, or it would have been too obvious to him. Of course Tom would make a copy. The question was whether or not the copy was at the hospital versus his home. The hospital would likely balk at the warrant, but since it was for information unrelated to any patients, it ultimately wouldn't be a problem.

Dylan looked up the number on his phone for the Copper Queen Hospital and asked for Dr. Emma Miller. When the answering nurse said Dr. Miller was with a patient, Dylan told the nurse who he was and that it was a matter of life or death.

He was on hold for about ten minutes before she answered.

"Dr. Miller here."

"This is Agent Curtis." Dylan shifted his stance. "We talked about Tom the other day, and the postcard he received from an old friend?"

"Yes." She sounded cool, and he wondered if she was perturbed by his call. She verified that when she added, "Is that why you took me away from my patient?"

"This is very important." Dylan pressed the phone tighter to his ear. "Did he mention making a copy of that card?"

"I'm not sure." Her words were brittle, as if she might be at the breaking point. "Is that all?"

Dylan tried to keep his cool, too. "Think a little harder, Dr. Miller. Please."

A moment of silence, and then she said, "I think he did. I was distracted at the time and in a hurry. It was so trivial that I didn't really think about it."

Dylan's heart beat faster. "Thank you."

When he got off the phone with Dr. Miller, Dylan called Trace. "We need a warrant to search Dr. Tom Zumsteg's office at the hospital. We're looking for a photocopy of the postcard mailed to him by Nate O'Malley. We might get lucky and he left a copy of the postcard at work."

"You've got it," Trace said.

"What is that?" Belle sat on the couch, an uneasy feeling crawling through her belly as Dylan holstered his phone. She looked at his handwritten list he set next to the spread-out copies of the postcards. She cocked her head as she scanned the page with the B & B insignia at the top. "Did you figure out something?"

"I don't know." He sat next to her and explained what he'd done by listing what words were wrong and substituting the correct word in the following column. "This could be interpreted any number of ways."

She nodded and looked at each postcard again. "You wouldn't think he'd make it too difficult, but he probably didn't want to make it too easy, just in case someone caught on."

Dylan tapped the capped end of the pen on the notepad. "I have George, our tech guy, trying his hand at figuring this out. He's a phenomenal code breaker."

They sat in silence and she could almost see the wheels churning in Dylan's mind. After a while, he leaned back and blew out his breath.

She studied him and couldn't help her mind from wandering and admiring his naked torso—all he had on was a pair of worn Wrangler jeans. Damn but he'd grown some muscle over the years. His hair was tousled from sleep but he looked wide-awake as he studied the pieces of paper in front of him. She wanted to run her hands all over that incredible body yet another time.

His muscles grew tenser and it was clear he was getting frustrated again. She wanted to do something to ease—at least temporarily—the stress he had to be feeling right now. Well, there was something she *could* do for him.

"I'm going to take a bath." A zing traveled straight between her thighs. Her nipples tightened in the cool air as she stood and let her robe fall open, exposing her breasts. "Care to join me?"

The look of hunger that swept over his expression was all the answer she needed. She turned away and let the robe drop to the floor.

She glanced over her shoulder and saw him pulling something from his back pocket before pushing down his jeans and stepping out of them. Her heart skipped a beat when she saw that he'd been commando beneath his jeans, and his cock was rigid and ready for her. The intense look in his gaze made her shiver.

He closed in on her before she could make it into the bathroom. She gave a delighted laugh as he swept her into his arms and held her to his bare chest. His skin was hot against hers, and the heat radiated throughout her own body.

She wrapped her arms around his neck, loving the skin-to-skin contact and the power of his embrace. It felt so good being carried by this big, powerful man, who happened to be the same man she'd fallen in love with in high school—only in a bigger package.

His eyes were smoky and he exuded the kind of intensity that made her feel like she was all he could think about. Just as he was all she could think about.

He placed a foil packet on a vanity table before he set her on her feet in front of the old fashioned claw-footed tub. "I think it's going to have to be a bath instead of a shower."

She grinned. "This might be a little tight."

"We'll make it work." He looked so serious, she almost laughed.

He put the stopper in the tub after running the water until it was warm. In the meantime she found a small bottle of complimentary bubble bath and poured it all into the tub. It wasn't long before bubbles were rising and the tub was filling.

She tested the water with one foot. "Oh, this is going to be heavenly." She turned off the water and climbed in, her back to the faucet as she sank blissfully into the bubbles. Her breasts were covered in bubbles and her hair wet from sliding down so far.

"Bubbles," he grumbled, but she could tell he was teasing. He stepped into the tub and eased down. He was so big that the bubbles were still below his chest. "Come here." He gestured to her with one hand.

She moved to him and he took her by the waist and had her sit astride him. She almost moaned at the feel of his rigid cock pressed against her folds. The urge to rise up and bring herself down on his erection was almost overpowering.

Water dripped from her hair and trickled down her breasts, droplets like tiny kisses on her skin.

He raised his wet hands, water rolling down his arms, and he cupped the sides of her face before bringing her in for a kiss. She wiggled closer to him so that her nipples rubbed his chest and her thighs were snug around his hips.

His kiss sent thrills through her body, and she trembled with need for him and only him. Last night hadn't been enough. Maybe she could never get enough.

He sucked her tongue before slipping his own tongue into her mouth. He moved his mouth over hers in a demanding kiss that nearly made her wild.

Water sloshed over the edge of the tub as she squirmed on his lap, grinding her hips so that her clit rubbed along the length of him. The friction shot spikes of arousal through her belly. She moaned with pleasure.

He brushed bubbles from her breasts before he lowered his head to suck her nipples. She gasped and slid her fingers into his hair, holding his head so that his face was pressed close. He moved his mouth to her other nipple and sucked it into his mouth. Her nipples were so sensitive that every lick and suck sent tremors throughout her.

She skimmed her palms up the hard muscle of his chest, over his shoulders, and down his powerful biceps. He gently tugged at her nipple with his teeth and she dug her nails into his arms and leaned her head back.

"I can't wait." He raised his head before reaching with one hand to grasp the packet off of the vanity. He tore open the packet and she shifted on his lap so that he could sheathe his cock.

Her heartbeat increased and her breathing roughened as she rose up on her knees while he placed the head of his cock against her entrance. Their gazes met and held as she sank down on his cock. Her eyes widened at the sensation of him stretching her, sliding deep inside her. Even though she'd had him last night, she was amazed at how full he made her feel.

She braced her hands on his massive shoulders and started riding his cock. She slid up and down the length of him, gasping with every thrust of his hips. The water around them splashed over their skin and sloshed over the side of the tub. Her knees and thighs were pinned between his hips and the slick porcelain.

"That's it, precious." He grasped her waist. "Ride me. *Fuck me*."

The way he said *fuck me* was so incredibly erotic that it almost shot her straight into an orgasm. She managed to hold onto the fine lines of control and rode him even harder than she had been.

"God, that feels good." Her words came out breathy and filled with the sound of need. "Don't stop."

"I don't intend to." He thrust up hard, causing her to gasp. "I plan on taking you until you can't walk straight for the rest of the day."

She groaned. Every word he said just made her feel like her body was going to burn up completely.

He eased one hand from her waist and moved it between their bodies to slide his finger into her folds. He stroked her clit and she couldn't have stopped the cry that tore from her if she'd tried.

She threw her head back, her hands clenching his shoulders, her fingers digging into his skin.

So close. She was so close to coming with his big cock inside her. She felt her orgasm growing like a ball of light inside her. Expanding, becoming bigger and brighter with every stroke of his fingers, every thrust of his hips.

And then she was gone.

Starlight fractured her mind. Shards so bright that she could see them behind her eyelids. She came with a shriek, her cry echoing inside the small bathroom.

Her body throbbed and her body felt so sensitive, like the lightest touch would make her come again.

He ground his hips against hers and it was enough that another orgasm hit her hard and fast. She cried out and could barely breathe from the wild sensations coursing through her body.

A moment later and he shouted as he came. He thrust his hips several more times before stopping. His breathing was harsh and ragged as he tried to regain control. And then he pulled her into his arms and brought her face against his wet chest as he stroked her damp hair.

His words came out husky but firm. "I'm never letting you go again."

CHAPTER 16

"I'm never letting you go again."

Dylan's words stayed in Belle's head, refusing to leave. It gave her a feeling of exhilaration, like she was running up a mountain, a fresh breeze on her face, and not one bit tired as she headed to the peak.

And then her stomach felt heavy, as if thick sludge slithered through her intestines. She had to tell him. But when she shared the truth with him, told him everything, he wasn't going to want her any more.

Maybe worse, he might try to kill her stepfather. Not that the bastard didn't deserve it, but she didn't want anything to happen to Dylan. She didn't want to see this brave, amazing man behind bars for the rest of his life.

"Is something wrong?" Dylan eyed her as she braced her palms against his chest and straightened on his lap, water splashing as she shifted.

"Everything is fine." She smiled and to her surprise she felt an instant warm bubble in her chest as he returned her smile—the way he looked at her was like magic. Maybe for a few minutes she could pretend that they could have a relationship…pretend that she really could be his and he could be hers.

The bubble burst and the heaviness returned to her belly. She needed to tell him.

She would wait, though. She had to find the right time, and now was not it.

God, this rollercoaster of emotions was going to drive her out of her mind. How could she feel such elation when she didn't deserve it?

As she let his cock slide from inside her, she reached for the small bottle of hotel shampoo.

He disposed of the condom and insisted on washing her hair himself. The feel of his big, strong hands massaging her scalp as he lathered her hair was heaven. Soap rolled over her shoulders and down her breasts in thick rivers of bubbles. When he finished shampooing her hair, he helped her rinse it under the faucet with clean water. He repeated the process with conditioner, working it into her hair and rubbing her scalp. Yes, it was heaven. She gave a sigh as he rinsed her hair beneath the faucet until the conditioner was out.

His touch was erotic, sending prickles of awareness through her at every touch.

When he was finished, she pushed wet hair away from her face. "My turn." After getting his hair wet beneath the faucet, she grabbed the small bottle and poured a dollop of shampoo onto her palm. She sat on her haunches to reach his head more easily. She slid her fingers into his hair and began working the shampoo into the wet strands and bringing it to a full lather.

When she finished washing his hair, she soaped his body with a washcloth and soap, loving the feeling of touching his big, powerful body. She rinsed him off, sliding her palms over his muscles, taking advantage of the time she had to explore the bigger version of his body that she had once known so well.

It was her turn next, and he took the cloth and soap from her. He soaped her in slow, easy motions, gently running the cloth over her breasts and down to her belly before rinsing her off.

Belle had never had such an intensely wonderful sensual experience. The way Dylan touched her was almost like he was making love to her all over again.

The water was cool once they had finished bathing each other. He climbed out and clasped her hand to help her out of the tub before taking one of the B & B's thick and fluffy towels and drying every bit of her body. They put one of the towels on the floor to soak up the water they'd sloshed everywhere.

Joe remained on silent vigil near the front door, as if intent on protecting them at all costs. His presence comforted Belle. Between Dylan and the German shepherd, she couldn't feel safer.

Dylan's phone rang and he retrieved it. When he disconnected the call, he told Belle that the agent had arrived with the change of clothing. Dylan had given Belle's clothing sizes to Sofia yesterday afternoon; he had clean clothes in his duffel bag.

Dylan finished dressing, put on his shoulder holster, and sheathed his weapon. He also holstered his phone and slid his credentials into his back pocket before heading downstairs to meet the agent.

While Dylan was downstairs, Belle stood in front of the bathroom mirror and dried her hair with the B & B's blow dryer. She wore only the towel secured around her and had to use her fingers to comb out the strands of hair as she blow-dried it.

Her hair was pretty much dry by the time Dylan returned. He laid a stack of clothes on the bed and then handed her a medium-sized duffel bag. She peered into the duffel and was grateful when she found a smaller bag with a toothbrush and other essential toiletries, and even a tube of neutral-toned lipstick that could go with almost any complexion. The agent who had gathered the supplies had to have been a woman who understood the power of lipstick.

It didn't take Belle long to pull her hair back into a ponytail, wash her face, brush her teeth and put on a touch of lipstick. When she was finished, she dropped the towel and went to the bed to check out the clothing the agent had brought.

Dylan watched her with hunger in his gaze, as if he was ready to take her back to bed. But it was time to get going, and she knew it as well as he did.

"I want to see Christie." Belle tore off the price tags and then stepped into the new jeans that the agent had dropped off. "I want to make sure she's okay."

Dylan frowned. "A couple of agents will be on your protective detail here."

"I'm going with you." Belle shook her head, her words hard and firm. "I refuse to be left behind."

For a moment he just studied her. "All right." He watched as she pulled on a dark blue cable knit sweater. "We're not staying long. I need to talk with Christie about her postcard and Nate, and then we'll head on out. It's too dangerous having too many of us at the same location."

"Thank you." She felt lighter from relief as she moved toward him, her bare feet sinking into the carpet. She'd expected him to argue more against her accompanying him. "I need to see her for myself and make sure she's okay."

"I do, too." He reached out and cupped the side of her face. "It's bad enough that Nate and Tom are gone, and Marta's in serious condition in the hospital. I don't want to lose anyone else."

She raised herself up on her toes and brushed her mouth over his. "I trust you to keep us all safe."

He slipped his hands into her hair and kissed her.

While Belle finished dressing, Dylan checked out and paid the bill. He felt edgy, uneasy. It was an intense, unusual feeling, and had everything to do with losing friends and needing to protect the living. The CoS had been family to him, and he knew the others felt the same way. Yes, they'd drifted apart over the years, but the true bond had never broken. Even when Belle was gone, he'd still felt somehow tethered to her wherever she went.

Belle was fully dressed by the time he returned, her dirty clothes in the duffel along with the toiletries.

"You're so beautiful." He couldn't stop himself from kissing her yet again. "I want you to stay by my side. I'm not taking any chances."

She offered a smile. "I'll be fine."

He studied her, feeling both exasperated and proud. She'd always been independent, but she was tougher now. She was a woman who knew what she wanted and refused to be coddled. She'd gone out into the world at a young age and had more than survived. It had taken a lot of guts to do the things she'd done and accomplish all she had.

While she checked to make sure they hadn't left anything, Dylan carried her duffel to the living room. He set it next to his own duffel and started to gather the copies of the postcards and the notations he'd made on the chart he'd created on the notepad.

Dylan turned to see Belle walking out of the bedroom, bringing a cell phone to her ear. Shit, he'd been so damned tired he'd forgotten to tell her to turn it off and keep it off. He started to tell her to give him the phone when clear concern caused Belle's brow to furrow.

"Christie?" Belle said. "You're cutting out." A pause and then Belle looked at Dylan and then at the phone. "The call disconnected."

Dylan took the phone from Belle and looked at the caller list. "Whatever number she called you on was blocked." He powered down the phone. "Are you sure that was Christie? She shouldn't have access to a phone."

Belle nodded. "It was her voice, but I couldn't understand anything she said."

"Hold on." Dylan's chest tightened as he dialed the number on his own phone for one of the agents protecting Christie and Salvatore.

"Davidson here." Trace's firm voice came over the line. "What's up, Dylan?"

Relief that nothing sounded amiss in the agent's voice relaxed Dylan. "Is Christie all right?"

Trace said. "She seems tired and on edge, but I chalk that up to the situation."

The tenseness in Dylan's muscles relaxed a bit. "Why didn't you take their phones away?"

"We did," Trace said. "Standard procedure."

Dylan tensed again. "She just called Belle from a blocked number."

Trace sounded puzzled. "That's not possible."

"Anything's possible." Dylan's jaw tensed. "Is she right there with you?"

"No," Trace said. "She went with Salvatore to their bedroom for a nap."

"Is anything out of the ordinary?" Dylan asked.

"Not until now." Trace had a frown in his voice. "We'll search for another phone in case Salvatore has a second phone."

Something didn't feel right in Dylan's gut. "I'd like you to check on Christie."

"Hang tight. I'll see if she's awake." Trace added, "I'll see if they have a phone we didn't know about."

Dylan's gut tightened as he waited for Trace to come back on the line. He heard muffled conversation.

Trace spoke into the phone again. "Everything seems normal other than Christie looking a little paler."

"Have them come into the living room." Dylan finished scooping up everything he'd brought with him, including the copies of the postcards, and shoved them into his duffel bag. "I need to talk with Christie. I'm on my way and we'll be there in fifteen minutes."

"You've got it. We'll do a search for another phone." Trace disconnected the call.

Dylan holstered his phone and saw that Belle looked worried. "Is Christie all right?" she asked.

"Things are fine according to Trace." Dylan zipped the duffel. "The call you got was odd. You're certain it was Christie?"

Belle cocked her head to the side. "It sure sounded like her."

Dylan nodded. "We'll talk to her ourselves."

"We know her well enough to tell if something's wrong." Belle picked up her bag.

"I'll get that." He took the bag from her and grabbed his own before they left the room and shut the door behind them.

Joe accompanied them to the SUV and hopped into the back seat with little urging from Dylan. When Joe was in the vehicle, Dylan helped Belle into her seat. Joe and Belle got settled as Dylan jogged to the driver's side and got in.

The place Christie and her husband were staying at was a modest house in Tombstone Canyon, not far from the Divide and the Mule Pass Tunnel, and a short drive from the B & B. The place was a little way from Tom's former home.

Normally, Dylan would have taken a while to make sure he wasn't followed. In order to get to the safe house in a hurry, he had to go directly there and do his best to ensure he didn't have a tail.

Belle thought she was going to go crazy with worry. She knew her friends were all supposed to have been safely guarded, but something was wrong. For Christie to call like she had and how she'd talked with Dylan… Was one of the agents there dirty? That was how it usually went on TV and in the movies—dirty cops, dirty agents.

She mentally shook her head. That was TV and movies. This was real life.

Dylan and Belle arrived at the safe house. Her stomach ached while her skin felt tight over her bones.

Clearly wary of his surroundings, Dylan strode to the front door with Belle at his side and Joe on the leash. Dylan had his pistol in his shoulder holster and had added another weapon in a holster on his hip. He went up to the front door but didn't knock. He un-holstered his phone and dialed a number.

"I'm at the front door, Trace," Dylan said when the man answered. "Everything okay?"

A moment and then Dylan said, "Good. Let us in."

The heavy-duty bolt locks made loud *thunks* as they were opened. Dylan re-holstered his phone as he glanced at Belle.

Trace Davidson was one of the agents and he bolted the heavy door behind them once they were all inside. The other was Agent Jennie Ortega, who Belle had met briefly at the DHS office.

Joe growled, drawing her attention. Joe's lips curled, his teeth bared. Belle followed his gaze and saw he was growling at Salvatore, who sat next to Christie on a loveseat.

With a snarl Joe lunged, throwing his body against the leash. Dylan was almost yanked forward from the unexpected charge, and barely kept hold of the German shepherd.

The dog fought against the leash, snarling and barking, his attention solely on Salvatore.

Looking terrified, Salvatore shouted at Dylan. "Control that beast."

Dylan crouched beside Joe and spoke to him in a low voice. Joe stopped barking and snarling but his body remained rigid, hair raised. His gaze remained focused on Salvatore.

A low growl rumbled in Joe's throat. The big dog was obeying, but he clearly didn't like it.

What was that all about? Joe had never exhibited that kind of behavior since she'd been around him.

Belle looked at Christie. Something was clearly wrong that had nothing to do with Joe. Hair at Belle's nape prickled. Christie looked pale and drawn, her gaze focused on something that Belle couldn't see. She refused to make eye contact with Belle, and she didn't seem to notice what was happening with the dog nearly attacking her husband.

A chill went through Belle as her thoughts turned back to how she'd been unable to make eye contact after Harvey had abused her. It had been so difficult to pretend everything was all right when she was with Dylan or anyone else in the CoS.

"Are you okay, honey?" Belle went to Christie and knelt at her side. "You don't look well." When Christie didn't respond, Belle put her hand on her friend's arm.

Christie jerked her arm away from Belle, as if she'd been burned.

Belle drew her hand away. Her chest tightened. "Christie?"

Christie's eyes were filled with fear as she met Belle's gaze.

"What's wrong?" The concern in Belle's gut rose like an angry wave.

Comprehension and recognition dawned in Christie's eyes. "Belle." Her throat worked. She seemed about to say something else but looked down at her lap.

"Tell me what's wrong." Belle put her hand on Christie's arm again.

Christie flinched but didn't jerk her hand away. She glanced at her husband, then back at her lap. "Everything is fine. I'm—I'm just a little worried is all." She mumbled the words.

"You don't look okay." Belle turned her attention from Christie to meet Salvatore's gaze. He appeared concerned, but at the same time she felt something was off. Like his eyes were saying something different than the expression he wore. Maybe it was the fact that a German shepherd had almost attacked him.

Salvatore smiled but his smile made her uneasy. "She has simply had a scare with all that has happened."

"Of course." Belle would have liked to sit next to Christie, but the loveseat was clearly made for two. Belle chose a seat that was closest to Christie's side of the couch.

"Why don't we have a cup of coffee?" Belle looked over her shoulder at Agent Davidson. "You do have coffee?"

Trace nodded. He was looking at Christie, his expression concerned. "I'll make a pot."

"I can do it." Belle got to her feet. "Christie, why don't you help me?"

Salvatore put his arm around Christie's shoulders. She seemed to stiffen, but didn't pull away. "My wife will feel safer with me."

"Safer from what?" Belle cocked her head. "We're in a safe house no one knows about with three agents. What's to be afraid of?"

Dylan watched the exchange between Belle and Salvatore who held Christie, his arm around her shoulders in a protective, loving way. But Christie, pale and drawn, had her head down again and was looking at her hands in her lap.

"Hi, Christie." Dylan tried to speak in a normal, casual tone.

She raised her head and he saw hurt and pain in her eyes. "Hi, Dylan." Her voice quavered.

Dylan couldn't help but frown. He'd known Christie most of her life and he'd never seen her like this. It was beyond fear...someone had caused her pain. His gaze moved to Salvatore and Dylan knew in his gut that her husband was the cause of that pain.

An urge to beat the shit out of Salvatore rushed over Dylan. He held back his anger and stared at the man. "How are you doing?"

Salvatore scowled. "Why are we being kept here like prisoners?"

"Prisoners?" Dylan stepped closer to the pair on the couch. "Your protective custody is voluntary. You can leave at any time."

A look of surprise flashed across Salvatore's face. "Then we will go now. Take us back to our home."

Dylan shook his head. "You can go. If Christie wants to stay, then she will remain in protective custody. Of course we'll have to move her."

Relief was obvious in Christie's expression, but Salvatore's scowl deepened. "My wife goes with me."

"Doesn't work that way." Dylan focused squarely on Salvatore. "If Christie wants to, she stays."

Salvatore snapped his gaze to Christie's, his arm still around her shoulders. "You *do* want to come with me."

Her expression turned from withdrawn to angry. "I'm staying." Her tone was defiant as she tried to pull out of her husband's grasp.

The living room window shattered.

Glass showered the room.

One of the women screamed.

An object was tossed in through the broken window.

With a clatter, a small metal canister landed on the floor, spewing smoke. The heavy white fog began to fill the room from the smoke grenade, obscuring everything almost instantly. Dylan couldn't tell where anyone was but Belle and Christie who were close.

"Shit," Trace shouted.

G.I. Joe started snarled and barked with an intense viciousness as he yanked his leash from Dylan's grip and leapt toward the window.

Dylan's heart thudded as he coughed. His throat burned and his eyes watered.

"Get down on the floor." Dylan got the words out between coughs as he went to Belle and Christie.

Salvatore was no longer sitting on the couch as far as Dylan could tell. Had Joe gotten to him? But Joe had headed to the broken window.

The women's terrified faces quickly vanished behind a screen of smoke as they coughed and choked.

He grabbed them by their arms and dragged them to the floor. "Crawl behind the couch."

With his weapon drawn, he kept low and stayed near the women as they used their hands to feel along the couch to find their way to the back.

Dylan's eyes continued to water from the smoke and he couldn't hold back the coughs.

"I've got Belle and Christie." Dylan's words seemed to bounce around the room. He had to protect the women at all costs and he intended to stay close to them.

"I got rid of the canister through the window," Trace shouted. "I'll get the back door through the kitchen."

Jennie Ortega yelled, "I've got the front—"

The door exploded inward.

Jennie's scream of pain immediately followed.

Debris rained down where Dylan, Belle, and Christie knelt behind the couch. Rage tore through Dylan. He rose and peered over the cushions. Smoke hung in the air, but the fog in the room was starting to thin.

Through wisps of smoke, Dylan saw Jennie on her back. She rose and pressed her left hand down on her right side, near a jagged piece of wood lodged in her body, where blood spread too quickly. With her teeth clenched, she raised her right arm, aiming her service weapon at the obliterated doorway. Even through the remaining fog, Dylan saw her arm shaking.

Dylan moved to the end of the couch, leaving Christie and Belle behind it.

A man rushed through the doorway and pointed a rifle at Jennie. Before Dylan got a shot off, Jennie hit the bastard in the neck. Blood sprayed from the wound. Jennie had clearly hit something vital and the man fell to his knees, his gun clattering to the floor as he brought his hands to his neck, his eyes wide.

Joe came out of nowhere and grabbed the man by his neck. Joe shook the man like a wild animal set to kill its prey. The man's body went slack, his eyes wide. The German shepherd dropped him and leapt toward the door.

Through the smoke, Dylan saw men entering, guns drawn. In the chaos that ensued, Dylan took down three more men while Jennie managed to get a second before she passed out.

Joe snarled, barked, growled, and took down more than one man. He attacked the men with a feral ferocity.

Just as Dylan shot a third man in the chest, dropping him, Belle screamed. He whirled to see Belle being carried over a fourth man's shoulder. Dylan hadn't seen the man go behind the couch through the remnants of the still hazy smoke.

Dylan set his jaw and aimed for the man's knee. The man screamed as his knee exploded and he went down with Belle. Dylan leapt over the arm of the couch as Belle scrambled away and the man started to roll over. Dylan shot the man in the chest.

When Dylan turned, he saw the room was quiet, bodies on the floor and no one moving. Jennie was in the same place, completely still. He hoped to God she was only passed out and that she was still alive.

"I stopped three men coming in through the kitchen." Trace spoke from behind Dylan. A sharp note of concern entered his voice as he added, "Where's Christie?"

Dylan spun to look at Trace as threads of smoke floated by him. Dylan's gaze swept the room. "She was here—"

A cry was in Belle's voice. "She's gone. Christie's gone!"

Trace gritted his teeth. "And so is Salvatore."

"Sonofabitch." Dylan pointed toward the bedrooms. "Check to see if she made it to another room," he said to Trace, who nodded and strode to the hallway, his weapon ready in case any of the attackers had gotten past them.

Joe stood beside Belle as if protecting her, his fur on end.

Dylan turned back to Belle. "Are you all right?"

"Christie? Where's Christie?" She flung herself into his arms.

"You're okay?" He wrapped her in his embrace.

"I'm not hurt." She leaned back, her face streaked with tears. "They got Christie."

He held her tightly to him one more time for a just a moment before releasing her. Belle was all right from what he could tell and from what she'd said.

"I'll check on Jennie." Trace walked past them and strode to where Jennie lay. He checked her pulse. "She's alive but she's losing blood. She needs an ambulance. Now."

One of the bodies twitched. Dylan wanted to shoot the man out of pure rage, but went to his side to question him. By the time Dylan reached the bastard, his eyes were wide in death. Dylan knelt and checked the man's pulse. Nothing.

With a growl, Dylan stood and looked at the devastation around him. He thanked God that Belle was all right and that Jennie was alive. But they had to find Christie. And fast.

CHAPTER 17

Christie's head pounded and ached. She tried opening her eyes, but her eyelids were so heavy she couldn't raise them. Drugged. She felt drugged.

A hard slap across her face caused her head to snap to the side. Pain shot through her cheek and head. Her eyes opened with shock and through blurry vision she saw a form in front of her.

She tried to raise her hand to her stinging cheek but found she couldn't move her arm. Dazed, she attempted to move her other arm, but it was tightly bound. She tried to move her legs and they were tied, too. Through the fog in her head, she realized she was tied to a chair. Her mouth felt dry and she felt tape over her mouth. She couldn't move her lips or her jaw. Lank strands of hair fell across her cheeks as she hung her head.

Memories rushed back and the terror that rose through her was swift and powerful. Her body trembled and her breathing started to come faster. She could only breathe through her nose and she thought she was going to hyperventilate.

The safe house. Belle. Dylan. Agents Trace Davidson and Jennie Ortega. The attack. Was everyone dead? Did they have Belle and Dylan?

Did they *kill* Belle and Dylan?

God, no.

Her thoughts spun as she tried to put puzzle pieces together. Where was she? She'd been grabbed, a hand clamped over her mouth as she was dragged out of the house. She didn't know how they'd found her in the smoke-filled room, but they had.

Did they get Belle, too?

Or had they killed her?

A sob rose up in her throat but it had nowhere to go with the tape over her mouth. She thought she'd choke like she had done when the living room of the safe house had filled with smoke.

She felt the remnants of a sting on her skin where a needle had pierced her flesh when she'd been drugged. She could remember fighting the man who had her, the prick of the needle as another man bent over her, and then everything fading to black.

Her vision cleared and she blinked. The figure came into focus and she felt as if she might pass out again when she saw the man was Salvatore.

Although, after what she'd been through, she found she wasn't surprised. He had orchestrated the attack from his phone.

Today he had nearly hit Christie again when he'd caught her using his phone to call Belle. If it hadn't been for Agent Davidson, who had come to the room where they were staying, Salvatore would have hurt her.

Her husband, the man she'd been married to for twenty years, was a monster like she had never known before.

He stared at her with cold calculation in his dark eyes. He perched on the edge of a metal table in a chilly concrete-walled room. She was strapped to a chair in front of him.

She closed her eyes for a moment, as if that might change her situation. Maybe it was a dream. A nightmare.

Cool air chilled her skin and she smelled something dank and dirty. Her head still swam and she swayed.

"Look at me." Salvatore's icy command jerked her back to reality.

Her skin prickled as she obeyed. Her throat felt raw from the smoke that she'd sucked in at the safe house, smoke that had filled her lungs when she'd opened her mouth to scream.

The fact that her husband had her tied to a chair in an unfamiliar room started to sink in. He reached for her and she flinched, expecting him to hit her. Instead, he grabbed the end of the tape over her mouth, and ripped the gray duct tape away. He dropped it onto the metal table. Her skin prickled unpleasantly, but she shook it off.

"Look at me, *mi mariposa*." Salvatore's voice cut into her fog.

The words came out thick and heavy as she said, "I'm not your butterfly." Not anymore.

He raised his hand.

"Salvatore." His name came out in a hoarse whisper. "What are you doing?"

"I've never thought of you as a stupid woman, Christie." He spoke in a slow, measured tone and lowered his hand. "Don't start now."

But she *had* been stupid. She'd been blind to who he was and what he was for the duration of their marriage. She hadn't known the true Salvatore until she overheard him ordering the murders of her friends.

How could she have been so foolish? She'd believed in him.

She'd loved him.

Their entire marriage had been a lie.

Tears burned at the backs of her eyes but she fought to hold them back. He'd already taken so many tears from her by raping her more than once after she'd overheard him.

Her heart ached while her mind raged. She'd given her love to a terrible man.

He was a horrible, horrible man who schemed and ordered the murders of people who got in his way. Her friends had become liabilities that he was discarding like pieces of trash. Had they been the first murders he'd contracted? Not that it mattered whether or not he hadn't done it before, but she knew inside that he had.

"Did you hurt Belle and Dylan?" Her voice shook.

"They're dead." Salvatore gave a slow smile. "They were slaughtered like pigs." He gave a dark laugh. "The fucking dog, too."

"Oh, my God." Christie's mind spun. She felt lightheaded, and she was close to passing out from the news. They couldn't be dead. Her friends. Two more of the most precious people in her life.

Dead.

At her husband's orders. Maybe even at his hands.

She looked at Salvatore and all she felt was hatred like she'd never experienced before. "You bastard."

"Language, my dear." He gave a smirk. "But don't worry. I'll be finished with you soon enough and you can join them."

Christie's head swayed. If she hadn't been tied to the chair, she would have slipped off and hit the floor.

Her friends were dead. The words repeated over and over in her mind.

Belle and Dylan are dead.

It didn't matter that he intended to kill her, too. She'd known that ever since he caught her when she'd overheard him. There was no way he'd let her live. He just wanted her to suffer.

"Next will be your friend, Leon." Salvatore smirked. "I think I'll have his whole family taken out for good measure. His wife. His kids. That leaves Marta who is clinging to life in the hospital." Salvatore shrugged as the horror in her body magnified. "She will be dead soon. I already have someone there who will finish her off. I expect a call any time now."

Even though she had no visible wounds, it felt like blood was draining from her body, leaking to the floor, forming a pool around her feet.

Salvatore gestured to her. "You I will save for last. I want you to suffer through every single death of your precious Circle of Seven friends." At that he sneered. "You kept me out, ignoring me in favor of them until Belle left."

Christie's mind was on overload. She didn't know what to say, what to think. He was still upset over that, all of these years later?

A knock came at the door. Salvatore didn't take his attention from Christie. "Come in." He said the order in a commanding tone.

The door scraped the concrete floor and Christie flinched from the sound.

A dark-haired man stumbled through the door as if shoved. She had a moment to see his face before he landed on his hands and knees in front of her. He cried out as his knees hit the floor. His body shook and Christie was certain his limbs would give out on him.

Her heart pounded faster as she looked from the man on the floor to the Hispanic man coming in through the doorway.

"Please, Mr. Reyes." The man on the floor's voice trembled, but he didn't look at Salvatore. "I'm sorry. I'll make up for it."

"Shut up, Carl," Salvatore snapped.

The man who'd shoved Carl through the door carried a handgun but tucked it into the back of his jeans. "What do you want me to do with him?"

"Thank you, Paco. But I'll take care of Carl." Salvatore kicked the man on the floor in the gut, a fierce, powerful kick. The man shouted in pain and rolled onto his side, his cry bouncing off the walls of the small bare room. "Won't I, Carl?" Salvatore said to the man he'd just kicked.

Carl was sobbing now. "I'll make up for it. I will. I promise."

"You failed me at the safe house and you ran while others died." Salvatore reached into his pocket and Christie's eyes widened. More fear burned her chest as he pulled out a small black handgun. "And you know what happens to men who fail me."

Carl's body shook as Salvatore took his handgun and pressed the barrel to the side of the man's head.

He wouldn't. Christie started trembling so violently her teeth clicked together. Salvatore wouldn't murder this man right in front of her.

At the same time the thoughts went through her mind, she knew that he could and he would.

Christie closed her eyes and turned her head away.

"You will watch, Christie." Salvatore's words came out more than cruel.

In the next moment she felt hands on the sides of her head, turning her back in the direction of Carl. Then the cold barrel of a gun was pressed to her own head and her eyes flew open involuntarily.

"I have to set examples." Salvatore's expression went hard before he moved the gun from her head and pointed it at Carl. "Goodbye, Carl."

Christie screamed, as the sound of the shot in the small room seemed to tear her eardrums. But it was the man's body that kept her screaming. The bullet had splattered blood and matter all over the floor and it had sprayed across her jeans and shoes.

She couldn't stop screaming. Salvatore slapped her so hard her chair tipped back. He caught her by her hair and jerked her forward, stopping the backward momentum and forcing her chair back where it was. She barely noticed the pain at her skull that radiated through her head.

Tears flowed down her cheeks but she knew there was venom in her eyes and her words as she spat words at him. "You're a horrible, sick monster, Salvatore."

He raised his hand to strike her again.

She stared at him, refusing to flinch. "A sick monster."

Pain burst through her head like stars as his hand connected with her head. This time she felt herself falling backward in the chair, with nothing to stop her.

Her head struck the concrete floor.

Everything went black.

CHAPTER 18

Dylan put his arm around Belle's shoulders, keeping her close to him as they left Agent Jennie Ortega's room at the Copper Queen Hospital, the same hospital where Marta was still in a coma. He wasn't about to let Belle out of his sight after everything that had happened.

It was late the same afternoon after the attack and Christie's kidnapping. The FBI would be getting a warrant to search Salvatore's home. Because it was a kidnapping, the FBI would be involved.

G.I. Joe was outside the hospital with Brooks, and Trace had already headed with a team to Tom's office with the warrant to search for a copy of the postcard, or even the actual postcard itself if by some chance Tom had inadvertently left it at the office when he went home.

That was doubtful, but they had to cover the bases in the warrant and nothing could be taken for granted.

"Thank God Agent Ortega will be okay." While speaking, Belle leaned her head on Dylan's shoulder. "She lost so much blood."

"She was fortunate." Dylan was thanking God, too. "If the paramedics had arrived any later, she wouldn't be here."

He felt Belle's shudder and wished he hadn't put it that way. He squeezed her to him and looked at her beautiful face. "Jennie is in stable condition, and that's what matters."

"What if they've killed Christie?" Belle's features were twisted with worry as she looked at Dylan while they walked down the hospital corridor. Her eyes were red from crying, her cheeks tearstained and smudged with something dark, her hair falling from her ponytail and hanging loose around her face.

"If they wanted her dead, they would have killed her at the safe house." Dylan realized his words sounded too harsh as he saw tears start to fill Belle's eyes again. He was blowing it big time in the consoling department. He squeezed her shoulders and pulled her more tightly to him. "In my gut I believe she's all right and we'll find her. We're pretty sure her husband is the key in all of this, and it's possible he won't hurt her simply because she's his wife."

"He always seemed to genuinely care for her." Belle shuddered in Dylan's one-armed embrace. "I am still having a hard time reconciling the man I thought he was with the man we believe he is now."

"That kind of betrayal is nearly impossible to comprehend for most people." Dylan shook his head. "When you trust someone and they aren't who you think they are…" He blew out his breath. "It's like a death."

He looked at her and her throat worked as she swallowed. "That's a good way to put it." A tremor was in her voice. "It's like the person we thought he was is dead and some other horrible monster has taken his place."

Dylan had been through plenty and had seen a lot in his life and in his career, but this one hit close to home. Christie was family, and the fact that her husband was probably at the heart of all of their losses would be almost too much to comprehend for many. Hell, he was having a hard time dealing with it.

But the pieces fit. When he thought about everything, they fit.

Belle moved out of his embrace and drew him aside in the hallway. "Have you heard anything about Tom? Are they sure that he was the one who died in the explosion?"

Dylan sighed. "Yes. Trace gave me the report before we saw Jennie."

The pain in Belle's eyes seemed to magnify. "I can't believe he and Nate are gone now. And Marta…" Belle's lips set in a firm line. "I want to visit Marta while you search Tom's office. I can spend some time with her wife, too. I would imagine she needs a friendly face and someone there who cares about Marta as much as we do."

Dylan's gut tightened. "I don't like the idea of you being out of my sight."

"An agent is posted outside of Marta's room." Belle put her palm on Dylan's chest. "I'll be safe there. It's you I'm worried about."

"Me?" A smile touched his lips. "I'm supposed to be the big bad agent. I'll be fine."

"Well, big bad agents are human, too." Her smile was forced. "Promise me that you will be careful, whatever you do."

"Of course." Dylan touched her beautiful but sad face, running his thumb along her jaw. "Promise me you'll stay in Marta's room."

Belle nodded, her soft skin sliding across his fingers as she did. "I won't go anywhere."

He lowered his head and brushed his lips over hers before taking her hand and walking with her toward Marta's room.

Rick DeLong was outside the room, an agent who was had just transferred to the DHS office in Douglas.

"Belle, this is Agent DeLong." Dylan in turn introduced Rick to Belle before adding, "He will take good care of you."

"Everything has been quiet," Rick said as he gave Dylan and Belle a nod.

Dylan opened the door to the room. Belle slipped inside after Dylan gave her a soft kiss. When he closed the door behind her, he braced one hand on the doorframe as if to steady himself. He had to stop feeling like he couldn't let her out of his sight. She was safe here.

He let his hand slide down the wood before turning to face Rick. "They're family to me." Dylan was surprised to hear the roughness of his own voice. "Take care of them."

Rick gave a sharp nod. "I won't let anything happen to them."

"Thanks." Dylan clapped Rick on the shoulder before heading to another wing, across the hospital, where Tom's office was.

When Dylan reached his destination, Trace was already conducting the search with two other agents. The murders, attempted murders, kidnapping, and an injured federal agent, made this case top priority.

Dylan stood beside Trace. "Find anything?" Dylan asked.

"Nothing even close." Trace shook his head. "We're going through everything with a fine-toothed comb and so far not a thing stands out."

After checking in with Trace, Dylan grabbed a pair of latex gloves out of a box on Tom's large desk and joined in on the search. He flipped through files, dug in desk drawers, and went over Tom's personal belongings. Dylan's frustration mounted the longer they searched. Tom would have kept a copy, wouldn't he? But he may have had it on him, planning on keeping the copy at home.

Feeling like he could punch his fist through a wall, Dylan sat in the leather office chair in front of Tom's desk. Once again he went through every drawer. He even went as far as to look beneath the desk, hoping for some kind of key to a secret drawer. When he found nothing, he riffled through papers in the wastebasket next to the desk. Nothing. Goddamned nothing.

He leaned back in Tom's chair and scanned the surface of the desk for yet another time, as if some new item or clue might appear out of nowhere.

A docking station for a laptop was at the center of the desk, but no sign of the laptop was in the office. Likely, Tom had had it with him when he'd gone home. Also on the desktop was a jade elephant paperweight that felt like it weighed five pounds. Next to the paperweight was a photo of Tom's son in a little league uniform, and beside it was another photo of the boy holding a soccer ball in one arm and a gold medal in the opposite hand.

A notepad with notes in what looked like a typical doctor's handwriting was to the right. Also to the right, near the notepad, was a white coffee mug with "World's #1 Dad" in crayon-like lettering in bright primary colors.

As he looked at the mug, Dylan felt like someone had punched him in the gut. The CoS hadn't just lost a friend, a part of their family… this young boy was now without a father.

Dylan's gaze drifted to the notepad. He stared at it for a moment without seeing it. When his eyes came back into focus, something about the pad caught his attention. He frowned and pulled it toward him with his gloved hand. The writing was virtually illegible, but when he took his time to study it, he was fairly certain that the note started with "Tom" at the top and then "Nate" was written at the bottom.

Heart beating a little faster, Dylan went over and over the note, finding he could pick out words here and there: "town", "good man", "fun", "ditch", "runoff", "mom", "help." One line was underlined, and in that line one word was circled—"mom".

"Did you find something?" Trace's low drawl caught Dylan's attention.

"I think so." Dylan tapped the notepad with his index finger. "I think Tom was trying to figure out his postcard message for himself by writing it out."

Trace braced his palm on the desk as he looked over Dylan's shoulder. "His handwriting damn near looks like a foreign language."

"I think doctor scrawl is a required class in medical school." Dylan looked at Trace. "We might have to get a code breaker to decipher it."

"We may have one or two here." Trace looked toward the doorway. "At least one of his nurses could give us a hand."

"Great idea." Dylan pushed the chair away from the desk and picked up the notepad between gloved fingers. "I'll make a copy of it and see if one of the nurses can lend a hand."

Dylan got up from the chair and strode out of Tom's office. He headed to the closest nurse's station. Carrie Prince, the same curly-haired brunette nurse he'd met yesterday, was at a desk behind the divider.

She glanced up from the file she'd been looking at. She got to her feet. "Agent Curtis," she said as she approached him. "What can I do for you?"

"I have something important that I can use some help with." He held up the notepad. "I think Dr. Zumsteg wrote out what we're looking for, but I can't read his handwriting."

"I'm pretty good at reading Dr. Zumsteg's writing." Carrie looked less teary and red-eyed today, clearly having pulled herself together for work. "As long as what is on here has nothing to do with any patients, I would be glad to help."

Dylan thanked her and she let him use the copier to print out a copy of the note. She took the copy while Dylan held onto the notepad. She sat at her desk and started making notes in the half page beneath the scrawl.

It didn't take Carrie long. She got up from the desk, holding the piece of paper. "It's a personal note and doesn't seem to have anything to do with any patients. It does have to do with a Natc. I think it fits the parameters of the warrant and I don't have a problem giving it to you."

Dylan gestured to the paper Carrie held. "Would you mind giving me a photocopy of what you've written out?"

"No problem." She went to the copier and in moments was back, handing him both pieces of paper.

He took the copies. "I appreciate your help."

"You're welcome." Carrie's expression held a lot of grief once again. "I hope this helps you solve this case."

He touched his fingers to the brim of his Stetson and gave her a nod before turning away. He felt a peculiar stirring in his gut as he read a note from a dead friend to a dead friend.

> Tom,
>
> It's great to have you back in Bisbee, and working at the Copper Queen Hospital. This town needs a good man like you for a local doctor.
>
> What fun we had playing in the ditch with the runoff water from the copper mines. _That was until your mom caught us._ We got our hides tanned for that one.
>
> People need your help. Glad you're there for them.
>
> Nate

The nurse had circled "mom" like Tom had, as well as having underlined the same sentence.

That was until your mom caught us.

Dylan considered Nate's reference to playing in runoff water. Had it been his dad and not his mom who had caught them and taken something to them—a belt, or a strap, or a paddle. Maybe a wooden spoon or shoe for all Dylan knew.

But he remembered Mrs. Zumsteg and she'd been a kind woman. However, Mr. Zumsteg was another story. He had an edge to him, and Dylan wouldn't have been surprised if he had done the spanking or beating.

"Mom versus Dad." Dylan spoke his thoughts aloud. "Could be father, but since he used mom, dad seems more appropriate."

He took the copy of the deciphered note, folded it, and put it in his shirt pocket before returning to Tom's office.

Trace and the other two agents were winding down their search. Dylan put the notepad and the copy with the nurse's handwriting into an evidence bag before turning the bag over to Trace.

Dylan pulled off his latex gloves as he spoke. "I think we got what we need." He nodded to the bag. "It's clearly a copy of the message Nate sent Tom on the postcard. I'd bet my truck on it."

"Good." Trace hooked his thumbs in his jeans pockets as he studied Dylan. "Does it make any sense to you?"

Dylan thought about the underlined sentence and the circled word. "As much sense as any of the notes make. Nate sure didn't make it easy on us. But he had to be certain that if anything happened to him, the CoS would compare the messages when we got together."

Trace nodded, wearing a thoughtful expression. "And knowing that you solve riddles for a living, solving crimes, probably made him confident you would figure it all out."

"Yeah, I'm betting you're right." Another rush of frustration tightened Dylan's muscles. "Damn it. What the hell did Nate get himself into?"

"That probably all rests on what Salvatore Reyes is involved in." Trace's features darkened. "Whatever he's done, he deserves to pay. It's clear he's done something to his wife and he needs to answer for that." Trace's words came out in a low growl. "Death would be too good for that sonofabitch."

When Dylan left Marta's room, Belle felt as if a connection tethering her to him had been severed. The sensation was like a hook had torn her guts out and left nothing but ice in its place.

Belle took a deep breath and faced the two women in the room. One woman lying so still in her hospital bed with a gauge sticking out of her skull while the other woman sat beside the bed.

"Hi, Nancy." Belle offered Marta's wife a little smile.

Nancy met Belle's gaze. "Hi, Belle." The blonde woman glanced at Marta. "Her eyes moved beneath her eyelids." Blue eyes brimming with tears, Nancy looked back to Belle. "It's a good sign. She's dreaming."

Belle went to Nancy, who got to her feet. Belle wrapped her arms around Nancy, who hugged her back with a fierceness that showed how much she needed the support. Belle felt the woman shake with a sob and warm tears wet Belle's shoulder through her shirt.

"I'm sorry." Nancy leaned back and wiped her tears away with her fingertips. "I can't seem to stop crying."

"Don't be sorry." Belle took Nancy's hands in hers. Belle's eyes were watering, too. "You love Marta. We all do. And you have every right to cry."

Nancy hugged Belle again before drawing away. "No one else from the CoS has come since you and Christie last visited."

"I know Leon would have visited if he could, and Christie would come back…if she was able to." More tears gathered at the backs of Belle's eyes. There was no sense in telling Nancy that Christie had been kidnapped…or worse. Not with Marta lying comatose in a hospital bed. For all she knew, Marta could hear, too, and it might cause additional stress to her system. Who could say?

Belle continued, "Because of what happened to Nate, Tom, and Marta, everyone is in protective custody."

"What about you?" Nancy tipped her head to the side. "Why are you here? You should be under protection, too."

"Dylan is in the hospital with me." Belle gestured to the door. "The DHS has an agent guarding the room, so we're all fine. Dylan will be here just as soon as he finishes up with something to do with Tom."

Nancy glanced at Marta. "I've been talking to her, telling her about the kids and asking her to return to me. I have to believe she can hear everything I say."

"I'm sure she does." Belle offered Nancy another smile. "She'll come back to you and the children. I'm sure she will." Belle had to believe with everything she had that what she said was true.

"I'm praying." Nancy sniffled and picked up a tissue from a box on a stand next to the bed. "Praying hard. Every minute."

"I'm praying, too." Belle tucked strands of hair behind her ear. "How are your mother and your sons?"

"Still in protective custody." Nancy sighed. "Mom has been allowed to call me on a secure line and I've been able to talk with the boys, too. The conversations are kept short, but it's good to hear their voices."

"I'm relieved to hear they're safe and well." Belle looked at Marta. "May I talk to Marta?"

Nancy moved aside and sat in another chair. "I know she'd like that."

Belle perched on the edge of the chair Nancy had been occupying and took Marta's hand in both of hers. Marta's fingers were cool in Belle's grip. Her eyes were drawn to the gauge in Marta's shaved skull, the neck brace that held her head absolutely still, and the breathing apparatus. Seeing it all caused a swimming sensation in Belle's abdomen. It was so hard to see her friend like this.

For a moment she just held Marta's hand. A tall vase of lilies, carnations, roses, and lilacs was on the opposite side of the bed and Belle caught the pleasant smell of the flowers.

"How are you doing, honey?" Belle squeezed Marta's fingers. "We miss you. It was so good to see you at the memorial and later at the Puma Den was fun. We'll have to do it again when you wake up."

Belle's lips quivered, but she wanted to keep it light, to say things that would make Marta happy if she could hear and understand. "I'm looking forward to meeting your sons. I bet the twins are cute guys and a handful." She imagined Marta smiling at the thought of her boys. "One day I'd like to join you in motherhood. It would be so much fun to get our kids together to play."

The words Dylan had spoken to her just that morning went through Belle's mind. *"I'm never letting you go again."* She could picture him so clearly as he said it.

Belle's chest ached and she swallowed. "I like the name Shane for a boy. What do you think?"

Movement beneath Marta's eyelids made Belle's heart pound a little faster. Could her friend understand her? Was Marta listening or dreaming? Or both?

"I've been thinking a lot of the things we did when we were young." Belle shifted on the seat. "We were good kids and teenagers, too, but we got into our share of trouble, didn't we?"

She continued, "Remember the time you and I got into Old Mrs. Swierc's pomegranate bush in her back yard? We were seven and went to Central School at that time. We sat in the alleyway, pulling the fruit off the bush. At that time I didn't know they were considered berries— the skin is so tough and there are so many seeds inside. But we loved sucking the pulp from the seeds and spitting the seeds out. Did you know that in the U.S. they can only grow in Arizona and California?"

The memory was strong and Belle smiled. "I'd been riding my pink bike with the white plastic basket on the front. Your bike was green with a black wire basket. I bet the boys could tell us what the makes were. I don't remember." She knew she was babbling, but she went on. "We each put pomegranates into our baskets, enough for the CoS to each have one. We were getting ready to ride to meet them when Mrs. Swierc came out of her house."

Belle laughed. "She seemed so ancient then, swearing at us in Polish. She marched us to your mom's house and between our parents we got into so much trouble." Belle shook her head. "We were so innocent in those days."

Marta's eyes darted beneath her eyelids, something that encouraged Belle to go on and she talked about other adventures in their elementary school years with a fondness that made her smile.

When she thought aloud about junior high, she said, "Now those were the awkward years. All those crazy hormones. I think our parents were wondering what they were going to do to us and if they'd let us survive until we grew out of those stages." She shook her head. "Remember how your mom put you into dance because she thought you needed a little refinement, and mine stuck me in softball with Christie just to get me out of the house?" She laughed. "Christie and I wanted to trade places with you so badly and take dance. You wanted to be the one playing softball. You always were the tomboy and I was such a girly girl." She grinned. "Still am."

Her grin faded and she sighed. "High school was different for us, but we still managed to stay close." She tried not to think about how much her life had changed because of her stepfather. "I'm sorry I didn't stay in touch when I left." Belle's voice thickened as she struggled to hold back tears. "I'm sorry about what I put the CoS through and how much I worried all of you." Her throat ached. "But I thought about you all the time. Christie told me what was going on with everyone. You know I love you, Marta. Don't you?"

A slight tremor went through Marta's hand. It was as if she was trying to say to Belle that she understood.

Belle nearly jumped out of her seat as she whipped her head to the side to look at Nancy. "I felt something. I think she was trying to squeeze my hand."

Nancy did come up from her chair, her eyes wide, hope in her gaze. "You did? Are you sure?"

Belle reached for Nancy. "I guess I can't be positive, but I think so." She took Nancy's hand and placed it over Marta's. "Maybe she'll do it again." Belle traded places with Nancy.

Nancy sat and held Marta's hand to her lips. "Come on, baby. I love you."

For a moment, both Belle and Nancy were still. Then Nancy's eyes widened. "I felt it. A slight pressure but it went away. She squeezed my hand." Nancy looked stunned, as if she couldn't believe it.

"I'll find the doctor or a nurse." Belle moved toward the door. "Dr. Miller, right?"

Nancy nodded, her gaze focused on Marta. "Yes."

Belle opened the door and slipped out.

Agent DeLong looked at her. "You need to stay in the room, Ms. Hartford."

"She moved. Marta moved." Belle glanced down the hallway. "I need to find the doctor or a nurse. I'll only be a moment."

The agent shook his head. "You need to stay."

Before he could stop her, she hurried to the closest nurse's station. She was aware the agent couldn't leave his post to chase her down, but saw him pulling his cell phone out of the holster at his belt. She didn't want him disturbing Dylan, but this was too important to not take care of right away.

Belle felt a little lighter. Some good news. The thought that Christie had been kidnapped crashed right back into Belle and she felt a thud in her chest, a pain so deep it almost drove her to her knees.

She paused in the hallway and held her hand over her heart, trying to maintain her composure. Dylan and the other agents would find Christie. They would. Belle was certain of it, just as she was sure Marta would come out of the coma.

Belle reached the nurse's station and saw a nurse with a badge that read Carrie Prince with the woman's picture on it. Belle felt out of breath and then she was talking rapidly. "Marta De La Paz just moved. I mean she sort of squeezed my hand and then she did squeeze Nancy's."

The nurse smiled, in a way like it was the first thing she'd had to smile about in a while. "I'll let Dr. Miller know and I'll send Marta's nurse, too."

"Thank you." Belle turned and hurried back down the hallway toward Marta's room.

The agent looked relieved when she came around the corner and walked toward him. "Dylan is on his way, and the nurse beat you here."

She was glad Agent DeLong had called Dylan. He would be happy to hear the news, too. "Thank you."

He opened the door and she stepped inside.

Belle looked at the bed to see a male nurse leaning over Marta, his back to her. She couldn't see Nancy. Maybe she'd gone to the restroom. Belle walked closer as the door shut silently behind her.

She opened her mouth to speak and then her mouth dropped open in horror. The nurse had a pillow over Martha's face.

He was smothering her.

"No!" Belle grabbed the vase of flowers from the side of the bed at the same time she shouted.

The nurse whirled just as Belle swung the vase at his head like a baseball bat.

Flowers flew across the room. The vase shattered as it connected with his skull. He staggered back and shook his head.

In a flash she saw Nancy slumped in her chair and the pillow still on Marta's face.

Belle was certain the oxygen tube was dislodged. She had to put it back!

The man lunged for Belle and he tackled her to the floor, knocking the breath from her. He wrapped his fingers around her neck and pinned her beneath his larger body.

Belle struggled but couldn't move her legs. She tried to scream, but no sound would come out. Stars sparked in her mind as she clawed at his face.

Why hadn't she screamed for the agent? It had all happened so quickly.

And now, dear God, she was going to die.

Vaguely she heard the door open and slam against the wall.

The sound of male voices.

Dylan's shout.

A shot echoed through the room.

Blood splattered Belle's face.

The man slumped on her chest. His fingers relaxed around her neck and then he was thrown off.

Dylan's face appeared over hers, panic in his gaze. He grabbed her to him, holding her tightly to his chest.

"Belle." He rocked her against him. "Thank God."

She gasped. "Marta."

He relaxed his grip and looked over his shoulder. "Belle needs medical attention. Now."

Behind him she saw people bending over Marta and she relaxed in Dylan's arms.

"I'm okay." Her words came out in a hoarse whisper. "You hugged me too tightly."

"You're not okay." Dylan looked at her with fierce intensity. "I am never letting you out of my sight again. Never."

"I'll have to go to the bathroom sometimes." She didn't know where the remark came from.

Dylan's features softened. "I'll go with you."

Someone knelt beside them. Belle recognized Carrie Prince from the nurse's station. "Let me see her, Agent Curtis."

Dylan held her hand in his tight grip as the nurse checked her vitals.

Nurse Prince looked at another hospital employee who was on one knee beside them. "Let's get her to a bed."

"No." It hurt Belle to shake her head and her throat ached as she croaked the words. "Marta. How is she?"

A third person stood over Belle. "She'll be fine. We got to her in time, thanks to you."

Belle realized the room was full of people now. "Let me up." She tried to push herself in a sitting position.

"We need to make sure he didn't hurt your neck too badly." Nurse Prince spoke in a reprimanding tone as she held Belle down by her shoulders.

"Do as she says, sweetheart." Dylan brushed his hand over her forehead.

"What about Nancy?" Panic lodged in Belle's chest once again. "How is she?"

"She was drugged." Agent DeLong was standing over them now. "They're taking her to a room now. They found a syringe by her chair."

Tears stung at Belle's eyes. "Is she going to be okay?"

"The doctor thinks so, but they won't say until they're sure what was in the syringe." Agent DeLong continued, "She was starting to come around, so they think she was just knocked out. They'll let us know as soon as they can."

Belle sagged with a feeling of hopeful relief. She had to believe that Nancy would be all right, as well as Marta and Christie, too. She couldn't give up hope on any of them. Not now.

Not ever.

CHAPTER 19

Salvatore stared at Christie where she lay on the floor, tied to the chair, near Carl's body. Salvatore's knuckles stung from hitting her and the side of her face was starting to swell and purple.

She stirred and moaned.

He crouched beside her. "*Mi mariposa*, you shouldn't have said what you did. I had to teach you a lesson. You know that, don't you?"

She mumbled something and he was afraid she was saying, "*Monster*," again, but he didn't want to hear that from her lips again.

His eyes narrowed. He looked at Paco and gestured to Christie. "Pick her up and keep her tied to the chair."

Paco looked unfazed as he took the chair and raised it so that Christie was again in a sitting position. Paco was a cold-hearted killer and that's what Salvatore needed. Paco didn't care if his target was male or female. He just did his job. "Do you want me to take care of eliminating her?"

"No." The words came out of Salvatore like pieces of ice. "I'll deal with Christie when I'm ready."

A smear of blood was on the floor where Christie's head had hit the concrete. Salvatore's gut churned involuntarily at the sight of her blood before he looked at his wife. She was dazed, blinking as if trying to regain focus.

Anger burned through him, making him hot enough to sweat beneath his shirt and trousers. *She* had driven him to hit her. *She* had provoked him. *She* was at fault for *making* him hurt her.

Salvatore stepped over Carl's body and walked around the chair until he was standing behind Christie and saw that her long red hair was dark where it was matted with blood. It pained him to see the blood. He reached out to stroke the hair he'd always loved and she flinched away from his touch.

He trembled with a flash of rage and almost hit her again. Instead, he moved to face her. He picked up the piece of tape that he'd laid on the table earlier, the piece that had been across her mouth. He put the strip back over her mouth so she couldn't speak the words that had cut him to his soul. If she said them again, he'd likely kill her right now.

"You're a horrible, sick monster, Salvatore."

Again the words chilled him.

He was not a monster. He was a businessman and this was all business. Mixed with a little revenge, he supposed. The damned CoS had always shut him out until Belle left. When she'd vanished, he'd hoped she had been kidnapped and that they'd find her body somewhere.

When Belle turned up years later and she and Christie had rekindled their close relationship, he'd been disappointed, but had put on a good show. Now the CoS had fucked up his life again and he was going to have to run. But first he'd make sure every last one of them died, preferably painful deaths.

His wife would be tortured by the agonizing deaths of her friends, and that would be pain enough for her. He'd be merciful and kill her quickly. Unless she provoked him again.

The look in her eyes when she'd called him a monster was unlike anything he'd seen from her before. He didn't like the strength he'd seen in her expression. She had always been quiet and gentle around him, like a beautiful butterfly. Despite never giving him sons, she had balanced him and he'd loved her.

Now... He had to do what he had to do. He was moving on and she'd be pushed to the back of his mind, a memory that he would eventually forget. He'd already separated from her in some ways.

Until death do us part.

Their vows to one another at their marriage ceremony were written in stone. And that's how it would end. With her departure from this life.

His private cell vibrated in his pocket, the one he'd used to set up the attack on the safe house. The one he used to conduct his *real* business.

He withdrew the phone from his pocket and looked at the display, expecting to see Oscar Garcia calling with the news that Marta was dead. Instead it was Jorge.

Cold washed over Salvatore. Jorge had been monitoring the situation with Oscar and Marta. That he was calling instead of Oscar could very well be bad news.

He bit out each word. "You have news for me?"

"Oscar is dead." Jorge's voice sounded flat, matter of fact. "Curtis killed Oscar after he smothered Marta and then strangled Belle."

"Was he successful in killing Marta and Belle?" Salvatore's voice rose. He saw Christie's eyes widen and he realized his mistake by letting her know Belle had still been alive.

"No." Jorge went on, "My resource says Belle stopped Oscar from finishing his job when she hit him with an object. He tried to murder Belle, but Curtis found them and killed Oscar before he could finish her off."

"Fuck." Salvatore spat the word. "I'll talk to Rodrigo and get Davies on the job."

"The feds have two agents on the room now," Jorge said.

Salvatore's hand shook. "Then Davies can bomb the fucking place."

"The hospital is being watched from the outside. He wouldn't be able to get close."

Salvatore struggled to maintain his composure. It would not do to have Paco and Christie see him lose control. "I'll get Rodrigo to lend me Davies to put on locating Leon and his family. I want you to track Curtis and Belle. Use whatever resources you need. Cost is no object."

"I will take care of it," Jorge said. "And I'll get Rat on the job, too."

"See that you do." Salvatore disconnected the call. Rat was nothing more than a shithead, but he did as he was told and was generally useful.

Salvatore dialed the phone to reach El Verdugo to request Davies's assistance. Rodrigo did not pick up.

Frustration ate through Salvatore's stomach like acid. He left a brief message that he needed Davies, and then disconnected the call.

When Salvatore looked at Christie, she had her chin tilted up and that look in her eyes that he didn't like. Not one bit. He'd always thought of her as that delicate butterfly he could crush if he chose to. She didn't look crushed. She looked angry.

He stared at her. She didn't look away.

Fury cut through his chest like a knife and he bent and clenched his fists on the tabletop. Nothing had gone as planned. Everything was falling apart and he had to pull it all back together.

He would, of that he had no doubt.

And every member of the CoS would die.

CHAPTER 20

It was the morning following the attack on the safe house, Christie's kidnapping, and the attempt on Marta's life.

Belle perched on the edge of the bed of the suite in the B & B, her hands braced to either side of her and her feet on the floor to keep herself grounded. Her skin felt chilled and her stomach tied in knots.

Nothing seemed real. It was all one big nightmare.

And then there was the secret she'd been keeping from Dylan.

She knew she had to tell him the truth. She'd put it off and put it off, and she knew there would be no perfect time to tell him.

Feeling overwhelmed, tears threatened at the backs of her eyes. She had to do it now. She'd waited too long.

Her thoughts whirled as Dylan used the bathroom in the suite they were staying in. The B & B was a large private home with two upstairs suites. Originally four bedrooms had been upstairs but they'd been converted into two suites when the new owners purchased the older home.

So much had happened since she got that first call from Dylan… Nate. Tom. Marta. Christie.

Marta's guard had been doubled and another team was watching the hospital. The FBI was now working with DHS to find Christie as it was considered to be a kidnapping.

Belle pushed her fingers through her hair, shifted on the bed, then tried to sit still. She wanted to be out there, helping find Christie. Dylan would be leaving soon to do just that.

Before he left, she had to come clean. After everything that had happened, she was going to hit him with a truth that would send him reeling. How was she going to do this?

The suites were nice and apparently rented out steadily, even though the owners did not advertise. Visitors to Bisbee learned about the B & B by word of mouth, and Dylan had decided it was an ideal temporary place to stay.

Agents had rented the two upstairs suites so no one was there but Dylan, Belle, and two agents Dylan trusted the most—Trace and Brooks. The owners kept to their private quarters and the kitchen on the bottom floor.

The two agents remained on guard in the hallway between suites, while Dylan stayed with Belle in one of them. G.I. Joe was in the front room near the door, sitting like a sphinx, his ears perked. He seemed to be intent on guarding them, especially after what had happened at the safe house. She wondered at how vicious he'd been to Salvatore and the other men, like he knew them. She had a feeling he did and that it had something to do with Nate.

Belle's throat and neck ached from nearly being strangled. Her skin had bruised, the purple marks stark against her naturally pale skin. Before she left the hospital, an agent brought her a turtleneck sweater at Dylan's request, which would help avoid notice of the bruises and avoid questions. Her eyes were red, a result of the near strangulation, but sunglasses had hidden the redness when she was in public.

She sighed, hating what she had to do. It was time—she had to tell Dylan everything. It was important that no secrets be kept between them.

When he'd finished in the bathroom, he looked distracted. "I hope to hell we have the warrant to search Salvatore and Christie's home by now."

He frowned as he saw Belle and sat beside her on the bed. "Something's on your mind." His gaze was intense. "And it's not just what's been happening. There's something else, isn't there." The last part he said as a statement, not a question. Like he somehow knew she'd been keeping something from him.

She looked down at her lap and saw that she was wringing her hands. She raised her eyes and met his gaze.

He skimmed her neck with his fingertips, a light feathery touch. "I hate seeing what that bastard did to you."

"Really, I'm okay." Belle sighed. "I'm lucky. I'm not like Marta, in a coma, with a gauge sticking out of my head." She swallowed. "And I'm not missing like Christie."

"What happened is nothing to dismiss, Belle." He cupped her cheek. "I haven't been so scared since…"

"Since I left in high school. I don't know if I can ever apologize enough for doing that to you the way I did." Belle bit her lower lip a moment before she continued. "I need to tell you something important that was one of the reasons I left. You might hate me for not telling you sooner."

Dylan frowned. "I could never hate you, Belle."

Her throat hurt more when she swallowed, and it was as if she could still feel the man's hands around her neck. "I will be honest. I can't say that I regret not telling you when you were a teenager. You could have ended up in jail, because you might have killed my stepfather."

Dylan's voice was harsh, anger clear in his expression. "Your stepfather deserves whatever he gets for what he did to you."

"Y*ou* didn't deserve to go to jail." She looked away a moment before meeting his gaze again. "And you still don't. What I'm going to tell you might make you want to kill him even more. Please promise me you won't go after him."

"What's going on?" Dylan's entire body seemed to go tense. "What is it that you need to tell me?"

For a moment she held her breath. *Just get it out.*

She let it out in a rush as she said, "My stepfather was responsible for your dad's death. Harvey killed your dad."

The shock that crossed Dylan's face sent a sharp pain through her chest. But the mask that replaced it scared her even more. It was like he'd shut down his emotions, shut *her* out.

His voice was hard, his expression even harder. "Explain."

She gripped his arm as if that might keep him from being lost to her altogether. "Promise me you won't go after Harvey yourself."

His arm vibrated beneath her touch, as if he was holding back every bit of anger he'd stored up since his father's murder. *"Tell me."*

"I overheard everything when my mother and Harvey talked about it. Before my mom died." Tears welled up in Belle's eyes. "The Jimenez Cartel put a hit out on your dad. My stepfather carried it out for the money. It was the one time I saw my mother stand up to him and tell him he shouldn't have done it. He hit her hard enough to knock her out. I slipped out the back door so he wouldn't know I'd overheard, in case he planned to take it out on me, too."

Dylan looked away. His entire body had gone rigid. "You should have told me."

His words were a cold slap. She'd expected it, but reality was far worse than what she'd ever imagined.

Then he did something that totally took her by surprise. He braced his elbows on his knees and buried his face in his hands.

"Dylan." She placed her hand tentatively on his shoulder. "I'm sorry. I really am. But you understand why I didn't tell you, don't you?"

He said nothing. She stroked his shoulder as he remained silent. "I'm sorry. Can you forgive me?"

After a long moment he raised his head, his forearms resting on his thighs as he stared forward, his eyes focused on something she couldn't see. Like a memory.

A cold look hardened his face and she jerked her hand back from his shoulder as if she'd been scalded.

When he turned to her, his eyes were slightly red but she saw no tears, only a mask that now shuttered his expression.

"Dylan?" She didn't know what to do. "I understand you being angry with me. But please don't go after Harvey by yourself. Do what you have to do to arrest him. But—"

When Dylan spoke, it was slow, measured, as if he was trying to maintain his calm. "I'm going to leave you here with Trace and Brooks. I trust them and they will protect you."

"Take one of them with you, please." She didn't care that she was begging. "They can help you take him into custody. I'll testify against Harvey. I'll do anything you need me to. Take *me* with you."

Dylan got to his feet and she rushed to stand, too. He gripped her shoulder with one big hand. "You will stay here." His face was still a mask, but as he looked at her, she thought she saw his sharp edges soften ever so slightly. He leaned over and kissed her forehead before grabbing his duffel bag, turning and leaving the bedroom.

The kiss stunned her. She didn't know if it was a goodbye kiss or something else entirely.

She hurried after him, fear for him making her heart ache as he strode to the door of the suite. "Please, Dylan."

He grasped the doorknob and looked over his shoulder. "You'll stay in the suite with Joe." He opened the door. "I have some business to take care of."

"Dylan." Even as she called out his name, he shut the door behind him.

She wrenched the door open and saw him talking with Trace. Joe came up to stand beside her.

Dylan looked at her and pointed to the room. "Get inside."

She set her jaw. "Come back."

With the duffel bag over his shoulder, he turned and jogged down the wood staircase and vanished from sight. She started to follow.

So that she couldn't chase Dylan, Trace stepped in front of her. "Go in the room, Belle."

"You don't understand." Tears burned at the backs of her eyes. "He's going after my stepfather. He wants to kill him. You have to stop Dylan."

Trace frowned. "What do you mean, Belle?"

"He was already furious at my stepfather for hurting me." Tears flowed down Belle's cheeks. "But now it's worse. I told him the truth." Her throat felt like it was closing in on her. "My stepfather is the man who killed Dylan's dad."

Trace looked as if his entire body had gone tense. "That's where Dylan is going? To your stepfather's?"

"I don't care about Harvey, but I care about Dylan. I don't want him to end up doing something he'll regret. Please stop him." She twisted her hands together. "Harvey lives in Galena." She gave Trace the address of the miserable home she'd grown up in.

"I'll call for someone to get over here." Brooks nodded to the stairs Dylan had just taken. "You go after Dylan."

"Back in your room, Belle." Trace's Texan drawl seemed deeper as he spoke and gave her a firm look. "Stay with Joe. Brooks will be outside watching the room."

"Okay." She put her fingers in Joe's fur as she pleaded with Trace. "Just hurry. Please."

It was still early morning, not even eight yet, and it was all Dylan could do to keep from throwing on Trace's SUV's grill lights and siren. He wanted to race far over the speed limit as he headed the vehicle toward Harvey Driscoll's home. But he needed the time to think and work out a plan before he arrived at the house.

The thought repeated over and over in his head. *Driscoll murdered Dad. The bastard murdered my dad.*

Too many things were happening all at once.

And Driscoll had murdered Dylan's dad.

Driscoll had not only killed Dylan and Aspen's father, but he'd taken away the man their mother had loved. For years she'd been haunted by Ben Curtis's death, until she finally gave herself permission to move on.

Dylan's skin burned and itched with fury. His face was flushed with heat. He gritted his teeth and clenched the steering wheel as he drove from Old Bisbee, around the pit mines, to the traffic circle, and then took the exit to Galena. The drive seemed to last forever. He wanted to get to the bastard who was responsible for so much goddamned misery and pain.

He wanted to kill Harvey with his bare hands. He could picture a dozen different ways he could kill the man. Make it look like an accident. Make it look like Harvey had killed himself.

But Dylan wasn't a murderer. He was a law enforcement officer. *Fuck that.*

He guided the SUV into the neighborhood and forced himself to slow down in case any kids ran into the street. The last thing he wanted to do was kill a child because he was on a mission to kill a murderer, a man who had raped his own stepdaughter when she was a teenager.

The woman Dylan had loved for as long as he could remember.

Belle had kept the knowledge from him, and if it hadn't been for Nate's death, she might never have told him. The better part of him understood she had just been trying to protect him. It was true that he could have ended up in prison for the rest of his life had he killed Driscoll. He'd been old enough that he would have been tried as an adult because he'd have known exactly what he was doing.

Another part of him didn't know how to deal with the knowledge that Belle hadn't told him before now. He knew she hadn't done it to protect Driscoll. She'd done it to protect Dylan because she knew what kind of temper he had. She'd probably been terrified of what Driscoll would do to her if he knew she'd overheard him telling her mother he'd murdered Belle's boyfriend's father.

The knowledge had tortured her all these years, of that he was sure. The thought that she had lived with such a terrible secret made his heart ache for her. No wonder she had run. Her stepfather had been sexually abusing her. Her stepfather had killed her boyfriend's father.

What she'd done by leaving had shown strength that many people didn't possess. Yes, there had been other ways to handle it, but she'd done the only thing she thought she could do. She had made a life for herself out of nothing and a lifetime of horrible experiences and knowledge.

Dylan had searched for his dad's killer ever since moving back to southeastern Arizona. He'd known the Jimenez Cartel had somehow been involved. It was a cold case by the time Dylan had been in a position to hunt for his dad's killer, but he'd been chipping away at it.

He'd never suspected Harvey Driscoll. The bastard had known Ben Curtis, but they had only met a couple of times as far as Dylan knew. It had probably been enough that Ben would have thought Driscoll had some other business. He never would have suspected the man was there to murder him.

Dylan pulled the SUV to the curb across the street from the house where Driscoll lived. A house where Belle had experienced the kind of trauma no child should go through. The house where a murderer still lived while the man he'd murdered had left behind a devastated wife and two sons.

For a long moment he stared at the house, trying to get his emotions under control. The house was in a state of disrepair that was worse than it had been twenty-three years ago when Belle left. Driscoll and Belle's mother had taken no pride in their home, the grass dead, the lone pine tree on the verge of falling down, the house in need of a new paint job.

Now the formerly yellow paint was gray and had curled and peeled until little was left on the boards. The wood steps sagged and the porch was in such bad shape it looked like it would collapse if stepped on. Dead grass and weeds choked the front yard, and in the midst of that sat the rusted and faded hulk of an old red Pontiac Grand Am. Dylan remembered that Driscoll had purchased the car new sometime after Ben Curtis's death. Driscoll had probably paid for it with blood money. Money made from spilling Ben Curtis's blood.

Dylan didn't know if Driscoll was home, but an early model 2001 green Ford truck was in the gravel driveway to the right of the house. Dylan wasn't even sure what he would do when he faced the sonofabitch. Truth was Dylan could easily kill Driscoll.

Teeth clenched, Dylan still gripped the steering wheel. He realized his muscles were shaking with the restraint it took to stay in his vehicle. He forced himself to calm his breathing. Whatever he did, it needed to be done with a clear head.

He let go of the steering wheel and swung open the door of the SUV. He climbed out before shutting the door solidly behind him. He let his gaze drift along the street.

Two doors down, a couple of identical looking boys, who were eight or nine, sat on the porch steps of a home in far better shape than

Driscoll's. No matter how rundown the area was, any house in the neighborhood was in better shape than Driscoll's. The boys' mother was likely tired of the kids playing video games all day and had probably chased them out of the house to play in the front yard.

A couple argued about finances as they came out of the house next door to the one Dylan stood in front of. The woman shouted at the man, telling him he needed to get a job because hers couldn't pay all of the bills. He told her to shut the hell up before he climbed into a newer Chevy truck and slammed the door behind him. The woman was still yelling as the man gunned the engine and peeled out of the driveway.

At the end of the street, a woman pinned laundry to a clothesline. In the early morning breeze, the clothes waved on the line. It made Dylan think of the times his mother had done the same thing on the ranch, and he pictured sheets billowing in a gust of wind. The sheets would smell of the clean outdoors as she tucked him in at night when he was just a young boy. His father would come in and tell Dylan and Aspen a story before bedtime. Often the stories were about farming and ranching, usually tall tales his father would make up on the spot. His father had been a gifted storyteller.

Dylan's stomach clenched at the memories. As he stared at Driscoll's house, he was conscious of the Browning semi-automatic in its shoulder holster over his T-shirt. The thought that he shouldn't be armed was fleeting.

Whatever happened, happened.

Dylan strode across the street. The fact that he'd be facing his father's killer was almost surreal. He'd been so close all this time. So close.

As Dylan pushed open the rusted metal gate of the hip-high chain link fence, it gave a rusted screech. His shoes thumped on the cracked concrete path to the wooden steps, which creaked as he took them two at a time. When he reached the porch, the boards were surprisingly sturdy beneath his weight.

He banged on the door with his fist, the sound loud enough to wake the dead and draw the attention of anyone in the street. When silence met his knock, he pounded on the door again. Likely Driscoll was still asleep.

Dylan pounded on the door even louder.

The door swung open. "What the hell do you want?" Harvey Driscoll slurred the words as he scowled at Dylan, face red, eyes bleary from alcohol and sleep.

Dylan studied the man who'd killed his father. He'd expected to feel even more rage, more murderous fury than he'd felt when Belle had told him. But now that he faced the murderer, Dylan knew that he wanted to make the man *pay*. Death would be too easy for the bastard. No, Harvey Driscoll needed to rot in prison.

The older man wore a dirty wife beater T-shirt, filthy pants, and no shoes. A bald patch on his head shone with sweat and his large beer gut hung over his belt. He squinted and looked from Dylan's holstered pistol to his face. His oily pockmarked face now had a cautious expression instead of a scowl.

"You a cop?" In his drunken stupor, he clearly didn't recognize Dylan. Or course, Dylan had changed in the past twenty-three years since Belle had vanished.

Dylan was aware of a truck with a powerful engine coming to a hard stop in the gravel across the street behind him.

"Harvey Driscoll." Dylan stepped back and gestured for the man to come out on the porch. "Step outside."

The man hesitated, then joined Dylan on the porch. He glanced over Dylan's shoulder and his eyes widened slightly as boot steps hit the asphalt. "I didn't do nothin'." Driscoll licked his lips. "What're you doing here?"

Trace or Brooks, likely had arrived. Belle had no doubt told the agents and Dylan's good friends the reason why Dylan left in a hurry. He ground his teeth. Both men should be guarding Belle, not just one.

The sound of steps came to a stop at the foot of the stairs. Dylan casually looked over his shoulder to see Trace standing with his arms folded across his chest. He gave Dylan a single nod but said nothing.

Dylan turned his attention back to Driscoll. The man's gaze narrowed. "I know you from somewhere. Who the hell are you?"

"So you like hurting young girls." Dylan said it as a statement, not a question. "You sexually abused your own stepdaughter. What other children have you molested?"

A look of fear flashed across Driscoll's face but then it was gone. "I don't know what the fuck you're talking about." He waved it away with a sloppy movement of his arm. "The little bitch is probably dead. Haven't seen her in over twenty years."

Dylan wanted to slam his fist into Driscoll's ugly face so badly that his teeth and hands ached with the force it took to hold himself back. Better yet, he should shoot the man and be done with it.

"I know who you are." Driscoll stepped closer to Dylan who took another step back to bring Driscoll further out onto the porch. "You're that punkass Curtis kid who was always sniffing up Belle's skirt."

"You're a pathetic excuse for a man." Dylan kept his voice low as he taunted Driscoll, aware that neighbors were watching now, which was exactly what Dylan wanted. "I hear you have a little dick and you couldn't even satisfy your wife. You even had to kill a man to get off."

"*Motherfucker!*" Driscoll bellowed the words as he stepped forward, his fist raised.

Come on, Driscoll. Take the bait.

"You haven't got the balls to do more than hurt little girls and kill defenseless men." Dylan braced himself.

With a roar, Driscoll swung his fist at Dylan.

Dylan didn't even flinch as the fist came toward him. Driscoll's fist connected with the side of Dylan's head.

Sparks lit up Dylan's vision for a brief moment, but he shook it off. Driscoll's fist came at him again.

This time Dylan whipped out his handcuffs with one hand as he used the other to grab the man's wrist. Dylan twisted Driscoll's arm behind his back, swept his feet out from under him, and slammed him down hard. The bastard's cheek rested on the porch. Dylan had his knee on the small of Driscoll's back with his hands cuffed behind him, the whole process done in five seconds flat.

"Let me go, you sonofabitch!" Driscoll struggled but Dylan had him pinned to the splintered boards. "Police brutality!"

Trace stepped onto the porch. "I'll take it from here."

The rage that Dylan felt toward Driscoll hadn't subsided. His body was still hot and tingling with the desire to hurt Driscoll. To *really* hurt him. Yeah, it would be better to let Trace handle the bastard from this point on. Dylan might just kill the man after all.

Dylan pushed away from Driscoll and stood. Dylan inhaled deeply then let out a harsh breath. He still shook from the force of his anger and had to take another deep breath. It didn't do much to calm him, but it gave him time to clear his head.

Trace settled his boot on Driscoll's lower back. Trace pressed his boot harder on Driscoll, causing the man to whine. Trace said in a low, exaggerated drawl, "Quiet down, or I'm going to have to let Dylan take over again. He's not as nice as I am."

Dylan relaxed his clenched fists. He turned away as he un-holstered his cell phone to call in the arrest of Driscoll for the federal crime of assault on a federal agent.

A crowd had gathered around. Dylan heard comments that told him Driscoll wasn't popular in the neighborhood.

"Did you see Harvey hit the cop?" asked a woman. "The old bastard got what he deserved," said a man. "I got it all on my phone," added a much younger voice.

Good. The recording would be proof of the assault by Driscoll. Dylan didn't look at the watching neighbors as he raised his own phone to his ear and made the call.

CHAPTER 21

The search warrant for Salvatore and Christie's home finally came through via the FBI as two agents with DHS took Harvey Driscoll away.

It was late morning by the time Dylan and Trace walked toward their separate vehicles. Trace was on the phone with Brooks, letting him know that Driscoll was very much alive but had been arrested and taken away, and why. Now they just needed Belle to go to the police, tell her story, and press charges for the sexual abuse. Dylan knew she would also testify about overhearing Driscoll bragging about murdering Dylan's father.

Next Dylan needed to build a case against Driscoll for Ben Curtis's murder. Dylan would need to work with other agents due to the fact that it was his dad who was murdered, but Dylan intended to do everything he could to make sure Driscoll was put away for a long, long time. Preferably for the rest of his life.

Once the wheels were set in motion, a search warrant would be issued to search Driscoll's home for the pictures and videos he'd taken of Belle when he'd raped her. They would also get a warrant to search for the gun that Driscoll had used to take Ben Curtis's life.

When Driscoll was hauled away in cuffs, some of Dylan's fury had lessened. Most remained in his mind and body like a too-high pilot light that would never go out. The bastard would pay. Dylan just had to be patient enough for the wheels of justice to turn.

Galena wasn't far from Salvatore and Christie Reyes's home in the Terraces. While Dylan drove to their home, he called George to see how he was doing with the memory card.

"Still working on it." George sounded frustrated. "My program has used every combination of the words that I can think of—together, individually, frontward, backward, flipped, first letters, last letters, first and last letters… Damn it, you name it, I've done it. The program we use is working overtime on it, too."

"Something must be missing." Dylan thought the words aloud.

"No kidding," George grumbled. "I'll stay on it."

Dylan thanked him as he arrived at the Reyes house. Trace pulled Dylan's truck up behind his own SUV that he had loaned to Dylan. Brooks was already there. Two other DHS agents had taken his place at the B & B earlier and were guarding Belle.

Male and female agents wore jackets with FBI printed on the front and in much larger yellow letters on the back. The agents were clearly preparing to storm the castle and conduct the search.

Brooks was turned away from Trace and Dylan. Brooks wore his agency jacket with FEDERAL AGENT in smaller letters beneath the large POLICE on the back.

DHS, ICE, EPA, and other agency acronyms were not as recognizable as FBI, CIA, DEA, or simply police to many criminals. Several agencies used POLICE across the back and on the front instead of their own acronyms for that reason. It was a matter of identification and safety.

Dylan and Trace pulled on their own jackets that matched Brooks's before they headed in the direction of the house. Brooks stood next to a woman who wore an FBI jacket. The female agent's black hair was pulled into a knot at the back of her head. It was severe enough to tighten her dark skin over her high cheekbones. Her eyes were black and sharp and it looked like her expression was likely perpetually serious. Dylan couldn't picture her cracking a smile.

Ahead of them was the pathway leading to the wrought iron security door of the Reyes home.

Brooks turned to face Trace and Dylan and nodded to them. Brooks made the introductions between the four when they met up. "This is Special Agent Laura Stillwater, the lead agent on the FBI's search for Christie."

After Dylan and Stillwater shook hands, Brooks said, "According to Agent Stillwater, they have a couple of leads." He glanced at her. "But they don't seem inclined to share them with us."

Dylan ground his teeth. The FBI could be so damned difficult to deal with.

"We'll fill you in soon enough." Stillwater drew her weapon. "Right now we're going to search their home and see if we can find clues to Christie's whereabouts."

Dylan's skin burned as his thoughts focused on his childhood friend and the need to find her. Christie had better be alive. If anyone had even hurt her, Dylan would tear the person or persons into shreds. If it was Salvatore, the sonofabitch was going to wish he were dead by the time Dylan got through with him.

Agents reported that wrought iron security doors were also at the back of the house, and all were locked.

Stillwater shouted out their presence and stated the FBI was coming in, but there was no response. Not that Dylan had expected any. Agents were posted at the front and back of the home, prepared for anyone who might run out.

Two agents took a hydraulic ram to the wrought iron, and it didn't take long before it was breached. Within seconds after opening the metal security door, the agents smashed open the front door with the ram.

Dylan's heart rate picked up as he, Trace, Brooks, Stillwater, and other agents entered the home holding their weapons in a two-handed grip, clearing room after room. When all of the rooms were cleared, agents began to methodically search the house for clues.

Trace and Brooks worked with the FBI agents, searching other parts of the house.

Stillwater and Dylan stood in the living room in front of a closed metal door that agents had been unable to open with the hydraulic ram.

"What the hell is behind this door?" Dylan said more to himself than anyone else. "Salvatore had to be hiding something important."

"We'll just have to find out what that is." Stillwater called for a hydraulic tool that would aid in opening a metal door. "If this doesn't do it, we'll have to call for more drastic measures."

Like explosives. Dylan frowned as the thought crossed his mind that just maybe Christie was inside that room. Even a strategically placed small explosive had the potential to kill or harm any occupants that might be too close.

Fortunately, the agents had the door open with the hydraulic tool within the next ten minutes. The time seemed interminable, but finally they were in.

When Dylan went through the door with Stillwater, he saw that it was an office. "Salvatore must have been hiding something important in here to warrant that kind of security." Dylan pulled on a pair of latex gloves before he began searching the room.

He started with the desk, his gaze drifting over the small gold globe of the world on the surface, the desk pad, a crystal eagle paperweight, and a framed professional wedding photograph of Salvatore and Christie. Dylan picked up the photograph. Christie looked so happy, her smile brilliant. Salvatore was smiling, too, but there was something in his eyes and on his expression as he looked at his new wife. A possessive look that was more than just a loving expression.

Dylan looked at the back of the frame and opened the hinged back. Nothing was hidden in the frame. He picked up the globe, which appeared to be solid, and then the crystal eagle paperweight.

He raised the lid of the humidor and the rich smell of expensive cigars drifted out. He'd never seen Salvatore smoke anything, but then he hadn't been around the man much since high school. Dylan pushed aside the cigars. A hint of gold flashed and he took several of the cigars out and set them on the desk. A gold key rested at the bottom of the humidor.

Dylan's heart beat a little faster. The key had to be for something Salvatore had used for hiding important documents or items he didn't want anyone to find. None of the desk drawers had locks on them. Dylan went through each drawer and checked for hidden compartments as well as skimming through documents in file drawers. He discovered nothing but copies of paperwork from the classic cars and real estate that Salvatore bought and sold. The originals were probably in his office in Old Bisbee. All of it looked legit, but the FBI would go through the documents.

Other than those papers, he found only personal receipts for normal items, including groceries, art, furniture, and a few other more personal things. Salvatore and Christie's marriage certificate was in the center drawer, encased in a plastic sleeve. He pulled it out and stared at it a few moments, thinking of the one line in a wedding ceremony that caused his stomach to churn with concern for Christie.

Until death do us part.

Would Salvatore kill her to keep whatever secrets he might have? What did she know?

He shoved the certificate back where he'd found it and slammed the drawer.

Dylan knelt to look beneath the desk, ducked in the kneehole, and ran his fingers along the underside of the desk in case there was a false compartment. He looked over his shoulder at Stillwater who was searching the office, her back to him. Other agents were also in the room now. "Do you happen to have a flashlight?" he asked Stillwater.

She dug in her jacket pocket and handed him a small flashlight. "We haven't found a safe behind any pictures or in the walls, or anywhere else we've looked so far." Stillwater put her hands on her hips. "Bastards like this always have a safe in their office. Especially one as secure as this place was."

Dylan thought about it. "Maybe Salvatore has a safe in his office in Old Bisbee."

Stillwater nodded. "That's where we'll be heading next. We have a warrant to search his office as well."

"Good." Dylan nodded. "I found a key in the humidor, but if there are any hidden drawers in this desk, they're well hidden. I'm going to take another look." He turned back to his task, clicking on the flashlight, shining the light, and searching the underside of the desk.

Muscles tense with frustration, he started to get up when he noticed a trace of white powder on the floor. He touched it with his gloved finger. The floor was rough beneath his touch, as if Salvatore's shoes had worn it down. Dylan raised his finger to his nose and sniffed the white substance before tasting it.

"Cocaine." He glanced at Stillwater who was watching him. "Looks like he spilled some beneath his desk."

"Interesting." Stillwater walked over to Dylan. "We'll have forensics analyze it." She marked the spot he pointed to with a placard.

"Almost finished here." Dylan shone the flashlight around once again and saw nothing.

He ducked out of the kneehole. Still in a crouch, he tried to think like Salvatore would, but considering he didn't know the man well, it wasn't easy.

Dylan got to his feet and showed Stillwater the key that he'd left on top of the desk. "There are no locks on the desk, so this has to go somewhere else."

"I wonder what it goes to." She pulled out an evidence bag and dropped the key into it before marking the bag. "We haven't found anything that needs a key so far."

The office was searched section by section, but nothing that would provide clues to Christie's whereabouts, or what Salvatore might be involved in, could be found.

When they felt that they'd searched the office top to bottom, and nothing of importance had been found in the rest of the house, Stillwater, Dylan, Brooks, and Trace headed to Salvatore's office in Old Bisbee to search it with another team of FBI agents.

Dylan shook his head as he climbed into the SUV. It was the middle of the afternoon and it had already been one hell of a day.

The office turned up nothing. No safe, no documents that showed anything illegal going on, nothing nefarious, and most importantly, no clues to where Christie might be. Stillwater still believed there had to be a safe somewhere, maybe a bank safe. Dylan had to agree.

When he'd had enough of coming up empty handed, he headed outside alone to clear his thoughts. It was starting to turn dark as he stood in front of the coffee shop in the Copper Queen Plaza, where Salvatore's office was located. It was just a few days ago that Dylan was in that office with Christie, Belle, and Salvatore. It seemed like a lifetime ago.

He couldn't stop working everything over and over in his mind. He had to solve this. He had to figure out where to go next.

From the start. He had to go back to the time this all began.

His mind turned toward the day he'd gotten the call. It had been pouring rain, Joe barking in his kennel, Nate hanging from a noose tied to a beam in the shed.

It was like a stab to Dylan's gut all over again. He could almost smell the rain and the stench of death as the German shepherd barked nonstop. The sound echoed in his head. After talking with the detective, Dylan had gone to the house, rain pouring down and mud slick beneath his boots.

He remembered the strangeness of the living room and his search there before going to Nate's office and finding the postcard in the baseball book. That book had meant a lot to Nate when he was young and he'd held onto it for decades.

Dylan frowned as he thought about the book. Could there have been more in the book than the postcard? Had it somehow meant more than just a place where Nate had stuck the postcard he'd never mailed?

What could the connection between Nate and Salvatore be?

Despite the fact that Dylan was tired and had no idea if his hunch was correct, he felt a surge of renewed energy. Maybe, just maybe, Nate had left more to go on than a bunch of postcards and a memory card.

A cold evening breeze chilled his face and hands, but he didn't let it bother him. He felt a strong desire to talk with Belle and make sure she was doing all right before he went to Nate's house. He'd left her when he was furious at Driscoll, and she probably thought he was angry with her.

God, he should have called her earlier in the day rather than letting Brooks and Trace update her. He wasn't angry with *her*. He was angry with Harvey Driscoll and Salvatore Reyes. He was frustrated with the fruitless searches. He was concerned about Christie.

But mad at Belle? No.

He pulled his phone out of its holster and dialed one of the two agents who had replaced Brooks and Trace in guarding Belle.

When the agent answered, Dylan asked to speak with Belle. Moments later, her soft voice came on the line. "Hi, Dylan."

His throat felt like it was going to close off. "How are you holding up, precious?"

A hesitation. "Aren't you mad at me?"

"No." He began walking toward the SUV he'd borrowed from Trace. "The last thing I am is angry with you."

He heard the sob in her voice. "I thought you hated me."

"I could never hate you." His gut ached at the thought that he'd left her feeling that way. "I should have called sooner."

"Are you coming back soon?" She had a hopeful note in her voice.

"No." He let out a heavy breath as he reached the SUV. "I'm going to Nate's house first to check on something. After that I'll come back to the B & B."

"Take me with you." A determined note was in Belle's voice. "I might be able to help." Her voice softened again. "I need to do something. Nate was my friend, too."

Dylan gripped the cold door handle of the SUV and squeezed his eyes shut. He wanted to see Belle. Would she be safe if he took her to Nate's house?

"I can't take that chance." Dylan opened his eyes and pressed the remote to unlock the SUV. "I don't want anything happening to you."

"You're not leaving me. Come get me." It came out like a demand. "I swear, I'll find a way out of this place. I want to help. I won't let you shut me out."

She'd managed to disappear as a teenager, what if she found a way to do that again? He couldn't and wouldn't underestimate her. She was a woman with such great strength inside her.

"I'll come and get you." He climbed into the SUV and started the vehicle. "But we're taking the agents who are guarding you and you will do as I say. Got it?"

"Just get here."

The B & B was five minutes away, but someone could be watching him, so he had to take his time and make sure he wasn't followed.

CHAPTER 22

Thirty minutes after Dylan had called Belle, he arrived. She'd been worried that he had changed his mind, but she couldn't imagine him saying something and not following through. He had always kept his promises when they were young. It was part of his honorable nature that had made her love him so much.

The moment he walked into the suite, she threw her arms around him and pressed her body against his. It felt so good being in his embrace, feeling his heat and solidness.

Her words were barely above a whisper. "I'm so glad you're not angry with me."

"I can't be angry with you." He drew away and it tickled a little as he brushed hair from her cheek. "Your stepfather is the one I'm angry with. You carried a heavy burden all of these years." She looked down but he put his finger under her chin and raised her face. "Don't let his actions hurt you. What he did—you shouldn't have had to bear the weight of it alone all of these years."

"Thank you." Her throat ached and it wasn't from nearly being strangled. It was from the lump that formed at his words. The fact that he understood and wasn't angry with her made her feel teary.

He hugged her to him. "I'm sorry I left like I did, and I'm sorry I didn't call. I should have talked with you sooner."

She hugged him back, squeezing tight, wanting to tell him how much she loved him. Because she did, more than she could ever imagine loving anyone. She held back from saying the words. It needed to be a special moment, not a casual "I love you" when they were about to set out on a task.

Joe nosed in and Belle smiled as she stepped back and looked down at the German shepherd.

Dylan crouched to face the dog. "I suppose you want to come with us."

Joe barked once.

"Then it's settled." Dylan scratched Joe behind his ears. "You're good to have around while we figure this all out." Dylan gave the dog a final stroke on his head before standing again.

"Thank you for coming back to get me." Belle smiled as he rested his hands on her upper arms. "Let's go get whatever it is you need from Nate's house."

Dylan lowered his head and gave her a long, slow kiss that nearly swept her off her feet and did take her breath away.

"Let's go."

After she put her jacket on, he took her by the hand and led her to the door before opening it and guiding her through. He looked at Joe and gave a nod to the open doorway and Joe padded past Dylan onto the landing between the two suites.

Belle had met the two agents, Jim Heber and Clarice Lutz. Dylan explained to them that they were heading to Nate's, and the two agents would accompany them.

The five of them, including Joe, were soon on their way to Nate's. It was dark and the houses were lit up on the hillsides of Old Bisbee.

It had been years since Belle had been to the Saginaw area of Bisbee and Nate's home, formerly his grandmother's.

At one time the homes in Saginaw had been in another part of town known as Jiggerville. Belle remembered from Bisbee history that somewhere near 1950, the copper mining company, Phelps Dodge, moved one hundred houses to a new settlement called Saginaw.

Moving the houses was necessary when the powers that be decided to dig an open pit mine to reach the ore where Jiggerville was located. The mine became known as the Lavender Pit Mine. The mine closed down in the early 1970's but the abandoned pit covered over three hundred acres and was over nine hundred feet deep.

The town of Bisbee nearly died when the mines shut down, but hippies moved into Old Bisbee and revitalized the area, turning it into an artists' community, and eventually a tourist attraction.

Belle thought about the days when Bisbee could have become a ghost town. She'd been young back then and she and her friends hadn't known how bad things were during those years. They'd just been like any other kids, living for the moment.

When they arrived in front of Nate's home and got out of the SUV, Belle gripped Joe's leash. Even through the leash, she felt how tense he was and heard his low growl, as if he was seeing and remembering the bad things that had happened here.

Dylan had grabbed a flashlight from the glove compartment and now he used it to light their way through the metal chain link gate and up to the house. The two agents who had accompanied them stayed close and on guard.

It was dark, but in the flashlight's beam, Belle could make out a shed in the back and a dog run to the left, near the shed. Joe growled as he strained against his leash as if wanting to go to the shed.

With Joe at her side, she followed Dylan up the steps to the door that was crisscrossed with yellow crime scene tape. He removed one of the pieces of tape, opened the door, and stepped through. He shined the flashlight over the interior before taking Belle's hand and helping her inside the home.

Joe followed and his growl deepened. She had a feeling something had happened here. Something bad.

She shivered and a sharp pain in her midsection caused her to put her hand over her belly. Nate had lived and died here. She didn't know exactly where he'd been hung, but she knew that it was on the property.

Dylan and the agents used flashlights to illuminate the home. *Nate's home* repeated in her mind. While Agents Heber and Lutz stayed in the hall, Dylan guided Belle and Joe to a room and pushed the door open. Once inside, Belle saw that it was an office.

Dylan went straight to a bookcase where one book partially stuck out from a bookcase, and he pulled the book out. Belle recognized it at once. It was an old book on baseball that Nate had often carried with him. She'd forgotten about that book and how much it had meant to him. If she remembered correctly, Nate's father had passed it down before he and Nate's mother disappeared. She saw the title, *Baseball, An Informal History.* Yes, Nate had been obsessed with that book, even though it had been seriously outdated by the time it came into his possession.

"Is that what you needed?" Belle felt like she had to whisper in the quiet of the room.

"Yes." Dylan gripped the book in one hand as he shone the flashlight on the cover. "The office has been combed through by the BPD and the DHS, but there might be something in this book that can help us that would mean nothing to them." He turned from the bookcase to meet Belle's gaze. "This was the book where I found the postcard Nate wrote to me."

The book had probably been one of the last things Nate had handled. Another shiver went through Belle as if his ghost was in the room with them, trying to tell them something and they just had to listen.

Dylan swept the light over the office and to the desk that probably once held Nate's computer. Dylan confirmed her thought when he added, "I don't know that there's anything left here that will help us. Forensics has gone through his desktop computer and has found nothing that is out of the ordinary. If there were records, he kept them somewhere else." Dylan frowned. "I'm sure Nate had a laptop, but one hasn't been found. I have a feeling someone got to it first."

Belle rubbed her arms with her hands, feeling a chill that her jacket couldn't keep out. "Are we leaving now?"

He looked at the book in his hand, then nodded. "I have what I came for. It's time to see what, if anything, this can tell us."

By the time they returned to the B & B with the other agents and Joe, Belle knew Dylan was flat out exhausted. Apparently after his confrontation with Harvey, he'd aided in the search of Salvatore and Christie's home before tackling Salvatore's office. Of course they'd also headed to Nate's to retrieve the baseball book.

She'd insisted they get some sleep before they tackled the book. He'd started to argue but relented and had gone to sleep as soon as his head hit the pillow.

Now she watched him shrug into a black T-shirt and pull it over his head. "I didn't mean to wake you."

"It's time to get up." She slid out of bed. "I want to help, not sleep."

He waited for her to pull on a pair of jeans and a blue T-shirt. "Are you hungry?"

She shook her head. "Let's get to work."

"I'll ask Jim or Clarice to grab something from downstairs." He left the bedroom of the suite and she followed.

Joe's ears perked forward and he rose from his sitting position as Belle and Dylan entered the front room.

As Dylan spoke to Agents Heber and Lutz, Belle sat on the couch in front of the coffee table where Dylan had left the book titled *Baseball, An Informal History,* written by Douglass Wallop.

The cover creaked as she opened it. She smiled, but it was a small smile, as she recognized Nate's handwriting as a kid on the inside of the front cover. The scrawl was messy, the letters scrunched close together, but she could still read the fading ink.

Property of Nate O'Malley

She lightly touched his script, the backs of her eyes aching with unshed tears at the thought of the boy and teenager she'd known. He had grown into a man and she hadn't been here to see it. And now he was dead.

Her throat still hurt from being nearly strangled, but from the desire to cry, too. She blinked rapidly, took in a deep breath, and slowly let it out before turning the first couple of pages. They were yellowed with age, and the book had the musty smell that older books tended to have.

She wanted to continue, but she knew Dylan would want to look at it with her. She flipped to the back and saw that it was 263 pages. Who knew how many times Nate had read the book from cover to cover when he was young.

The book jacket slipped off as Belle started to close the book. She started to put the jacket back the way it belonged when she felt something beneath it, on the back of the book.

Dylan closed the door, but she barely heard it as she removed the book jacket and looked at the back.

Her lips parted and her skin prickled as she stared at a disc that had been slipped into a handmade pocket made of ledger paper that was taped to the back of the hardcover book. BOB DYLAN was printed with a black marker on the gold DVD.

Her heart rate picked up. She didn't look away from the DVD, as if it might disappear, as her own Dylan sat on the couch beside her.

Wordlessly, he pulled the book closer to him. He carefully slipped the DVD out of the pocket and held it by the edges, careful not to touch the surface

She looked from the DVD to the Dylan who sat right beside her. "Do you think he wrote 'Bob Dylan' on it to throw off anyone who might see it?"

Dylan gave a slow nod. "Sometimes, when we were goofing around, he'd call me Bob. Likely anyone who saw this wouldn't think twice about it being me that it referred to. They would just think it was music."

Belle studied the unreadable expression on Dylan's face. "I didn't know he called you Bob."

Dylan shook his head. "He didn't do it often, and just when we were alone." He slipped the DVD back into its paper pocket. "Hold on." He got to his feet and strode across the room to the door.

He opened it and spoke to Agent Lutz. Belle couldn't hear their conversation but watched as the agent nodded and responded before turning away. Dylan stayed in the doorway until Lutz returned and handed him something. When he turned and closed the door behind him, she saw that he was holding what looked like a slim laptop.

When he sat on the couch beside her again, he set the laptop on the surface and booted it up. As he waited, he retrieved the DVD from its pocket.

Belle realized she was holding her breath and let it out slowly. Her heart pounded even faster as he slid the DVD into a slot in the laptop.

A directory came up and she saw a list of MP3 files, all of them with a Bob Dylan song title.

Just Like a Woman
Like a Rolling Stone

Visions of Johanna
Blowin' in the Wind
Tangled up in Blue
Every Grain of Sand
Mr. Tambourine Man
Rainy Day Women
I Want You
Positively 4th Street
Knockin' on Heaven's Door

"This one." Dylan used the touchpad on the laptop to move the cursor over *Tangled up in Blue.* "If you look at this little icon, you can see it's not a song. It's a video."

"Hidden in the middle of Bob Dylan's songs." Belle looked at it in amazement.

Beside her, Dylan clicked on the title. "*If* this isn't actually a video of Bob."

Belle watched as a screen opened. For a few seconds the screen was black—and then Nate's face appeared on the screen.

An ache hit her full force in her chest as she stared at her friend. He was older, but the same eyes looked back at her that she'd known well.

Nate looked directly into what had likely been his laptop's or desktop computer's camera.

"Hey, Dylan." Nate grinned, but then it faded a little. "If you're listening to this, then likely I'm dead." He gave a smile. "I hope you tossed my ashes over that ridge in the Mule Mountains, where the CoS used to hang out."

Belle put her hand over her mouth to hold back a sob. That was where they'd had Nate's memorial.

Nate looked serious. "And I hope Belle's sitting right next to you, buddy. Where she belongs."

Belle's stomach flipped as she lowered her hand and she looked to see Dylan's gaze on her before they both looked again to Nate's image.

"Let's get down to business." Nate held up a ledger. "Two ledgers have gone missing from my office." His expression turned serious. "You're not going to like this, but I think Salvatore Reyes took them." Nate hesitated. "I think there's a good chance that he's going to try to kill me."

A noise of protest escaped Belle. The thought that Nate expected an attempt on his life by Salvatore was another knife to the gut. She'd had a feeling, but hearing it from Nate was worse.

"You're probably wondering why I didn't let you know in some other way, Dylan." Nate's throat worked as he swallowed. "You were undercover and I didn't want to do anything that would lead Salvatore to you. That's why I sent the postcards. If I die, I figure you'll get with everyone in the CoS, and you'll put all the pieces together. I'm sure that's why you're here."

Belle looked at Dylan and saw his hand fisted on his thigh. She touched him with her fingertips and he took her hand in his but didn't look away from the computer screen. She felt his tension through their connection, but she wondered if he felt a little more grounded like she did as they held hands.

"I may have made one mistake." Nate rubbed the bridge of his nose with his fingertips before looking at the camera again. "By now you know that I sent Christie a postcard, too." He shook his head. "I didn't want it to be obvious that I wanted you to find out Salvatore was involved by leaving Christie out. But the more I consider it, the more I think I screwed up. Damn, but I hope not."

You did, Belle thought with a sadness that tore through her like a knife. *But you never could have imagined what Salvatore would do.*

Nate looked at the screen with an earnestness that made Belle squeeze Dylan's hand tighter. "Find those ledgers, Dylan. They're important. I'm certain Salvatore has a safe in his office. When I was there once, he went into his office and came back with ledgers Edmund had worked on."

A pause before Nate continued. "G.I. Joe…" He trailed off. "He and one of the ledgers have the keys. That's all I'm going to say in case the wrong people discover this DVD." Nate looked grim. "And there are a lot of the wrong people around."

His Adam's apple bobbed as his throat worked again and he sounded choked up. "Salvatore forced me to kill a man not long ago." Nate dragged his hand down his face, which had gone white. "He said he'd kill my friends if I didn't do it and he put a gun to my head." Nate's eyes looked watery. "The guy's name was Edmund Salcido, and he was Salvatore's accountant. Apparently he was skimming off the top. Salvatore used him as an example of what he'd do to me if I didn't help him and if I tried to cheat him, too."

Nate rubbed his face with his hand. "Salvatore made me slit the guy's throat. Right in my living room. It was like Afghanistan all over again. After I killed Salcido and the man bled out, Salvatore made me clean up the blood while he watched. Blood had sprayed everywhere, Dylan. Fucking everywhere. Salvatore made me paint the walls and told me it would look like I tried to cover up the murder. I don't know what they did with the man's body, but I'm pretty sure they planted the weapon somewhere on my property. They did it so that they'd have more leverage against me."

Bile rose in Belle's throat the whole time Nate spoke about the murder. She was certain she was going to throw up.

He looked away from the camera, clearly choked up before returning his gaze to the camera again. "Your postcard is in the book and I hope that helps you find this. I just have to slip the DVD into the pocket and put it on the shelf and I know you'll find it. I have no doubt you'll remember how much I loved that book. I carried it everywhere and you know me well."

A dog's ferocious barking started, sounding a little distant, like the dog was outside. "G.I. Joe is going crazy." Nate moved away, disappearing from sight for a moment, then returned in front of the camera.

A panicked look shot across Nate's face. "Oh, shit. Salvatore just drove up with his men and they're getting out of their cars. See you, Dylan."

The screen went black.

Belle's stomach churned and she barely kept from vomiting. "That was probably when they came for him—when they killed him."

Dylan squeezed her hand so tightly she felt like the bones might break. "Nate probably just had enough time to burn the DVD before putting it in the book and stuffing it on the shelf."

A tear rolled down Belle's cheek. Dylan released her hand then cupped her face with both of his. He used his thumb to brush away the tear. "We're going to get Salvatore, Belle. And we're going to get Christie back. I promise you."

Belle closed her eyes for a moment before opening them again. "I believe you." He slid his fingers down until his hands rested on her shoulders. She sniffled. "Nate said we had to find those ledgers."

"Yes." Dylan looked like he was considering it. An expression crossed his face, as if something had just dawned on him. He moved his hands from Belle's shoulders. "I think I know just where the ledgers are."

Chapter 23

Heart thumping, Dylan took Stillwater's business card out of his wallet and dialed the FBI agent's number.

When she answered, he said, "I need you to meet me at Salvatore Reyes's home. Bring the key I found in the humidor. I think I know where the safe is."

"It's not a safe key." Stillwater had a frown in her voice. "Not to mention we combed that place top to bottom, twice."

"Trust me." Dylan felt a flash of irritation. "I can't go into it now. Just meet me there."

"Give me an hour to get the key and meet you at the Reyes home," Stillwater said before disconnecting the call.

Belle stood. "I'm going."

Dylan considered it. Salvatore wasn't likely to return to his home—or would he? He would want to get whatever it was out of the safe. Dylan believed Nate, who had been certain the safe was in Salvatore's office.

After he arranged for Brooks and Trace to accompany them, along with Agents Jim Heber and Clarice Lutz, they all headed to Salvatore and Christie's home. Both Belle and Joe went with them.

Stillwater took forty-five minutes to get there instead of an hour. She tore down the police tape covering the door and they entered the home. Clarice stood inside the doorway, Jim outside, while Brooks took the back and Trace stayed by the door to the office.

Belle and Joe walked with Dylan and Stillwater into Salvatore's office.

"I'm hoping you're right, Curtis." Stillwater handed him the key when they were in Salvatore's office.

"I'm sure." Dylan took the key and started toward the desk as he pulled a small flashlight from his pocket. "I'm betting Salvatore spilled his coke when he was putting it away." The chair was already pushed back and Dylan knelt in the kneehole beneath the desk and illuminated the space with the flashlight.

He ran his hands over the floorboards, which he had figured were worn from Salvatore's shoes. Dylan felt a slight ridge and paused as he felt it. It was thin, not much bigger than a knife blade, and when he aimed the flashlight at it, he couldn't see anything at first. But then he thought he saw a slight, virtually invisible line running horizontal to the vertical floorboards. Clearly a craftsman had been at work here if this was where the safe was located. Dylan would bet almost anything that he'd found the safe.

He pulled out his pocketknife, flipped it open, and ran it along the vertical floorboard on the right, where the tiny gap was slightly bigger than on the other side and the horizontal end. When he moved the knife, it hit an obstruction. He wiggled the knife around. The way the knife slid around it, he guessed it was small, smooth, and round. He pressed the knife against it.

A section of the floorboards started to rise.

"Holy shit." Stillwater was crouched beside him. "I think you just struck gold."

Beneath the floorboard was a square hinged door with a keyhole. Dylan tried to lift it, but it was locked. He held his palm up in front of Stillwater. "Key."

She dropped it into his palm. He slid the key in the keyhole and felt a click. This time the door rose when he pulled up.

"I'll be damned." Stillwater sounded amazed as a safe came into view. "This thing would take some time to get out of here. We'll have to get some guys down here with a torch."

The safe had a keypad. Dylan stared at it. "Maybe it's something simple since the safe was hidden so well. He's a cocky sonofabitch, so it's possible he didn't put a lot of effort into his password."

"Try Christie's birthdate." Belle spoke up from behind Stillwater.

Belle gave him the date and he tried it on the keypad. He put in two digits for the month and date and used the last two digits of the year. When that didn't work, tried all four numbers in the year then other combinations. "Nothing's working." He looked over his shoulder to Belle. "Do you know Salvatore's birthdate?"

She shook her head and frowned.

"It's in the database we use." Stillwater took a big phone out of her pocket that was almost the size of a tablet. She swiped it and then pulled up information. "Here it is." She called out the date.

Again Dylan tried various combinations but none worked. He dragged his hand down his face. They'd have to wait for the damned torch, but even then, this one didn't look like it would be easy. They were running on a clock. They needed to find Christie, and maybe what was in this safe would help.

"What about Salvatore and Christie's wedding date?" Belle had a bit of excitement in her voice. "He doted on her and called her his bride, even though they'd been married for some time. When I think about it, it seemed like he thought of her as a kind of prize that he'd won."

Dylan glanced over his shoulder again. "Do you know it?"

"Christie told me it was a June wedding and that Salvatore had gone all out. I wasn't there of course." She shook her head. "But I don't remember a date."

The marriage certificate flashed in Dylan's mind. It had been in Salvatore's center drawer. "Hold on a sec."

Stillwater and Belle backed up as Dylan came out of the kneehole and opened the center drawer. The certificate was still there. He looked at the date before ducking back under the desk and keying in the numbers on the pad, using two digits for the month, two for the date, and two for the year. Nothing.

Next he tried the same, but four digits for the year. A heavy click and the door unlocked.

"I'll be damned," Stillwater said again.

"You and me both." Dylan used his flashlight to illuminate the contents of the safe. It wasn't very deep and he'd easily be able to take out items. He set down his flashlight. "Do you have gloves?"

"And evidence bags in my SUV." Stillwater stood. "I'll be right back."

Dylan shone the flashlight in the safe as he waited. Stacks of cash, passports, what looked like the spines of ledgers and a thin laptop. In one corner he saw a bag of white powder. Salvatore had a bit of a coke problem, and that's where he'd screwed up. Dylan wouldn't have thought about the safe being there if it hadn't been for the traces of cocaine beneath the desk.

Stillwater returned in moments and handed Dylan a pair of latex gloves, then donned a pair herself.

He slipped the gloves on and reached into the safe. The first things he pulled out were the passports. He flipped through them and saw they were under various other names for Salvatore and Christie. "Looks like he had contingency plans." He handed them to Stillwater who also viewed the passports before dropping them into an evidence bag.

Dylan continued to pull items out of the safe. A laptop that he recognized as Nate's, but with a missing hard drive; stacks of ledgers—some in Nate's handwriting; a small stash of cocaine; and stacks of one hundred dollar bills. It looked like at least a million in cash had been hidden in the safe.

When he flipped through some of the older ledgers, he saw names of criminals he knew and others he didn't. The ledgers had likely been passed down because some were too old to have been Salvatore's.

Dylan stopped and his skin grew cold when he saw Harvey Driscoll's name. Next to his name was the sum of $10,000.

Driscoll. It was likely the payout for Ben Curtis's murder. Dylan's dad had died for ten grand and a family had been destroyed. Not to mention Belle's life had altered drastically with the knowledge when she had heard her stepfather discussing it with her mother. It wouldn't have mattered if Ben Curtis had been murdered for a million or more. The results were the same.

Dylan's throat nearly closed off as memories of his dad slammed into him.

Followed by images of his dad's funeral.

Dylan handed the old ledger to Stillwater to bag. "Put that one in a separate bag. In it is evidence of a payout for a murder. My father's murder."

Stillwater said nothing as she slipped it into another bag and marked it.

When the safe was empty, down to the last quarter found at the very bottom, Dylan backed out from under the desk and stood. He hadn't expected that he would find pain beyond Nate's murder in that safe.

Gunfire erupted from an automatic weapon.

The sound of glass shattering.

Shouts came from the living room.

Dylan grabbed Belle and took her down to the floor. He leaned over and shut the safe beneath the desk before forcing her into the kneehole.

"Stay here," he ordered.

"Please be careful." With a terrified expression, she grabbed his hand. "I could never handle losing you again, Dylan. I love you."

"I love you, too, Belle." He loved her with everything he had. He'd never stopped loving her. "Don't move. I *won't* lose you again."

He looked at her one last time before leaving her behind.

Dylan heard Stillwater calling for backup.

"Agent down!" Clarice shouted from the living room.

More gunfire from the front and then from the back of the house, too.

Adrenaline pumped through Dylan as he peered around the office doorframe. Jim Heber was sitting on the floor, his back to the wall inside the front door, a grimace of pain on his face. He'd made it inside from his post outside the front door, but not before being injured. The right shoulder of his shirt was soaked bright red with blood and he was holding his right arm to his side. He set his jaw as he clutched his service weapon in his left hand.

Clarice Lutz crouched on the opposite side of the door, her weapon in a two-fisted grip. She met Dylan's gaze, her voice calm although her tone was elevated. "At least three men are in front. I don't know how many in back."

More shots peppered the house.

Then silence.

The sudden silence was almost unnerving.

Like the calm before a storm.

Belle had never felt so afraid in her life. She could barely breathe and heard her blood race in her ears as everything went silent.

The desk she was hiding beneath was at the opposite end of the room from where Agent Stillwater and Dylan were crouched beside the door. They were focused on what was happening in the rest of the house.

A whisper of a sound met Belle's ears in the otherwise abnormal silence. Her eyes widened and a silent scream rose up in her throat as she saw a bookcase swing open just feet from her.

G.I. Joe stood to the left of the desk, near Belle's position. He went stiff as he watched the bookcase.

Her heart thundered as Salvatore came through the entrance, his arm around Christie's neck, a gun to her head.

A man stepped out from behind Salvatore—the same man she'd seen watching her just days ago. He caught sight of Belle beneath the desk and pointed a pistol at her.

Belle froze at the sight of the gun pointed at her. Her heart thundered as she stared at the weapon.

One more man came through the doorway, one she didn't recognize. He was compact and short, and he had a mean look in his eyes. He, too, held a pistol.

Christie whimpered as Salvatore pushed her forward, the barrel digging into the side of her head.

Joe snarled.

From her side vision, Belle saw Dylan whirl at the helpless sound Christie had made and Joe's snarl. Dylan immediately had his gun leveled on Salvatore. His gaze darted from Salvatore to the man behind, who had his gun pointed at Belle's hiding place, and then to the third man.

Stillwater turned when Dylan had, and Trace had entered the room at the same time.

Joe snarled again, his body in attack mode.

The look on Dylan's face was fierce, a killing rage in his gaze. "Let Christie go and get that gun off Belle."

Salvatore stared at Dylan. "You are going to give me every single thing that was in that safe."

"No." Dylan's voice was cold. "You will turn over both women or you and your two men won't make it out of here."

Belle's mind spun as her heart raced. How were any of them going to get out of this alive?

Salvatore's smile was grim and her skin went cold as he spoke. "Give me my property and call off reinforcements or Jorge kills Belle now. I only need one hostage."

Dylan's heart had gone into overdrive the moment he'd seen Christie and had realized Belle was in another man's sights. A third gunman backed up Salvatore and Jorge. Dylan recognized the man as a thug nicknamed Rat.

Dylan's mind flashed through the options. There were none.

Jorge would murder Belle and Salvatore could kill Christie as well, if Dylan and the other agents didn't cooperate.

There had to be other options. Dylan had to come up with something.

Christie's face was even paler than before, yet Dylan saw not only fear but bravery in her gaze, too, as Salvatore gripped her around her neck.

He looked at Dylan. "You'd better call off any reinforcements on the way. Remember, if anything happens to me, Belle dies."

Dylan had never felt so damned helpless in his life.

Trace had managed to get between Dylan and Stillwater so that all three of them faced Salvatore and his men.

"You won't succeed, Reyes." Stillwater's hard voice came from beside Dylan.

"Shut up, bitch." Salvatore narrowed his gaze. "I told you, Dylan, call anyone off who's here or on their way."

Joe was crouched on his haunches, as if waiting for his opportunity to lunge at Salvatore, who didn't seem to notice the dog.

Dylan slowly withdrew his cell phone and hit the speed dial number for Sofia.

Trace said in his heavy drawl, "No one here is messing around. You injure these women and you and your men will pay the price." There was steel behind his tone.

Salvatore ignored him.

Dylan had put his phone to his ear. Sofia answered and he said, "We have a situation at Salvatore Reyes's home. Reyes and one of his men are holding two hostages. Christie Reyes and Belle Hartford. We need all agents to stand down immediately."

"Shit. I'll call the FBI." Sofia's voice was ice cold. "The hostage rescue team will be on its way."

"Done, Salvatore." Dylan lowered the phone as Sofia disconnected. "I've called them off."

"Take that garbage bag out of the wastebasket and put all of my belongings into it." Salvatore nodded toward the desktop where everything had been laid out. "But first all of you drop your weapons."

"You know we can't do that." Dylan never wavered his aim. "This isn't TV." A law enforcement officer never intentionally lost control of his or her weapon.

"No, it's not TV." Salvatore scowled as he stared at Dylan. "You have no options, Dylan. None at all. You do what I say."

"You shoot either one of them and you're dead." Dylan's voice was low and cold. He realized the open door behind Reyes and the other two men was probably an escape route that could go out anywhere. If Reyes made it back behind that door with the women, things could be bad. Real bad.

"Do as I said." Salvatore narrowed his eyes. "My things. Now."

Dylan kept his weapon trained on Salvatore, never taking his gaze off the man as he pulled the bag out of the wastebasket and set it on the desktop. One handed, he started putting the evidence-bagged items into the larger garbage bag, his movements slow and deliberate.

"Hurry," Salvatore said.

When the garbage bag was bulging, full of the findings from the safe, Salvatore relaxed his grip on Christie. He released her neck but still kept the gun pointed at her head. He held out his free hand. "Toss it here."

Joe was clearly waiting for his opportunity to lunge at Salvatore. But the man had his gun pointed at Christie, his finger hovering over the trigger. If Joe went after the bastard, the dog could cause the gun to go off and shoot Christie.

A distraction. Dylan needed something to take their attention from Christie and Belle. He hoped what he planned to do was the right thing and that they were stupid enough to fall for it.

Dylan took the bag off the desk. "It's all here."

Salvatore's eyes were greedy and triumphant.

"Here you go." With a powerful upward swing, Dylan flung the garbage bag filled with Salvatore's items, aiming it between Jorge and Salvatore.

Both men reached for the bag to catch it, taking their eyes off of their victims.

With another snarl, Joe lunged at Salvatore.

The dog sank his teeth into Salvatore's arm, forcing his aim down at the floor.

Salvatore screamed as the dog's teeth penetrated his skin.

The gun went off.

Stillwater grunted with pain as the bullet slammed into the upper arm of her gun hand. Her gun flew from her grip.

Joe drove Salvatore down.

Christie fell with Salvatore to the floor.

The German shepherd shook his head, digging his jaw into Salvatore's arm.

Trace dove for Christie, grabbing her and rolling her away from Salvatore.

Trace pushed her behind him and put Rat in his gun sights. He took one shot and dropped the bastard.

Joe shook Salvatore's arm even harder and the gun flew from his hand.

The weapon spun across the floor toward Belle.

Salvatore tried to fight off Joe, but the dog's grip was too tight.

At the same time Salvatore was going down, Jorge grabbed the bag in one hand.

Dylan shot Jorge, aiming for center mass.

The man moved a fraction before the bullet hit him, striking him in the right side.

Jorge cried out and dropped the bag, but still had hold of his weapon.

Belle scrambled out from beneath the desk and reached for Salvatore's gun.

Her fingers closed around the grip.

Jorge turned his weapon on Dylan.

Dylan pulled the trigger again but Jorge had dropped to his knees, gun still aimed at Dylan.

Belle pointed Salvatore's gun at Jorge. She squeezed the trigger.

Dylan took a third shot just as Belle took hers.

Both bullets hit Jorge, blood instantly soaking his clothes at his neck and his chest.

Jorge screamed but didn't let go of his gun.

Belle and Dylan both shot Jorge again.

He collapsed, face down, his gun falling from his hand.

Dylan rushed forward and kicked the gun across the room, far from Jorge. He kicked the gun away from Rat, who lay still.

Jorge didn't move. Dylan checked his pulse and found none. He rolled the man over and Jorge's eyes were wide and sightless. Dylan checked Rat for a pulse. None.

Belle had Salvatore's gun still trained on Jorge. Her hands were shaking but her aim was good.

"Put down the gun, Belle," Dylan said.

Visibly trembling, she laid the gun on the floor.

Dylan wanted to go to her but had to deal with Salvatore, who was still screaming.

Brooks was holding back Trace, who looked like he wanted to kill Salvatore.

Dylan approached Salvatore. Joe released the bastard when Dylan grabbed him by his collar.

With everything he had, Dylan slammed his fist into Salvatore's face. Blood poured from Salvatore's nose, over his mouth and chin. Tears flushed from his eyes from the pain.

Dylan started to hit Salvatore again, but Stillwater grabbed his arm with her good hand.

"Let the courts put him behind bars." Stillwater gripped Dylan's arm tighter. "I want to see him rot in prison."

Dylan lowered his arm and shoved Salvatore away from him. Salvatore stumbled back and fell on his backside. Still shaking with rage, Dylan leaned down and grabbed Salvatore by his collar again and dragged him to his feet.

The desire to hit Salvatore again was so strong that Dylan almost did. Instead, he turned away, leaving Salvatore with Stillwater and another agent who had walked in. Apparently backup had arrived and had taken care of whoever had attacked the house while Salvatore and his men came in from the hidden bookcase entrance.

Behind him he heard Christie. Her voice trembled, but she said clearly, "I will testify against Salvatore about all I know of what he's said and done. He killed a man right in front of me."

Dylan walked to Belle who was standing now and staring down at the body of the man she'd help shoot.

She looked at Dylan, shock on her face. "Did I kill him?"

"It doesn't matter." Dylan took her in his arms and drew her stiff body close. "We both shot him. He won't hurt anyone ever again."

Belle clung to him, a sob escaping her. "He deserved it, but to kill a man…"

"Shhh, precious." Dylan rocked her. "You helped save all of our lives. Without your help, things could have gone bad, very bad."

Her body relaxed and she tilted her tear-stained face to look at him. "I love you, Dylan. I love you so much."

"I love you, too." He kissed her gently on her lips before drawing back and looking into her eyes. "I'm never going to let you forget it. I will never let you leave me behind again."

CHAPTER 24

B elle's stomach churned as she brushed her hair and thought about
what she was about to do. She thought she was going to be sick.

No, she couldn't let him have that power over her.

She didn't want to do it. But she had to. She knew it was the only
way she'd ever find true peace. She wanted every part of her free of
the past so she could move on and face the future without emotional
baggage.

With a sigh, she set down her hairbrush by the sink. She held her
breath as she used the hairspray then slowly let her breath out as she
put the can next to the brush.

It had been three days since Salvatore had been arrested. Tomorrow
the sick bastard would be appearing before a federal magistrate judge
in Tucson. It would take some time for the case to go to court, but
eventually he'd face a jury and she was certain it would not be a good
end for him.

In addition, there was the chance that he would be considered
a flight risk. Not only due to his business and personal relations in
Mexico, but also the fake passports that had been found. He had clearly
already been planning something. The feds were working on tracing

money Salvatore had in offshore accounts now, thanks to the ledgers. If he wasn't granted bail, Salvatore could very well await trial in prison for as long as it took.

The FBI had whisked Christie away into protective custody until she could testify against Salvatore in federal court. Belle hadn't seen her since the day Salvatore was arrested. Apparently there had been death threats against her that the FBI was taking seriously. The threats could have come from the Jimenez Cartel or Salvatore himself, but whatever the case, Christie's life could be in danger.

Belle adjusted the turtleneck sweater she wore as she looked into the mirror. It hid the remnants of the bruises on her neck that had yellowed in the days since she'd nearly been strangled. The traces were almost gone, but she didn't like to see the leftover marks.

The fact that the rest of the CoS and their families were safe now was such an incredible relief. It was like she'd been anchored to a cement block in the middle of a lake through everything that had happened. Now she was above the surface of the water and free, breathing in the sweet, fresh air.

When she thought about Nate and Tom, however, the sadness was deep and profound, a heaviness in her soul that wouldn't ever fully go away. She was grateful Marta was awake now, and according to the doctors, should make a full recovery.

Belle put on her coat that had been lying on Dylan's bed. In moments she would step out into the cold with him and make the journey to Tucson. It was a journey she knew she had to take to fully heal.

G.I. Joe was back with Leon and his family. The dog seemed happy to be with Leon's kids, appearing to have adopted them as his own instead of the other way around.

The memorial for Tom would be tomorrow. The remaining members of the CoS would be able to scatter Nate's ashes over the ridge, too, with the exception of Marta who was still in the hospital recovering, and Christie who was in protective custody. Belle, Dylan, and Leon had sworn to stay in touch. Belle knew that Christie would, too, after the trial, as well as Marta once she was out of the hospital.

Absently, Belle pulled her hair out of the collar of her jacket and let it fall down the back of the coat. She took a deep breath and faced the bedroom door. Dylan was waiting for her in the kitchen.

Salvatore was likely going to go to prison for a long time. Hopefully he'd be there forever. Once Christie testified to the murder she had witnessed, and all that she had heard him state about the murders he'd contracted for everyone in the CoS, that should be enough to put the nails in his coffin.

The clues Nate had left had finally paid off. The key to the passwords was inside the front cover of one of the ledgers in Nate's handwriting, just like he'd said.

Just two numbers and two symbols, and then the first two letters of the incorrect word, had to be used and each folder on the memory card opened when the passwords were keyed in.

The folders had been filled with documents, receipts, money trails, payoffs, and other crucial information.

There was even old proof that her stepfather had been paid off for murdering Dylan's dad.

Her stepfather.

She closed her eyes. It was now or never.

Belle waited in the hard plastic seat to be called in. Dylan sat next to her, holding her hand, anchoring her.

She looked at the face she loved so much and smiled. "Thank you for being here with me."

"You don't need to thank me." He touched the side of her face with his fingertips. "I will always be here for you. Always."

"I know." She put her hand over his. "And I will always be here for you."

Harvey Driscoll was still in the custody of federal agents, not only for assaulting a federal agent, but also for the charge of murder after being contracted by a Mexican cartel, across international borders. Proof had been found that Harvey had also transported drugs from Mexico into the United States. Later today he would face the federal magistrate judge.

He would also be tried for the sexual abuse of his stepdaughter in the Arizona court system. There was no statute of limitations for statutory rape in Arizona. Not only would Belle be testifying, but the photographs and videos of the abuse had been found when a search warrant had been issued for Harvey's home.

Belle wasn't straight on how the federal court system worked versus the state court system, but she was certain of one thing—Harvey would never hurt her or another minor again.

How would she react to seeing him face-to-face? She didn't know if her body would tremble from rage or she would charge up to him and spit in his face.

The emotions running through her made her stomach clench harder as she waited to be taken into the room where she would face her abuser.

That young, traumatized girl was no more after the years of therapy she had put herself through. She'd grown to accept that the abuse had not been her fault. She was a stronger woman now than she had ever been.

Dylan had been at her side every step of the way. He gave her even more strength than she already possessed.

When it was time, she stood, ready to be escorted into the room where she would face Harvey.

Dylan wore a fierce expression. "Are you sure you don't want me to go with you?"

"Yes." She laid a hand on his arm. "I need to do this alone."

He studied her and gave her a single nod. "I love you," he said before she turned away and was escorted into the room.

Her stomach settled as she sat on one side of the window and looked at the empty seat on the other side. She felt a stillness in her heart that hadn't been there before.

When he was escorted into the room she was only mildly interested in his bruised and battered face.

He sat in the chair opposite her. "If it isn't the slut." He sneered at her as he spoke. "I thought you were dead."

She studied him. She felt no emotion, only a calmness she hadn't expected.

"What the fuck do you want?" he reached down and she knew he was grabbing his crotch. "Come back for more of this, didn't you." It didn't come out as a question.

"I wanted to see the pathetic excuse for a man who sexually abused a defenseless teenage girl." The words came to her easily and firmly.

"You asked for it." He leaned forward, a leer on his bruised, ugly features. "You wanted it."

"I hope you enjoy prison, Harvey." She tilted her head to the side. "It looks like you have already made new friends."

His face grew red, making the swelling, cuts, and bruises look even worse. The fact that she wasn't responding to his goads like she used to clearly rattled him.

He snarled the words. "If you came back to beg for forgiveness, slut, you're not getting any."

She leaned forward, her forearms folded on the table. She was glad the barrier was between them but she wasn't frightened of him like she had been when she was young.

"I don't forgive *you*, Harvey, and I don't feel the least bit sorry for you." She watched his expression shift as she spoke. She got to her feet and a little smile came out of nowhere. "Enjoy your new boyfriends."

Her back was already to him as he spouted words that simply bounced off of her. The words didn't register, she only knew they were hateful by the way he screamed them as she walked away.

She stepped through the doorway into a much brighter future.

As Dylan walked out into the sunshine with Belle, he felt a moment of the only satisfaction he could get out of everything that had happened. Dylan had let a couple of things slip. Not only had Harvey Driscoll killed two boys' father, their mother's husband, but he'd molested a young girl, his own stepdaughter.

One thing about it—child molesters didn't last long in prison. Even criminals had standards and child abusers were the worst of the worst.

Yes, Driscoll was going to get exactly what he deserved.

CHAPTER 25

Belle cuddled in Dylan's arms in front of the fireplace in their cabin at Diamond Peak Ski Resort near Lake Tahoe. Outside the big picture window, snowflakes drifted lazily down from a gray sky. Beyond were beautiful white slopes and a thickly forested skyline of trees heavy with snow.

Inside, the fire crackled in the hearth, heating her skin deliciously. Almost as wonderfully as the warmth of the man she was entwined with. The smell of cedar and pine filled the room.

She tipped her head back and smiled at him. She'd never felt so happy, so complete as she did in that moment.

He lowered his mouth to hers and gave her a soft, sweet kiss. "How are you feeling, Mrs. Curtis?"

"Sore, Mr. Curtis." She snuggled closer to him. "Other than that, I feel wonderful."

The first day of their honeymoon had been spent with Dylan teaching her how to ski. According to him, she had done fairly well for a beginner. She'd used muscles she didn't think she'd ever used before, and no doubt she'd be even sorer over the next few days.

New Year's Day had been the perfect wedding day—a wonderful day to start their new life as husband and wife. It had been just a little over a month since Belle had come back to Bisbee. They hadn't wanted to waste any more time getting married after everything had gone down. Twenty-three years had been long enough.

A real estate agent was in the process of selling Belle's home and after their honeymoon, she and Dylan would move all her belongings to Bisbee.

"I love how you remembered that we used to talk about snuggling up someplace warm while it snowed outside." She put her palm on his chest. "Having grown up in southern Arizona, where it rarely snows, it always sounded like such a treat."

"How could I forget?" He touched her face with his fingertips. "After you left, I dreamed of you, snowflakes in your hair and on your lashes. You would be smiling up at me and telling me you loved me."

The backs of her eyes ached. The words "I'm sorry" sprang to her mind, but she didn't say them. Dylan had told her time after time that there was nothing to be sorry about, nothing to forgive. She had made the only choice she had felt she could make at the time. That was the past and now they had a future to look forward to, a future together.

"Your mom looked so happy with her new husband." Belle thought about Dylan's family. "It was good to see Aspen, too."

"They're your family now, too," Dylan said softly.

"I'm glad." Belle smiled. "It was so good Christie was able to make it to the wedding to be my maid of honor." Belle moved her palm over Dylan's T-shirt. "It wouldn't have been the same without her, if the FBI hadn't figured out how to get her there and back safely. Back to wherever it is they're hiding her."

"It meant a lot that Marta could make it, too." Dylan let his fingers slide down to the hollow of Belle's throat. "She's looking better."

Belle nodded. "And Leon being there was important. All of us who are left in the CoS." They would always think of themselves as the Circle of Seven even though there were only five of them now. "G.I. Joe being at the wedding felt like a tribute to Nate."

They were quiet a moment, and Belle thought Dylan was probably wishing, like she was, that Nate and Tom could have been at the wedding. The irony was that if Nate hadn't died, she and Dylan would probably never have ended up where they were now.

"Fate wanted us together." Dylan seemed to read her mind or her expression, and his voice was low and earnest. "One way or another, we would have found each other."

She smiled, feeling the truth of his words in her heart and soul.

Dylan grinned and shook his head. "The best man is in trouble though."

"I'll never forget the look on Trace's face when he accidentally caught the wedding bouquet." Belle giggled. "Total shock and then complete embarrassment."

"He won't live it down." Dylan's grin broadened. "Brooks captured it all on video. He has probably already shown it to all of the guys at the office."

"I'll bet Brooks has let everyone see it." She tilted her head. "Now we just need to set Trace up with the right woman since he's supposed to be the next one married."

Dylan shook his head. "Now you're matchmaking?"

Belle sniffed. "*We* are."

He held up both his hands in a "not me" motion. "No way. I'm staying out of this."

"We're in everything together now." She poked his chest with her finger. "Don't you forget that."

He groaned and rolled his eyes toward the ceiling as if begging for guidance. She poked him again and he wrapped his arms around her and kissed her ear.

Then, with a thoughtful note in his voice, he said, almost as if to himself, "If there was anyone I'd like to see happy it would be Christie."

"You're brilliant!" Belle clapped her hands, delighted. "She and Trace would be perfect together."

Dylan buried his face in one hand. "Me and my damned big mouth."

"No doubt it would have to be a while." Belle tapped her bottom lip with her finger. "Christie will need time to heal. And of course it will have to be after she testifies."

He raised his head as he lowered his hand. "Please forget I ever said anything."

"Yeah, right." It was her turn to roll her eyes. "You just had one of the most brilliant observations ever."

He gave an exaggerated sigh. "Promise me you won't say anything to Trace?"

She gave him an impish grin. "I make no promises." But then she grew serious. "Considering Christie is hidden somewhere, and Trace is still in Bisbee, it's not likely anything is going to happen." She perked up. "But once the trial is over…"

"One day at a time, sweetheart." Dylan stroked a strand of her hair. "Let's just wait and see what the future brings."

She nodded. "Fate happened for us. You never know how things will work out."

"Back to us." Dylan shifted Belle so she was straddling his lap. "I have something for you."

She watched him as he dug in his pocket and pulled out a small brown felt bag. Her stomach flipped as she held her breath in anticipation. He opened the drawstring and poured a small silver chain onto his palm.

A lump caught in her throat as he took her right wrist and fastened the bracelet to it. The bracelet he'd given her for her sixteenth birthday, the one she had left for him with her goodbye note. She stared at it and the pink heart dangling from the center of the bracelet. *I love you,* was engraved on the backside of the heart.

Tears filled her eyes and she flung her arms around his neck. "I am never taking this off again. Never."

"I know." He stroked her hair. "But, I do think we have something to work on."

She straightened and wiped tears from her eyes with her fingertips. "And what's that?"

He trailed his index finger down her nose to the tip. "What do you say to growing our little family? Beginning now."

A burst of joy rose inside her. They had talked about having one or two children, but so much had happened that they hadn't discussed when they would be ready to start.

"I say yes." She gave him a hard kiss then leaned back. "Absolutely yes. Now."

He grinned and stood, sweeping her up in his arms. He held her close and she clung to his neck, comfortable in his embrace. He hugged her to him.

It surprised her when he sounded a little choked up. "I love you, Belle."

She snuggled against his chest. "Then get us to the bedroom so that I can show you just how much I love you, too."

ALSO BY CHEYENNE MCCRAY

~Romantic Suspense~

"Lawmen" series

Hidden Prey
No Mercy
Slow Burn

"Riding Tall" Series

Branded For You
Roping Your Heart
Fencing You In
Tying You Down
Playing With You
Crazy For You
Hot For You
Made For You
Held By You
Belong To You

"Rough and Ready" Series

Silk and Spurs
Lace and Lassos
Champagne and Chaps
Satin and Saddles
Roses and Rodeo
Lingerie and Lariats
Lipstick and Leather

Cheyenne writing as Jaymie Holland

"Tattoos and Leather" ménage

Inked

Branded

Marked

Stranded

"Hearts in Chains" BDSM Series

Wounded

"The Auction" Series

Sold

Bought

Claimed (with bonus novella *Taken*)

"Taboo" Series

Wicked Nights: three Erotic Tales
Taboo Desires: three Tales of Lust and Passion
Playing Rough: three Stories of Sensual Submission

Paranormal

The Touch

EXCERPT...HIDDEN PREY

"Lawmen" series
By Cheyenne McCray

Almost absently, he rubbed his thumb along Tori's delicate jawline while they both remained quiet. He liked the way she fit in his arms. It felt...right.

It was the right time to tell her about what happened with Brian. Landon knew he should do it now.

And then every good intention vanished as she tipped her face up to look at him. Her eyelashes glittered from the remainder of her tears and her brown eyes seemed even darker than normal. As their gazes met and held, he didn't think he'd ever be able to look away from her again. She drew him to her in so many ways and he was helpless to stop himself from wanting to get closer to her.

The other agents were downstairs and he was upstairs, alone. With Tori.

This wasn't smart.

Hell, it was a long, long way from smart.

He held his breath, then let out a slow exhale as he lowered his mouth to hers.

The moment their lips met, she gave a sigh, surrendering herself to his kiss. That sense of surrender fueled him, somehow making him desire her even more than he already did.

He moved his lips over hers, hungry for the taste of her, the feel of her. Her scent filled him, as if a part of her was now inside him. Her lips were so soft, her taste exquisite on his tongue. God, he knew he could never get enough of her.

She leaned into him as their body heat melded, fusing them together in a way that defied explanation. Her sighs turned into a soft moan as he moved his hands over her shoulders, down her arms, and to her waist. She was wearing one of her new T-shirts and he pushed the hem up just enough that he could feel her soft skin along the waistband. He gripped her slender waist in his hands, his fingers brushing the base of her spine where she'd been tattooed.

Her hunger and his grew in matching intensity. She moved her palms up his chest to his shoulders and gripped them like she was afraid she would slide away if she didn't hold on tightly.

He slipped his palms from her waist to her ass, feeling the perfection of it as he squeezed her closer to him. His cock was impossibly hard, pressing against her, straining to get free from behind the tough denim of his jeans.

Their clothes—too much cloth was between them. He wanted to feel her warm silky skin against his, nothing keeping them apart. He wanted only to slide between her thighs and drive his cock deep inside her heat.

The rumble that rose up in his chest was like a lion staking a claim on his territory, and she made an answering purr, giving herself completely to him. Not just surrendering, but offering herself for his pleasure. She asked for nothing, just gave him everything she had.

She sighed again as he slid his lips along her jawline to her ear. She gasped when he nipped at her earlobe and shivered in a delicate way that told him he'd just found one of her erogenous zones. He sucked the soft flesh into his mouth and nipped at it again. He felt another shiver run through her body.

He moved his lips down the column of her neck to the hollow at the base of her throat. The soft purring sounds she made caused his cock to grow even harder and he rubbed himself against her in a slow deliberate movement, like what he'd do when he was inside her.

A gasp escaped her as he cupped her breasts and flicked his thumbs over her taut nipples that pressed against the fabric of her T-shirt. She slid her fingers into his hair and encouraged him to lower his head so his mouth was even with her breasts. His body was close to shaking from the power of his need for her as he circled her nipple with his tongue, wetting the T-shirt and causing her to suck in her breath. She gave a small cry and gripped his hair tighter as he moved his mouth to her other nipple.

He had to taste the salt on her skin, feel its softness in his mouth. He pushed her T-shirt over her perfectly sized breasts and licked each of her nipples through her satin bra. She caught her breath as he pulled her bra beneath her breasts so they were bared for him.

She pushed his head down again, guiding him so that his mouth was directly over her nipple. He skimmed his lips over the hard nub and she moaned as he sucked it and flicked it with his tongue. Her nipples were hard peaks as he nipped at each one. God, but he loved the way she tasted. He loved that she wasn't afraid to show him what she wanted. He loved everything about her.

Excerpt…Silk and Spurs

~Rough and Ready Series~
By Cheyenne McCray
Silk and Spurs ebook available FREE at all major ebook retailers

"Can I help you?"

A deep, masculine drawl from behind her send a shiver down her spine and she lowered her camera and let it hang around her neck. She turned to face one hell of a fine cowboy, easily one of the sexiest she'd seen in all of her twenty-nine years.

At least six-three with broad shoulders and a cowboy's build, he had blue flame eyes and black hair that curled slightly beneath his cowboy hat. His skin was well tanned and his arms roped with muscle.

"Sure." She smiled. "You can help me anytime." He raised an eyebrow and she grinned as she held out her hand. "Jessica Porter," she said. "But please call me Jessie. I'm here to photograph the ranch and the upcoming wedding."

"You're my kid sister's friend." The cowboy took her hand in a firm grip. "Welcome to the Bar C."

Jessie's heart started to pound like crazy as the cowboy's warm touch sent fire through her body. Her mouth grew dry and she bit the inside of her lower lip. It was the most enticing reaction that she'd ever had to a man.

Before he released it, he said, "I'm Zane Cameron."

The disappointment that swept through her was a surprise. She didn't even know Zane, so what difference did it make that he was getting married in just weeks?

What a shame. All of that hot man flesh would soon belong to some other woman.

The green-eyed redhead was so sexy that he'd damned near gone hard when he'd clasped her hand. She had a cute grin and shapely body and her nipples were hard, poking against the light cotton of her T-shirt.

She wasn't wearing a bra.

For one moment Zane thought about carting Jessie off to the ranch house and taking her six ways 'til Sunday.

Well hell. He mentally shook his head. He had no business thinking about another woman and his body had no damned excuse to react the way it had.

Except that Jessie Porter was one hell of a woman. And he was a red-blooded American male and he'd just had a natural reaction to her.

Keep telling yourself that, Cameron.

"Congratulations," she said. Her smile was enough to make him crazy.

For a moment he didn't know why she was telling him congratulations, but then he regained his senses.

"Thanks." He hooked his thumbs in his belt loops, feeling like he needed to anchor them to make sure he kept his hands off of her.

She tilted her head to the side, which caused her dark red hair to slide away from her elegant neck. "Is the bride-to-be here?"

"Phoebe's at her place." He dragged his hand down his face then gave a nod in the direction of the house. "You can photograph anything you'd like to around here. Danica wants to give the album to our aunt."

Jessie nodded. "Danica mentioned that your aunt took care of the two of you along with your three brothers. Raising five kids is quite a feat for one woman."

"Sure as hell was." He glanced at Jessie as she fell into step beside him.

"Danica said two of your brothers are twins," she said. "Wayne and Wyatt."

Zane nodded. "Yep, and our youngest brother is Dillon."

Her smile was pure sunshine as she looked at him.

God only knew why he found himself comparing Phoebe with Jessie.

He'd begun to feel a little uneasy about his relationship with Phoebe and he'd managed to put off the wedding another couple of months, but here it was, creeping back up. To him Phoebe had been the picture of sweetness and intelligence, but lately it seemed that there had to be another side of her that others had seen but he hadn't, but then maybe it was the pressure of the wedding. It did concern him, though.

Ah, hell. Maybe his concern was just a case of pre-wedding jitters. Although he had a good mind to move the date again.

He glanced at Jessie and thought how different she looked from Phoebe who was pale blonde and petite at five-one. Jessie, on the other hand, was no shorter than five-eight. Both women were beautiful as hell, just as different as sunrise from sunset.

He ground his teeth. He'd never been one to compare women, especially not now that he was about to be married. It was time he settled down and had a couple of kids to carry on the Cameron name. No one else in the family seemed to be inclined to head down that road. Someone had to do it.

EXCERPT... BRANDED FOR YOU

"Riding Tall" series

by Cheyenne McCray

Branded For You ebook available FREE at all major ebook retailers

The afternoon was cooling off as it turned to dusk and then darkness descended on them. They each grabbed a light sweat jacket from the camper and slipped them on.

Ryan took a couple of steaks out of the cooler to cook over the fire. Megan sliced the potatoes and wrapped them in foil with butter and seasonings and put them in the coals first. Ryan buttered, salted, and peppered the corn on the cob and wrapped them in foil, too. When it was time, they placed the corn along the edge of the fire. Ryan had cored out the onion and put butter in the center and wrapped it in foil and put it in the coals, as well. The steaks went on last, when everything else was just about finished cooking.

When it was ready, they sat on the camping chairs in front of the fire and ate dinner.

"This is unbelievable," Megan said with a smile.

Firelight flickered on her pretty features, casting shadows in the darkness as they ate. He thought about what he'd said to her earlier.

"I might be falling for you, Meg."

He didn't regret his words. He'd dated a lot of women in the past but there'd just been something missing. Something intangible that he hadn't been able to name.

He'd never been a love 'em and leave 'em kind of guy, but some thought so. He just wasn't going to hang in there with someone if he knew she wasn't the right one.

He'd never felt the same way with anyone that he did with Megan.

Last night he'd taken her hard and rough, and the memory caused his groin to ache. Damn she'd been amazing. But she needed to know that he wanted more from her than a night of good, hard sex.

When they finished dinner and had cleaned up, he brought a blanket from the camper and handed it to her before he put out the fire. After he extinguished the fire, he lit a candle within a glass and metal hurricane lantern.

He took her by the hand. "I've got something I want to show you." Her hand was warm in his.

She smiled up at him, her smile causing something deep inside him to stir. He led her into the forest, candlelight from the hurricane lantern lighting the way. The candlelight was much gentler than a regular camping lantern and the shadows from it bounced from tree to tree.

"I saw a place somewhere over here," he murmured as they walked through the forest then came to a stop. "Here we go."

A small clearing lay on the other side of a fallen tree, a bed of leaves at the center of the clearing. They stepped over the tree and then he found a sturdy place to set the hurricane before taking the blanket from Megan and spreading it out on the leaves.

He slipped out of his jacket and set it on the fallen tree. "I'll keep you warm," he said as he held out his hand.

She looked up at him, slid off her sweat jacket, handed it to him and he set it on top of his own.

He sat on the blanket and beckoned to her. She eased onto her knees beside him and he cupped her face in his hands and lowered his head and kissed her.

Her kiss was sweet and his desire for her kicked into full gear. He wanted to take her hard again, right now. But more importantly, he wanted to show her that it wasn't only about rough sex with him. It was all about her.

When he drew away from the kiss, her lips were parted, hunger in her pretty green eyes.

"You're an incredible woman." He brushed his thumb over her lips, which trembled beneath his touch. "I've loved every minute of this weekend."

"So have I," she said, her voice just above a whisper. "I wish it didn't have to end."

"It doesn't." He nuzzled her hair that was silky now that it had dried. "When we return, we just pick right back up where we left off."

She smiled and he kissed her again. She felt so soft and warm in his arms. He slid his hand under her T-shirt, pleased she didn't have her bra on as he cupped her bare breast and rubbed his thumb over her nipple. He watched her expression as her lips parted and her eyes grew dark with need.

He drew the T-shirt over her head and set it on the fallen tree. Candlelight flickered, gently touching her bare shoulders and chest.

"You know how much I love your body and how beautiful I think you are," he murmured before stroking her nipples with the back of his hand.

He cupped her breasts, feeling their weight in his hands before he lowered his head and sucked a nipple.

She gasped and leaned back so that her hands were braced behind her on the blanket, her back arched so that he had better access to her breasts. He pressed them together and moved his mouth from one to the other, sucking one nipple before moving his mouth to the other one. Her nipples were large and hard and he loved sucking on them.

"I want you on your back, looking at me." He adjusted her so that she was lying on the blanket. Her eyes glittered in the light, desire on her features.

He was surprised at how she made him want to go slow with her, to be gentle and show her how much he cared. She stirred things inside him he'd never felt with another woman.

19332614R00175

Made in the USA
Middletown, DE
17 April 2015